TELÉMACHUS

Note: This novel, *Telémachus* (pronounced: Tuh·**leh**·muh·kuhs), takes its title from the name of the hero's son in the *Odyssey*, and its section titles from that epic poem; a work of the imagination, it is not based on real people or events.

Acknowledgments

The lines by Mark Rothko are from "A Symposium on How to Combine Architecture, Painting, and Sculpture," *Interiors* 10 (May 1951), Museum of Modern Art, New York, 1951.

Lines from Joseph Brodsky's poem "Odysseus to Telémachus" are from *A Part of Speech* by Joseph Brodsky. Translation copyright © 1980 by Farrar, Straus & Giroux.

Lines from *La Divina Commedia*, Purgatorio, Canto XXXI, ll.10-30 (Grandgent edition, Harvard, 1972) are in the author's translation.

Thanks to *Story Houston* for publishing an excerpt called "All We Like Sheep." My thanks also to those friends and close readers who've encouraged this book to creep along over several years: Pat Hawley, Finn Wilcox, Frank Moffett, Jack Estes, Theo Daley, Kathy Prunty, Mark Schreiber, Kathleen Alcala, Bill Ransom, and especially, for her enduring support for *Telémachus,* Lauren Grosskopf. I also wish to acknowledge the ghosts of Savoy Enterprises, as well as to offer my lifelong gratitude to friends who've inspired me to write some of these tales: Chelle Roberts, Jim Tordoff, Joey Nee, Tim McNulty, Ken Cline, the late Jewel Schwitters Cline Atwell, the late Jim Malloy, and the late Eleanor Daley.

for Tex

ISBN 978-1-7370520-6-7
Library of Congress Control Number 9781737052067

Cover art by Gae Pilon
Cover and Book Design by Lauren Grosskopf

Pleasure Boat Studio books are available
through your favorite bookstore and through the following:
Baker & Taylor, Ingram, Amazon, bn.com &
Pleasure Boat Studio: A Nonprofit Literary Press
www.pleasureboatstudio.com
Seattle, Washington

To paint a small picture is to place yourself outside your experience, to look upon an experience as a stereopticon view or with a reducing glass. However you paint the larger picture, you are in it. It isn't something you command.

—Mark Rothko

Telémachus, my son! To a wanderer the faces of all islands resemble one another. And the mind trips, numbering waves; eyes, sore from sea horizons, run; and the flesh of water stuffs the ears.

—Joseph Brodsky

TELÉMACHUS

MICHAEL DALEY

PLEASURE BOAT STUDIO:
A NONPROFIT LITERARY PRESS

Table of Contents

MENTOR

1.

THEY FOUND MY FATHER, a famous man, sitting upright on a hundred-year-old bench, at an unfrequented subway stop called Andrews Square in South Boston. Medics determined the cause of death to have been his heart and that he'd been dead twelve hours before anyone realized he wasn't waiting for a train, asleep, a vagrant, or a mound of rags beneath a hat. That image, which appeared on the front page of a major newspaper, still haunts me with its caption: "poet warrior's heart stopped underground two miles from his birthplace." I've tried again and again to paint him, but the minute I begin to mix the gray and silver oils to paint his form leaning against those dull yellow wall tiles, I'm bothered by the question I've been trying to answer since his death: did he find the last piece of his own puzzle before he sat down in that station?

Before that picture reached the newspapers, one of his lawyers called me—Johnny. I had only talked to Johnny on the phone once or twice back when Mac was attempting to pay my tuition fees, but I had a pretty clear image of what he looked like. In my mind, at least, he always wore a baseball cap with his three-piece suit. Took it off for court, of course. He was thin as a rail and moved as fast as he talked. He didn't drink or smoke and while we were on the phone he told me he was slowing down his Peloton to give me this regrettable news.

"Bobby, I'm so sorry." He was only slightly out of breath. "Nobody knows what happened to him. I mean leading up to the heart attack, you know?"

"Yeah, I guess. Um. Why did his heart fail on that particular night? Any idea? Had he been seeing a doctor that you know of?"

"No, I don't think he would do that unless—well, you know how he was—unless he was dragged there in an ambulance. He still smoked and drank like a fish, as far as I know, Bobby."

"Could he have mouthed off at someone who pulled a knife, or a gun and had a heart attack from terror?"

"Oh—well, yeah. I mean, that's your Dad. Who the fuck knows what he might do from one moment to the next."

"Ironic isn't it? I mean after a decade in every warzone on earth he dies on a quiet bench at a subway station? I wonder if it was grief?"

"Grief? What do you mean, Bobby?"

"Well, maybe he just got tired of seeing so much. He saw enough war and death, you know? Maybe he stopped being able to separate death in the world from his own? Or maybe he was just too lonely to keep going."

He had abandoned us and the creaking family home for the last time, as well as our little town in the Pacific Northwest, and "returned," as he put it, "to the scene of the crime," the Irish-Italian maze of triple-decker houses and potholed streets in Dorchester where he spent the last ten years of his life.

"How long since you've seen him, Bobby?"

"Yeah, you're right. I'm not the best son in the world. All these years and I couldn't make myself do the right thing and visit him. Well, I don't know if you know it, Johnny, but, apart from the summer when I was thirteen, I've only known him through phone calls and letters. Im*por*tant letters, I'll grant him that—to him *and* to me—and they came regularly beginning after my sixth birthday until that thirteenth summer. They picked up again after that—I've saved the next twenty years of his letters from some pretty grizzly locales too—famine, refugee camps, friggin' bullets flying around. You name it, he was there; I'm sure you know all about what he was paid for poems he wrote in the danger zones. Remember when he sent me to the Parisian art school and couldn't meet me there because he was in Libya?"

"He changed, you know," said Johnny. "He just wasn't the same happy-go-lucky guy after the accident. So, I guess when he started diving into those hotspots he thought he found a way to shake off the misery and guilt. Found some other 'Mac' to put out there in front of the world. You know he was all about his reputation, right? Hey, you know what I remember about Mac? It was probably one of the first times I ever met him, and I think he might have been testing me. He was drinking and he was happy. Oh, boy, could he get happy when he wanted to."

"I thought you didn't drink."

"I don't. Not anymore. But I was kinda young then and I was meeting this famous guy. So, you know, I thought I could keep up."

"What happened? Did he get you drunk?"

"No, not really. Like I said, he wanted to test me, I think—to see how low I could sink before I realized he was putting me on. 'First thing I ever learned, Johnny,' he said, 'and I'm gonna show you—first you get a good flame off'n that cigarette lighter, so you can heat the bottle and what molecules cling to the inner walls will just drip down for one or two more tastes, or at least enough to pass around because, after all, the liquor store's closed, the truck's outa gas.' I just stared at him as he fanned this lighter over the bottom of a bottle with some kind of grin I never saw before, his eyes lighting up. 'There,' he said, 'what d'ya know? Wanna try some, Mr. Attorney?' I shook my head. I didn't want what he was selling, and I think that's why he hired me after that. Then he said, 'Some days you have to put your eyeball to the mouth of a drained bourbon. That's revelation, when you crawl down into the mirror. An empty bottle's never really empty.'

"Anyways, that's the old Mac. He quit playing like that over the last I don't know twenty years or so. And back in the day, he needed someone he could trust to be his lawyer when the lawsuits were coming at him like flaming arrows. You might have been too young to remember now, but he got famous by excoriating celebrity poets around the country in his reviews. Thanks to me he never lost. Turned out the dark secrets he uncovered about those folks were actually true. He got even nastier when he started in on the politicians."

I'VE ALWAYS WANTED to recapture what I thought couldn't change but did or seemed to; the real Mac already seemed far away, when I was thirteen. He wasn't the Dad he was when I was little, that's for sure. But—and I held onto this as a kind of belief in him—he was Mac and Mac had to be Mac. That's all. Yes, he had the rep as a poet, then there was the insufferable literary critic who was long forgotten by the time he died. When I was thirteen, his personality had dimmed; what was left of the Dad I remembered from childhood had turned down to barely a flicker.

So, here I was at thirty-five with a career painting miniature landscapes almost supporting me, and I set out to find my father. And where better to start, but a small funeral parlor? I was too cheap to spring for GPS in my rental car from Logan Airport, so got lost within a mile of the place. I did have my cell phone and the kind lady's voice from their front office guided me through neighborhood streets to arrive at Scully's & Sons Mortuary. Cynical as I am, I saw theirs as the business of kindness that dealt in the studied habits of concern and delicacy. I just wanted to grab his stuff and get out. I'll take charge of his ashes, I was thinking as I parked, although I had no idea where or how to disperse them. I hoped someone, maybe Scully himself would have Mac's personal effects, whatever he had in his pockets when they found him. I hoped whoever his Literary Executor was had already archived his papers. Which, frankly, I thought of as a fire hazard. With this in mind, I squirmed out of the rented minicar, and there in the parking lot stood Moses Aimes, Mac's lifelong friend, more dignified than ever in the black suit and waving both hands, grinning at me; seeing him swept me back to my thirteenth summer three thousand miles from this grimy city where Mac chose to make his last stand.

"It's so good to see you, young man. I wish I could tell you how deeply sorry I am your Dad is gone. I saw him that same night and, you know, he was quiet and sedate but gave no sign something like this might happen. He apparently took off in the night and went walking to the subway."

"Great to see you again, Moses. You look in good health."

"Yeah yeah, I get by. Well, what are we all gonna do with ourselves now, I wonder. No more Mac to kick around."

"I haven't been able to do that for a long time, I'm afraid."

"Oh, I know. I know. He told me, Bobby. He was delighted to take out all those letters you sent him and the drawings, and the clippings of your gallery shows. He paid somebody to buy a few of your paintings; did you know that?"

"No, I didn't know that. Wow. I'm kinda shocked, you know? He could have *told* me or something. I wonder which ones he has."

Turns out Moses *is* the Literary Executor, and he's already collected Mac's papers. He's well suited to the task; he has that 'friend of the family' status from back in the day; he knew everything there was to know about all of us, and now he's a renowned medieval scholar, recently retired from some university in the Midwest.

"Well, it certainly is good to see you again now that you're all successful and established and all that, Bobby."

"Established, maybe."

"I do wish I could stay longer, but I have an appointment with your dad's publisher in New York this afternoon. So, I must hop back on the Expressway in a few minutes. In fact, I'm a bit behind schedule. I stayed here for just this chance to see you. I'm glad I did."

We found out then that both of us had the habit of scuffing gravel in the driveway and looking down as if interesting goings-on were just below our feet.

"You know, this neighborhood has totally changed since your dad was a kid here. Lots of multi-colored individuals now, and families."

He stretched out his arms and pointed toward a hill to the east.

"Used to be, right over there, where I grew up in Roxbury, if a white family drove through, we always knew. They'd mostly keep the windows rolled up and nobody would look out except maybe some kid in the back seat like Mac. The Dad at the wheel looked like he was taking a big risk, holding his breath through enemy territory. Two worlds, Bobby. Two worlds back then."

"It feels like a different world to me just standing in this parking lot, Moses. I want to get back on the plane as soon as I can."

"Yeah, your dad was like that with most places, I'm afraid." He had opened his car door and was crouching down into the seat. He'll have to hurry to get to the airport in time, I thought, for the shuttle to New York. Meeting with Mac's publisher. Ugh. Not something I ever wanted to be part of.

"Sorry, you have to take off so soon. Can we keep in touch?"

"Absolutely, my friend. I'll write you soon. I gotta tell you about those cops who came to your dad's house. I was his house guest. They were just a little surprised."

The car's ignition was a smooth whirr, and he looked straight ahead at nothing in particular. "I miss him, you know? I really do."

"Yeah."

He turned and looked up at me. I tried to find an expression with my eyes that might let him know I had many mixed feelings about all this. "You do too?"

"Well. I guess. You know, I haven't seen him in twenty years. We kept in touch, but that was about all."

"Yeah, I know. I might have been his only friend. Did you know that?"

"I would have guessed that, yeah."

"I came here to see him, and we walked and talked, but that was about it. The days of going anywhere or doing anything that seemed halfway important were over."

My regrets were insignificant, in a way, compared to the feeling I was left behind, and I didn't want to let Moses go away thinking what Mac left undone really mattered all that much.

"He left when I was six and I didn't see him until I was thirteen. Then he stayed for the summer and took off again."

"Yeah, I know about that. Taking off like that when you were a teenager he told me he figured he had done all he could, and it was important to him to make amends. That's why he drove himself to go all over the place looking for famine and war. He did, Bobby. He wanted to somehow make up for what he had done in his life, for the people he hurt. And I believe he didn't think he hurt you, but he did think you would be fine or at least better off without him hanging around, telling you what he thought of whatever you were doing. He sent you to Paris because that's about all he thought he could do, and he thought he could help you find out what it was like to be you."

"Yeah. I get it. Deep down he was just 'Dad' like always. Thanks, Moses. Hey, it's been good to see you. I know you gotta head out. Okay, so long."

"Bobby, you should find out what happened to him. Find out what changed him. He was different after Albuquerque; you knew that, right? That summer was make it or break it time for him, and I think he broke it. He wasn't the same Mac you knew. You should find out."

"Okay. Yeah, I guess so."

"I gotta hit the road now, but I'll write to you. I know a few things about his past you might like to know."

SCULLY'S WAS A sprawling and faded white affair with what might have once been lawn paved over in crackled tar. A few scrawny hedges blocked part of it from the street where a seemingly endless array of plumbers' vans and concrete trucks crawled past. Inside, the lady whose kind voice I remembered from the phone greeted me. She hardly spoke, though, other than to commiserate over what distress I must have been feeling. She was sorry for my loss. I wondered how often in a day she uttered those words. She wasn't the embodiment of kindness I had expected, greeting my sudden entrance in the cold vestibule. She didn't offer to take my coat or serve me tea or anything; she indicated I could follow her along a carpeted narrow hallway where we made a turn into yet another corridor, a long and mauve space that looked as though it would go on for miles with panel doors one after the other on both sides. At the seventh of these, she stopped, opened the door on the left, and beckoned me to enter. She said, "I'll give you a few minutes, Mr. Bacca," and closed the door so that I was alone in the room with a small card table and a large gray cardboard box. An envelope rested on top of the box with my name on it. A letter from M.M. Bacca to me, Robert Hieronimo Bacca.

"Dear Bobby, I don't know when I died, but I made all the arrangements with the Scully's so you wouldn't have to. This should accompany something like an urn with my ashes. I knew Judith Scully in grade school, so they were delighted to get my business. Here's the gist: though disposing of ashes is illegal apparently unless you go miles out to sea, find the best-looking bridge without a streetlight that crosses the Neponset River at high tide on the dark of the moon and deposit half my ashes in the river. Take the rest of me back with you and drop them in the Pacific. I loved you all my life, Mac."

It was a cardboard box with Scully's printed logo, as dry and subtle as "memento mori." Releasing the four flaps of the lid, I saw the transparent bag, thick plastic, filled nearly to bursting with ash. They were silken to the touch, with hard knots of what I could only have thought were remnants of his bones, Mac unburnable to the very end. I couldn't take my hand away, the ash between finger and thumb, the ash rubbed into my palm, steeping my hands down in there, embedding him within the creases of my knuckles, lifelines of my palm, finally awash in the death of my father.

2.

Dear Bobby,

SORRY I HAD to rush off and didn't have time to tell you about the morning they found Mac. I was serious, though—you really should find out what happened that changed him. Those were some lost years, most definitely. They were losses to the both of you. I can assure you he thought of you often and felt bad about having to take a job so far away when you were still a little kid. I knew some of the things he was up to in New Mexico, but we were both gainfully employed, and I was working my way through grad school there, so we lost touch. One guy I'd recommend to you, who worked pretty closely with your dad was his T.A., Winston Roblé. What a trip he was. Still is, I'd imagine. You should look him up and find out what went on with Mac back then. Anyway, when the EMT came to the train station to take your Dad to the hospital, where of course he was pronounced dead on arrival, a perceptive policeman located his ID in the billfold, which led that officer to the house; I don't think anyone suspected foul play, but, since I answered the door, having spent the night on his couch, and since I am rather a large black man, he strongly suggested I come down to their pleasantly bright precinct office and answer a few questions. Just for your own edification, I'm including my little record of the conversation I had with the constable:

"Mr. Aimes, we found you at the apartment of a Mr. M.M. Bacca. Is that correct?"

"I was lost?"

"Excuse me?"

"You found me."

"Yes. Ha! That's funny. No, I get it..."

The Detective looked up from his pad of yellow-lined paper, Bic poised, teeth too large for his smile.

"So. Yes, when we arrived at the residence at..."

He looked down with relief.

"Number 12 Annabel Street in Dorchester. You were inside."

With these last words, Detective Meares looked up again, squinting as if to solve a problem.

"I answered the door when someone in a uniform politely rang the doorbell."

"Yes. Why were you there?"

"Why was I there? Or why was I there?"

"What? Just answer the question, please." Detective Meares tapped the blunt end of his pen against the pad, where he kept his eyes focused.

"Which one?"

He looked up at "Mr. Aimes" now.

"Why were you there? Why were you there? What the fuck difference does it make? We found you in his house, he was dead, you were there. So, why?"

Meares leaned back, tossed the pen onto the desk as if to convey, 'Alright, I get it. I can listen. Just tell me.'

"Isn't there another question you want to ask me?"

He rolled his chair back up to the desk, grabbed his pen, and sighed.

"Look! Aimes, what the hell are you doing? Okay, okay. You're the professor. What question should I be asking?"

"How did I know Mac Bacca?"

"You knew the deceased?"

He started to write, eyes darting between me and the tip of his pen as he scribbled on the pad.

"Good question."

"Well?"

"I was in his apartment. I answered the door in a bathrobe, holding a cup of coffee and a newspaper when your young officer rang the doorbell."

"So?"

"Did the officer think I was robbing that apartment?"

"Now, wait a minute. Nobody's accusing you of robbery. The officer didn't mention any details about your appearance."

"Would you read the report?"

Turns the page, sweeps over the handwritten report with his index finger.

"Aloud?"

"'A large black man answered the door.'"

"And?"

"That's it."

"You had a question?"

"Yes. You still haven't said what you were doing there."

"I was holding a newspaper and a cup of coffee, and I had gotten up from the kitchen table to answer the doorbell where a polite young policeman was ringing."

"Yes, yes, but WHY were you in M.M. Bacca's apartment?"

"He was a famous writer, a well-known critic, and a TV personality. Did you know that?"

"Yeah, sort of. Someone put something to that effect in the report. What are you suggesting? Is that why you were in the apartment? That's a good one. You were interviewing him, or something like that? Wait a minute. You were in a bathrobe, you said, so you spent the night. With him? Are you telling me...?"

"I knew him."

"When did you meet him?"

"1961."

"What? I thought you just said..."

"You said."

"What were you doing in his apartment and why did you spend the night?"

"I knew him."

"Where did you meet him?"

"Proctor's"

"Who's that?"

"Not who. What."

"Alright, what's that?"

"It was a school."

"Where?"

"Ipswich."

"You're telling me you've known this guy, this famous writer, since 1961 in Ipswich? What kind of a school was that?"

"Private."

"Did you work there?"

"No. I didn't work there. Much."

"What was Bacca doing in a place like that? And what were you doing there? This is starting to sound weird. Wait! Are you a writer?"

"No."

"Alright, alright. Oh—hey, what do you know about this? Right beside him, on the subway bench was this white box with a large chocolate truffle. Did he bring that with him? Was it at the house?"

Long pause.

"White box. White ribbon? Truffle shaped like a heart? Yeah, I knew that once. But he only described it. It was a gift."

"Oh? For who?"

Pause.

"He never said. And it's 'For whom?'"

"What? Oh. Okay, so, he was up in Ipswich at this school called Proctor's. Doing what? Teaching?"

I leaned forward; hands clasped together to contemplate how best to phrase the next bits of information.

"Have you considered the math here? How old was Bacca? What year was he born? Go ahead, take a look at that record. No, I can tell you, if you want. He was born in 1947. In 1961, he would have been fourteen. I was also born in 1947. So, I suggest to you that the math can tell you what each of us was doing in Ipswich in 1961 at the Proctor's Academy. And, yes, it was named for some old Puritan. We were students. I did do schoolwork, but not much, as I said. I wasn't there as an employee, nor was he. I met him in 1961 when we were both sophomores, and on scholarships. We've been friends since. I was staying at his place in Dorchester. I slept on the couch last night, and I don't know what happened to Mac. He must have gotten up during the night and wound up on that bench, but I don't know how. I didn't hear him leave the apartment. I can go now?"

P.S.

Now, Bobby, I think there's a whole lot you never knew about Mac because he didn't tell you much about himself or his early education. I'll get to that probably in some other letter. I don't have time right now to tell you *all* about that part of his past, but here's something I've wanted you to know since I saw you at that funeral parlor. It's one of the memories about your dad that keeps resurfacing lately. I don't know why this one memory in particular from our old school days, but I thought it might give you a little insight into how we became close friends.

The way I'm recalling it now, Mac and I were part of a group of high school seniors standing in a circle around a man who called himself 'Red Cap.' He was a black man. So, in this circle, where I was the school's only black kid, there were five other guys, white guys from all different backgrounds, mostly well-to-do—the tuition was steep and I had a scholarship—and directly across the circle from me was your dad, sixteen or seventeen like me and a scholarship kid as well. Not that everybody knew or cared whether we were there because the school was paying, and paying because for one reason or another we both scored high on the entrance exam and made a good impression in our application letters, which were actually essays in letter form about, let me see—I don't know, probably about something like 'why I want to have a good education'... or 'what I want to be when I grow up'...'the benefits of higher education to the community.' Stuff like that. Standard back then. Anyway, here was this Red Cap as we all stood out on the lawn, and he regaled us in a semi-literate gravelly voice. I was certain—and I remember thinking this as I looked around the group—each of the others, except for maybe your dad, was intent on every word old Red Cap said because they never met much less talked to an adult black person before, at least not up close. And this guy didn't much care who he was talking to. That is, he was extremely personable, a trait I'm sure helped him get along with all sorts of employers, supervisors, and guys on the job. And he was old, or that's how it seemed. You know, a short, gray-haired black man, kind of squat, strong muscles and rough complexion, missing a few teeth, and talking, laughing, shuffling his feet all the while he went on and on. Sort of like a monologue because he wasn't really interested in anything we had to say. I don't even know if he completely understood the kind of place we were in or why we were standing there on the baseball field in jackets and ties. He was just used to being around a lot of different kinds of people and seemed to really like us, maybe mostly because we were all teenagers, and all males, so he could say anything. It seemed as though he didn't realize we were the most innocent group of young men he'd ever been near, didn't know that half of what he said we didn't quite pick up because he spoke so fast and used a kind of patois, it seemed to me, rarely encountered in the prissy suburbs, or even in my own neighborhood. His dialect was unabashedly Southern. I did understand him to say his parents had been freed when they were just "chil'ren." They were sharecroppers, and he was too, till, you know, one day he *put the white man's milk truck in a ditch and that wife of his came to the door when he went up to the farmhouse? To confess to it? She didn't have but nothin' on under that silky little white robe. There was nothin' he coulda done about it,* he said. He came north on a freight train. Eighteen. After that, he never saw his family again.

He was there at the school to do a job, but when he found us, it seemed like he didn't have anything at all to do. Maybe his job was the set-up and later the tear-down of the big tent on our school grounds for...let me see, I think it was a Dog Show, but that seems hard to believe now. A Dog Show at our school back then—hmm—must have been small potatoes because as I remember the tent wasn't huge. Just big enough to accommodate a ring and a couple tiers of bleacher seats. I do recall, though, that while he gabbed, there was a loudspeaker or a megaphone intoning and a great deal of applause in the tent. At any rate, it had very little to do with us, and with what went on in our day-to-day school life. This was a Sunday, and we were sort of captivated by all the people, especially the women in bright sundresses who'd arrived all together with poodles and Weimaraner's.

As I say, he never seemed to realize—and I finally have come to understand he wasn't trying to shock us for some reason—that we were total, utter innocents. That we had no experience whatsoever of the world, especially how a story could suddenly turn so personal, even intimate. The guys might have asked questions to keep him talking. He'd start a story about his life, even about where he lived now and his own family, and then without prompt veer back to his parents the sharecroppers or complain about the cost of cigarettes...*out here in y'all's sticks.*

So, when they pressed him with questions, it was in earnest, a wanting to know more. I knew more and though the others had to find out what kind of life this man led, I had no idea what was coming or why. We had assumptions about adults who came on our campus for any reason, those who were let into our life. We assumed they all shared the values that so far we had no reason to question. None of us—well, possibly this was less true of Mac in the early days—but most of us were not morally rebellious. We not only worked to absorb the very difficult material of a Classical education, and your dad certainly did too, but we accepted that a virtuous life was its own reward and that those virtues were conjoined to the knowledge our scholarship and our learned teachers inculcated. Your dad, I guess because of the deep grain of irreverence he'd nurtured even as a youngster, could separate learning itself from the moral high ground we were given to believe was our path through the mirk of corruption that even our guest speakers called 'the world,' even while preparing some of us to become its major players.

So, when he spoke about his daughter, and perhaps there was more than one, we thought he'd tell us admirable family stories about struggling in the poorer classes to survive. We assumed, that is, he had something to tell us we could use in our barely formulated worldview, a pathway toward becoming those men we knew we wanted to be, who would make an important contribution to struggles such as his and his family's. He told us she was pregnant, and we dutifully nodded our congratulations. Once again we assumed that certainly, a grandchild would have been a great joy to him, a source of happiness for his daughter and, we also assumed, her husband. Then he told us he had wanted her to wait. This may have been when we started to exchange glances around the circle, when some of those white boys looked quick across the grass over at me and I began to look down. That she hadn't waited, he said—not, as we already had become aware was a false assumption, to get out of school, or to live a little, have a job, even go to college for Christ's sake, ticking off all the 'good things' she could have waited for...to just move out to the suburbs—but she hadn't waited...for him. And he chattered on and on, but not as if he thought he had to explain this to us, but as if it was a common truth, that we would agree with him and that anybody would because that was just what she was supposed to do, to *give it to me, not go off like some skank looking for it someplace else,* that his virgin daughter should have gotten pregnant, because it was her first time, by him, and not by some stranger.

After a few minutes with nothing more to say, after we all nodded as if we understood and could be thought to agree completely with him, our new best friend, everyone slowly turned back toward the big tent or found we had something important we were supposed to have finished an hour or so ago. Victor Sinclair was the only one in the group who gave any reaction. He sort of shrugged, then waved, and made a grim distraught face as he turned away and lumbered alone off the field.

Mac and I headed in the direction of the lake. I was uncomfortable, not only because of the story and what this more-or-less anonymous black man represented to my fellow students about the community I came from but that they all would now be thinking of me a different way, that their stereotypes had been deepened and widened from the more positive image I gave them as their one and only scholarly black boy, to this recognition of something sinister in

Red Cap's family history.

We didn't say anything to each other until we got to the water. Some ducks shot up and fled across the murk of that little lake. Then Mac started talking abruptly.

"When he mentioned he had family members he knew who had been slaves, and then he started telling that story, I remembered the tradition of *Droit du Seigneur.* Remember that?"

The geese, I remembered the geese, for no reason, and the day one of our teachers—a nut-bag from Romania—organized us to circle the field and charge, swinging baseball bats, tennis rackets, nets, rocks in a sock, hockey sticks, old shoes, anything we could find to kill one or two of the thirty-five Canadian geese that'd been grazing on the baseball field for a month. That creepy memory comes back to me once or twice a year still—the first truly cruel mob activity I was ever recruited for. Then, my happy thought: all thirty-five of them lift off and fly just above our heads, and that fool—who for all I knew may once have had to kill wild geese for his hungry family—was the only one with his baseball bat still swinging at them; each one of them honking as if outraged, insulted, stokes the evening air—I could feel the breeze off their wings—and in unison, they left our yard, left us, and didn't come back the next year.

Mac, who seemed a little impatient I hadn't answered him or admired his insight, said, "Remember? The Lord fucks the bride. It was a law. I don't know, maybe it's just a legend, maybe it goes all the way back to King Arthur and Storytime. Nobody's gonna be telling *us* any of the kinky sides to those stories. But in America, the Lord becomes the Slave-Master and anybody growing up with or descended from somebody who grew up with a chain around his neck might try to do anything to keep The Master away from his family. So, I wonder if Red Cap is just so used to telling that story and talking to folks who recognize his right, even in the sense of a race memory, to protect his family, the right to keep his daughter and the gene pool free from the white man's taint. What do you think?"

The ducks had alighted on the opposite bank. Reeds were swaying. I could hear the booming megaphone from the tent, and when I looked, I thought I saw Red Cap himself slip through a flap in the tent, but I don't know, it could have been anyone.

"So, you think it was an act to protect...that got passed down... and became a pattern of...behavior? An almost understood... what?...A right?"

"I think I read about it in Engels, believe it or not. It's an anthropological trait. The slave-and-master relationship has its accommodations. It may have been revenge at some point, but really I think it was an act of survival."

"Oh! Oh, yeah, I see. I see what you're driving at. And Engels, well. Wow. Hmm. I don't know."

"What do you think?"

"Well, I can tell you what I *don't* think. I don't think you and old Commie Engels know what the fuck you're talking about. I think old Red Cap just told us he did *not* abuse his daughter, and maybe he thought we already had a low enough opinion of him so he might as well go ahead and rub our noses in it. A bunch of white boys with nothing better to do than listen to bullshit. I think he already knew he was suspected of doing god-knows-what around a place like this, so we better be keeping an eye on him before he pilfers the silverware. Might as well shit all over us with one of these bigger-than-life scandals, since there wasn't anybody in that crowd who was going to question a thing he said. He knew right from the start that a pack of high school innocents like us would hang on his every word, and we could even hold him up to the light in all his grit against any of our so much more sophisticated stuffed shirt authority figures and he'll come out on top. So, why not give us a taste of what we might have been thinking about in the first place? Yeah, he knew who we were alright, and he played us pretty well, I'd say. So, you and Engels can go snort up a line of coke and make all the wise comparisons your own distance from reality will allow, but the more you drag in King Arthur and his filthy knights, the more your class consciousness shrivels into a dream world, and your petty prejudices get equated with DNA vendettas that can't hold up in the face of pure ego, plain and simple, spitting in your own fucking face..."

I think it was about halfway through this little speech of mine that your Dad started throwing things at me—pinecones and pebbles and waving twigs at my head, until he finally just covered his ears and sat down on the ground, head swinging back and forth, so that when I did finally stop, he was whispering, "...please, please, please, Mr. Moses, I'm sorry, but will you *please* shut the fuck up...?"

More Later, Bobby
~Mose

3.

MY FATHER WAS a "sonofabitch" or so his biographers have reported on his later years: vicious to us his family and to anyone who had the temerity to interview him or seek his opinion on other American poets. I didn't spend many years with him, but I have a different memory; during that summer I turned thirteen, for instance, he was if anything befuddled, almost willfully confused, baffled by the universe of the worldly Seventies—and kind to a fault. I got away with most anything I wanted. I never tried the marijuana he left lying around in the small lunchbox rescued from his Fifties childhood, bearing the "heroic figure" of Hopalong Cassidy. He allowed that "getting hopped up on Hoppy" couldn't do him any harm, but he didn't encourage me—in fact, pointedly said I should keep my "fucking hands off Hoppy." Which, of course, might have been an invitation, as later that summer when he left the keys to his Citroen on the counter, and let me know with a smirk I'd "better not take that beast for a drive." He seemed a little proud of me when he bailed me out of county jail.

I hung around him that summer, but always went home to my mom's house—"Seven-Seventy-Seven," he used to call it; he still owned it—where I always felt I had to fight for floor space; there were so many people coming and going, especially after the bars closed when she got off work. She didn't smoke or drink, but when she locked up at the *Little Friend*, a tavern downtown on Sea Street, it was two in the morning and she was wide awake; so, she invited the "Night People" to sit around her dining room table. These were some very odd characters—shy introverts who slept by day and awakened to catch the late afternoon light. They painted or composed musical scores, and one guy worked out all numeric possibilities in his perfectly clean deck of cards. She would sit up with them until she got tired, her long fingers waving beside her head when it was getting near time. She'd be finishing a thought, opposing the Nietzschean painter's faith in the capacity of men to function without ideas, and suddenly grow frustrated with her own sentence, or shift into French, her native language, then wave that hand somewhat like shooing mosquitoes. Which didn't mean she wanted everyone to leave, she would say, but it did mean she had had enough of words and the shooing was directed toward endlessness itself, the reverberations of distraction and argument. And there they might be, three or four of the gangliest, nerdiest fellows in our little town, sitting each in his remote inward concentration around the big oak table until they became embarrassed by their own silences, and waddled out into a predawn haze.

I remember when they brought that table home. I was probably five or six, and a street cat had shown up one day, literally throwing his body against the front door, which my father opened thinking someone had knocked. It was a bull's-eye tabby, he said, gray with that black target etched on each side. A full-grown cat, but skinny, and it responded happily to a bowl of milk he set down. The cat stayed for months, until one day he disappeared. He was gone two weeks before they realized they missed having a strong male cat around, enough that they decided to get another. They would have preferred if he just came home, or if someone responded to the many beautifully designed posters in my mother's elegant penmanship, with cat faces she encouraged me to draw with bright crayons. She used plastic push pins to hang them up on telephone poles. One afternoon I watched a man in jogging tights and a turquoise t-shirt stop to ask if she needed help. She was stretching her long bare arms as high as she could. I was just a kid, but I instantly worried why my mom would need help pushing a pin. He was, I see now, not interested in the cat at all, but he read the flourish that said, "...answers to 'Larry'." Mom's accent always stressed the second syllable when calling the kitty to his dish, and many emphatic words came out *en français. 'LarrEE!'*

"Really?" the guy asked, "You got a cat to answer to its name?"

"No," she said, "Moe and Cur*lee* work *just* as well."

AT THE HUMANE SOCIETY, they both felt sympathetic toward an old, toothless Persian whose croak when they got him home inspired little affection. They set him up on the couch, along the top of which Mom draped a blanket she used to wrap me in when I was an infant. She fed him well, but he was so thin and uncomfortable, petting made him more miserable. Then Larry came back, throwing himself at the door again. The problem now was they needed another couch so that each cat could have one, and they wound up at a yard sale where they did find a couch, but also the big oak table. My father was certain some group of political organizers had sat at it and hammered out plans for demonstrations against the War, or organized Coops and farmers' markets before someone hauled the table away from the big city.

"See that gouge, Bobby?"

"Yeah?"

Maybe he thought I had slipped up whittling. He had shown me a few tricks he learned at Boy Scout camp, and he thought I should try, but I got bored pretty fast. He even purchased a... as he preferred to call it... a Bowie Knife for me to have a crack at putting a fine point on some rotten old stick. But I lost the knife.

"Well, I'm reasonably certain that's where one of the Marxists who hoisted too much rotgut got into it over political theory and jammed a steak knife right into this table. What do *you* think?"

I might have smiled a little, but I went back to eating his sticky linguini. However he'd invent its past, the work he wanted to see done at that table never really did take place, since they split up two years later. The table still wobbled because he never figured out how to screw the top onto the base properly. As she got up to say goodnight to the "Night People," the table always tilted dangerously, threatening for a moment a coffee mug, its steam shuddering upward.

4.

WHEN I WAS SEVEN, my father took us to live in Paris for the year of his first Fulbright, a place I'd read about in Victor Hugo and Alexander Dumas thanks to Dad constantly pushing their books on me. I guess he had a long-range plan. As soon as we arrived, he made sure to take me around to every museum; we spent days in the Louvre. Now so many years later I realize why my mother never returned to France, her birthplace, to her family, and why instead she chose to remain in the same little town where my father lived. (Well, "lived" only in the sense that he maintained a mailbox and a tiny monk's cell of an office above the novelty/hardware store. It had been his so-called studio, but after they split up at the end of our Fulbright year, he crammed his whole life of papers and books in that tiny space. It was his storage room for the five years he was teaching in Albuquerque. His landlord who ran the novelty store got a regular check in the mail and didn't complain. When Mac did return, it was his squat, as he liked to call it—right in the middle of downtown Sea Street, where tourists and bars collided. I never understood the novelty store's attraction for tourists, because it was haunted as well by local Vets who came into town to stock up on kerosene, batteries, and the 'sundries' his landlord hoarded while casting a morose eye as both the Vets and the sunburned tourist kids moped through the aisles. Down from the hills, the Vets creaked along Sea Street in beater pickups; they rumbled out of well-fortified homesteads miles away from town. He had an 'office-slash-apartment' with a bathroom down the hall, on the top floor, with a view of Admiralty Inlet that would bring an artist's heart to his throat. At least it always did for this artist—my craving to capture it and lay it out upon a canvas was that stirring.) After they divorced she stayed in that town and not until late in life, did she leave America to see Paris again. As I got older, I often wondered why. When I began to travel or as a teenager when I spent fewer and fewer nights with her, I began to think of her as a victim of inertia or call it habit—the steady contact with friends, the routine of our town. But now I see it was in fact only for me—only for me that she spent so much of her life in this foreign place, only because I was born here, because my father, who she believed would eventually return to town for good, wanted to "at least see my own kid every coupla days." It never occurred to me that he could live just about anywhere else and so could I, or that I could have grown up in Paris, had Parisians for cousins and friends.

But it did recently, while I was in Paris and walked past my old *L'Ecole* where *mon mere* had carefully enrolled me for the year of the Fulbright. School had just let out onto the streets of Montmartre. A tourist this time, and unnoticed by all, I heard a little boy about to climb into the back seat of his father's car where it was parked along *Rue Lepine. "Bonjour, Cretien,"* and receiving no reply from little Cretien who was also, his hand in one or another of his parents', about to board his own family's car, he called out again just a little more desperately I thought, *"a bonjour, bonjour, Cretien,"* with this time a sweet impish grin. Cretien's parents, a bit less sentimental than a spectator like me, don't so much as smile at the cuteness of it all. *Maman* has already slipped behind the Peugeot's wheel, and revs the engine, but Papa buckles the little boy in, his face half-turned, and sends a telepathic giggle to the other boy's parents, a pair of gigantic claws scrambling along beside the boy to the cobbled parking area. *Papa's* eyebrows risen show he and *Maman* are humbled and honored acolytes in this daily ritual of the boys' farewells.

WHEN WE LIVED THERE, my father held a grant to research the poet Rimbaud for one year, and later volunteered to lecture. It was a chance for my mother to see her family again, and—very occasionally—exhibit the product, me, of all those years she'd lived in the United States. I don't remember my grandmother apart from a green sweater and thick gray hair, but she did live in Montmartre and my mother took me to visit once or twice a week that year. My mother never took her hand off me, touching my hair in an unusually preoccupied manner, squeezing too intensely my shoulder as she stood next to me to say goodbye at *chez grand-mère*. I don't recall any of their conversations, just that my mother seated me next to her on a velour couch and insisted I not walk around. When we strolled down the hill—always during a half-hour break from *L'Ecole*—I could see my grandmother's bony face looking at us through the glass doors that led onto an exceedingly small balcony with cast-iron railings. Although her face gave me no hint of her feelings at our departure, the way she moved her fingertips to her lips, then held them against the inside of the glass made me think she was a prisoner or at the least incapable of leaving that tiny flat.

As I said, my mother returned to France in her later years, and sometimes I accompanied her. She came to visit her brothers, nieces, and nephews and me, besides visiting, to resume my passion for French and French museums. My interest in art began the year they enrolled me in the little Atelier at the foot of Montmartre. My career now is certainly ludicrous compared to well-known artists, but I sell enough of my work to live comfortably. It was on one of these trips that I began to paint my grandmother framed by the glass doors, her hand gesturing. I wanted to capture that elusive half-smile that gave away nothing. My uncle came into the studio where I was flummoxed for the right mix of colors to contrast her thin face in slight afternoon shadow with her sweater.

"Olive," he offered. "That's what that sweater was. It was her most formal and she saved it to wear for you."

He was older than my mother and I knew his memory might be faulty, but I asked him anyway if he could tell me why my mother was so possessive of me back then, why she never let me get too close to *grand-mère* or be alone with her; why for that matter our visits were timed to take place during the brief periods I had off from school and why she would always use the school schedule to inform her mother we had to go. He studied the painting some more. I knew I didn't have the shading on the left side of her face right, but he wasn't looking as critically as I might have.

"I remember that railing," he said. "You've done it perfectly. The scrollwork was just that way."

He looked up, his hands dancing the shapes in iron along the air and smiling at me. Then he stopped, held his right wrist.

"When your mother was eight, the rest of us had moved out, had jobs, or were in school. Marie was married already, I think. Our mother had just given birth to Cecile."

"My aunt Cecile?"

He asked if I was ready to take a break and offered to tell me 'the whole story' at the nearby café which would be relatively quiet since it was early afternoon, and we could sit outside not far from the Seine. My uncle, Auguste, was at that time in his eighties, spry and tall. His grace of movement was that of a once-renowned athlete. Yet I didn't want to tire him. I offered to meet him some other time when it might be more convenient, but he told me to clean my brushes, lock up the studio and meet him at the café.

"I can't talk about her here, Robert, not with this likeness you've made. I remember that gesture of hers quite well from whenever my children and I—well, your cousins, *Luc et Marisal*—would pull away from the little curb where I always parked. I didn't like to look up at her there, but they would wave and wave until they could tell me her sweater in the distance was like an olive in a martini."

WE WERE SITTING under the heater in that outdoor café on the *Rue de Trois Ponte,* but my hands were cold as they often are when unoccupied with sketching or painting. Even when I practice my art out of doors in late fall, I find I am warm to my fingertips. I don't know what to attribute it to but desire—to my true belief. I have this one art to consume me in its obsessive way, as if an obnoxious party trick, through the warehouse of my veins, down to my fingertips. Which themselves seem barely to have anything to do with guiding the brush or pencil but are controlled without reasoning. My brain is my hand, my hand my brain.

But this afternoon I am not drawing or painting, and my fingers are somewhat cold, though I wrap them about the glass of *Vin Chaud* which I have not yet sipped. Uncle Auguste knows that I rarely drink any longer, and then only to relieve duress. Yet he has insisted I accompany him and ordered us both a glass of hot wine. My fingers around the glass, gray I think is close to their color, skin roughened by time and the tools. Across the bridge is the ruined shard of *Notre Dame de Paris* which I have attempted to sketch many times with no real luck.

"SO," SAYS MY UNCLE. Now that he is ready, I'm not quite sure I want to know, and his one word tells me he thinks the story has been worth waiting for. Of course, his ordering the wine tells me he thinks I'm in for a shock.

"I'll just blurt it out, okay? Because you really ought to know that your mother had a good reason to distrust your grandmother and it started when she was a little girl.

"I suppose all of this is third-hand information. I was away in the Czech Republic when it happened. I was fighting forest fires that summer, too. But that's neither here nor there."

"Wait, you were a firefighter in the Czech forest as well as in Paris? I didn't know you fought forest fires over here too. When did you go to work on the Arson Squad? Was it after that?"

"No, before. I stopped for two years and was smoke-jumping—that's what we called what I did America—that summer, you know when. How old were you then?"

"That summer? That's when I was thirteen."

"Ah. Well, after that I returned to the arson work."

He was full of surprises. I knew him through my entire youth and most of my adulthood and still, his résumé took new turns.

"But, let me tell you," taking a sip from his wine. "Okay. Your mother distrusted your grandmother, do we understand?"

"Of course. That was perfectly obvious whenever she took me there. I was little, not stupid."

"No, of course not."

He couldn't look at me as he began then. Instead, he gazed across the bridge toward *Notre Dame.*

"One day that summer when your mother was eight, she was standing on that wide veranda we had in the old house."

Some talkative American women at the next table began to laugh about something and he stopped, not I hoped because he'd lost his train of thought.

"Wait. Let me back up a little. I need to tell you about your grandfather. You never met him, did you?"

I had absolutely no memory of my grandfather, although from time to time my mother would quote things her father always used to say.

"He was a composer, although not a wildly successful one, I'm afraid. He did manage to sell several of his pieces and, if you recall, his symphony was performed here in Paris two years ago. But he did indeed work at his music for days at a time, alone, in a room with the door closed and not to be opened except by him from inside with the pianos, where his composition drafts were strewn about on the floor. He was a quiet man. He smiled as if he were a cat while standing perfectly still. Tall and thin as a pipe, he never hugged us or her as I remember. At least I cannot imagine, when I think of them, ever hugging or when I have looked at the old photographs, ever showing affection to one another in our presence. My mother, though, did have a baby that winter, Cecile, and soon thereafter my father retreated to his room to compose, he said, a celebratory 'Sonata to Newly Born.' And that summer when the baby was six months old and your mother was eight is when my mother, I think, was feeling the stress more than she ever had. And let me remind you that she had already raised quite a handful of us—five to be precise and obviously, many years apart, all of us, in age."

"Auguste, how old was my grandmother when Cecile was born?"

"Cecile, yes, she was the baby girl who left the family, and you never heard her story before she came to your town, none of us knew everything about what happened to her. Well, let me tell you as much of the story as I know, and it might explain why you didn't meet her sooner. My mother's stress in raising this baby was so great, *Robert*, that she had a mental breakdown. And on a ridiculously hot summer evening, she came out onto the veranda with the screaming baby wrapped quite tightly in a blue blanket. Yes, blue. I am sure of it, at least so I was told by Solange. Your mother, the little girl then, and Solange were already on the veranda. Solange was our neighbor. She was twenty-four. My mother, who was thirty-six then, by the way, came up to them, holding the baby and she had tears in her eyes. Solange asked if she could help. Could she try holding the baby for a while? My mother said no—indeed, this was her lot in life, her small skill, to take care of children. No, she could not compose or make great art, but this child was certainly a symbol, such a clear, vibrant, throbbing, screaming symbol of his love, of *his* love for her. When I asked her, Solange said she couldn't tell if my mother was being sarcastic or if she really did worship my father so much that she believed totally in what she was saying. Solange did say, though, that her voice was rising as she spoke this. She was in fact screaming the word 'love' to Solange and then she took three steps backward and began to rock the child so fiercely, savagely even, her eyes wide, that Solange stood up and came toward her very slowly. It was then my mother rushed over to the railing—very much like the one you painted so well, Bobby—and told Solange to stay where she was. She held the baby up higher now; she was threatening to fling our little sister from that height, down onto the street. Solange remained calm. Your mother was standing behind Solange, standing still, not moving. Remember, *she* was a child.

"Solange spoke in a soothing voice and kept asking my mother to please let her hold the beautiful child. She told me she repeated that as often as she could, 'the beautiful child,' 'the lovely baby,' 'the innocent,' 'this newborn.' And yet she knew she would fail if she mentioned my father and how much he would be hurt by this... she did not know what to call what my mother might have been contemplating.

"My mother, after about fifteen minutes, became as if numb. Both she and the baby had stopped crying. She sat down on the floor of the veranda and allowed Solange to take the child from her arms. Your mother almost instantly took the baby Solange held out to her, and hurried away, off the veranda and out of the house."

5.

ONCE, EARLY IN that year, my father came home to our third-floor flat, his hat on with a bit of Parisian snow along the brim. He was carrying a small bundle of groceries, a baguette protruding past his shoulder, and he had that grin, his awkward toothy expression, when he spoke to my mother and me, both of us sitting on the flowered couch in the softened light of a reading lamp. I was just learning to sketch with pencil and had succeeded in getting the neighbor's dog to lie still on the plush rug. She was an old mutt. I forget her French name, but Butch was the name I gave her. I was sketching the curls of fur the way they hung from her wide neck, and she was sitting still until my father came in, so I was predisposed to look unfavorably at him. My mother who had been reading quietly for an hour or so, barely looked up when he brought in the cold air.

"Guess what?"

Butch hoisted her old gray body up, back legs weak, and toddled over to my father even though I lamely grabbed at her fly-tail fluff and shouted: *"Couchon! Merde!* Stay!" and my mother looked up, her finger on the line she was reading, "What?"

"Well, I've had an interesting day," and he set down the bag on the table beside the couch. Then began to take off his wet coat and hat but kept talking.

"I was walking aimlessly around in the Left Bank, and I've never been there before so I wanted to see every shop and get a good sense of the streets—you know, smell every smell. Basically, I was looking for a place to sit at a table and write for a while, but I also, more importantly, needed a bathroom bad. I did not want to just sit in any café, just so I could use the Gents, though. I wanted a table with a view. Mostly of the street and of people walking by. So, I figured that would come all in good time, but I *had* to pee. So, I was looking for a public facility out on the street. Anyway, I kept walking and walking and really had to pee like a racehorse..."

"Massimo, do you have to? All these details? Please, no."

"But wait. I came upon an art school, a college, and entered through the large gate, walked through a wide-open area thinking I was bound to find...what I was looking for here, and began to wander the hallways, through empty classrooms, art studios, upstairs and down, all the while thinking what if some official or a security person asks what am I doing here, who I am and so forth? I thought I'd tell them I was the guest lecturer in Poetry. That's about as far as I got. If they wanted to know whose class, I would have said I didn't know the professor's name.

"So, no one stopped me, and I finally did find the *L'Hommes.* Then I had to wend my way back out through various corridors, and this is when a white-haired gentleman greeted me, and we struck up a conversation. When he learned I was here on a Fulbright and researching Rimbaud, he wanted to know if I might, in fact, come talk to his classes.

"Anyway, long story short, he's asked me to give a series of lectures, my choice of topics, to his art students trying to acquire

English. He can't pay me—and I probably couldn't accept anyway with all the rules of the grant—but he's offered to give a full art course at the college to you, Bobby."

The dog did, finally, manage to slink away, toward the apartment door. It was time for her to go home for dinner.

BECAUSE I WAS a little fearful of being around college people, I stayed as close to him as I could. He would walk me to each workshop and class and present me to the teacher or the artists in the studio. And I attended his lectures, which began with a small group of listeners, but which grew steadily every week. These lectures several years later would lead to his well-known book of essays, *An Autopsy on American Poetry*. I don't know much about its reception or about reviews, but I think it's safe to say just from the title that his reputation for caustic criticism began here. At least as far as I know, it was his first book of critical essays and soon after, his books of poetry were published, his Rimbaud translation and some short pieces of fiction, all of which, according to him, the major hotshots couldn't wait to get their hands on "to shred and burn."

Since his audiences were primarily art students, he based his remarks on comparisons with artists, especially French artists. His theory of regionalism he applied to Monet, for instance; the world's leading Impressionist who created his own environment and observed continuously the play of beauty over his own ponds and lily pads. He insisted that if Monet had traveled to the extent other French artists of his day had, or earlier than he, Gauguin, for example—whose work my father found distasteful—then his art would have suffered and thus art, the study of beauty, would have never reached the stages of investigation mankind had achieved through Monet. Even as a kid I recognized the irony of his lectures in favor of staying in one's own region—"biome," he kept calling various places, as if he and his French audience knew what he was talking about—while he was living in what was obviously a foreign culture and one to which his own predilection for sarcasm, harsh criticism and manipulation could not hold a candle. Somehow, he applied his theories to contemporary poets in America who seemed to have lost interest in beauty as they perceived it where they lived, and who in his words, "pretended to find art while reading their cereal bowls, ashtrays and tatters of burnt newsprint."

QUITE APART FROM my father's authoritarian views on art and beauty, I've managed to formulate my own notions to the extent beauty has become a religious obsession. For a while, I taught art classes at the local community college. I was surprised most students were not adults. Before teaching there, I'd imagined community colleges were attended by people returning to school. From a career or the workforce, or a marriage, after child-rearing or to earn citizenship or learn the language or a skill for better employment. But many students, among those who could afford the time or credits to take a class like "Art," were either still in high school and floating between both institutions or had recently become high school graduates. They seemed like kids to me, and I was only twenty-five when I taught. Maybe they were so thrilled at being college students they registered for a class whose course description reminded them of grade school. Or the universal need of expression guided them to easels and brushes. Since I've always deluded myself, I am now prepared to recognize there might very well be no such need and artists are only ever talking to other artists. But I don't think that demonstrates that I've internalized an "art for art's sake" bias. We speak to the best minds, and, to get back to my point, that was not what I had in my Art class. Young people, teenagers still—they would spend so much "non-instructive time," when I hoped they would paint or draw or sculpt, talking in pseudo-intellectual loops. Few having read a book by a reputable philosopher, psychologist, or theologian, they rattled on, "solving," as we used to say self-deprecatingly, "the problems of the world."

Yet, to be honest, their topics occasionally drew me in. Questions of the Day: "Does a working-class man need a 'self?'" "Is interdependence a possibility in post-evolution society?" "How can there be pain *and* a Supreme Being?" Maybe they came to my studio directly from "Intro to Philosophy" or "Modern Ethical Problems." One day someone asked "How about you, Mr. Bacca? Do you think there's a God?" I'm never prepared for that question, but then again, I'm never asked my beliefs, rarely consulted even about my feelings.

When I answered, "I don't know..." Phillip Castro who did at least strike a pose at the easel, brush in hand, interrupted with a good debater response:

"Agnostic is the easy way as they say at church. It takes courage to believe or to disbelieve, doesn't it?"

He liked to needle, or attribute an offhand remark to any authority, some author he found on a webpage. He turned back to his easel and swiped a brave elliptical brush stroke.

"I don't know," I continued, "how to define Supreme Being. There's a standard definition that seems to define 'limitless,' 'all this and all that.' I don't like 'all powerful' or 'all just' because they seem superstitious. Also, I don't know if I want to define a Supreme Being as my opposite, or opposite all human community. I'm not agnostic, I'm areligious. The definition of god makes the Supreme Being an abstraction. 'Limitless, absolute, necessary.' Remove all the physical metaphors, the story of Christ, the mytho-history of the Jews, and God is Abstraction Itself, which presumably Socrates defined as the Highest Good. An abstraction no different from Beauty, which awaits the mind to acknowledge and replicate in another mind. What we call 'Art'."

6.

I DON'T KNOW anything about Mac's basis for criticism or how he launched his "autopsy" because I was, as pointed out above, a little kid—but also because poetry never interested me, and in fact, I've never read any of his poems. I'm certain my mother rarely read the things he wrote. But I do remember that she was incensed by some of his reviews, by their meanness, and one of their arguments is etched into my bad dreams. My parents would argue. I'm certain most couples argue over money or sex, but they argued over her belief that he was using his critical work to settle scores with poets who snubbed him. That he was shallow and unethical, were her accusations. This went on for some time in tones at once subdued and fierce, voices from the Parisian living room when they thought I was asleep. My mother would never have brought up these things if I were around because she knew how much I idolized him, and how I too hoped to be an intellectual who could scald the cultural soup of my generation. But one night I heard her reading to him pieces of some of his latest reviews.

"Massimo, how can you say things like this about other poets? Listen to this..."

"Now wait a minute, Natalie, that's just the way I go about making my point. It's not personal. I'm trying to read a poet's work objectively and I'm certain they appreciate having someone tell them why what they're doing isn't quite as strong as the blurb-writers keep blabbing about and..."

"Here. I'm going to read you a few things I found that I...really can't stand. I just don't see how you can be so mean to say this to anybody, or about anybody else's writing...Listen:

'Pablo Salimontez's' Bad Dodos *is a bad book. The so-called verse he's collected in this slim pastiche is missing any evidence of its ever having been emitted by a human mouth, let alone having origins from a human soul. These are both diatribes and catatonic nursery rhymes spawned by someone whose undisguised self-absorption gives rise to immoderate loathing of one's own species. These are poems that reek of clumsy foreplay and a history of personal trauma seeking a cure in an artform this pretense of a poet has never been anywhere near.*

'Here's an example:

Why do I, forever a joker,
see that crack-up on the dark back road
as the only symbol within Western Civ
to kill off and maim you and me?

'You may love this stuff, dear reader, but this critic finds it and the editors who promote it, the award-givers who applaud it, bookstores that display it, as well as those 'followers' who fork over their cash for it, as reprehensible as any fascist government's scheme to undermine culture itself where it abides in the oldest of artforms, poetry, which Bad Dodos *is not.'*

"That's horrible, Massimo! The poems can't be as bad as you say they are and even if they are no one deserves to be treated this way in public. How can you write like this? How? Tell me."

"Well, I do have a reputation to keep up, you know. I can't just give half-hearted praise like everybody else and slip in a few polite words to critique. That's just not the way I do things. You know that. I'm all in."

"What about this?

'It's not the MOST atrocious book I've ever read but this Formula for Baby Poets *by Maude Liptauer is one that no amount of revision could help one arrive anywhere close to adulthood.'"*

THEY SEPARATED AT the airport. Soon to divorce, they headed off in opposite directions when we landed at Kennedy. It was one of those moments. They stay with you, one or two scenes from the narrative of personal history. For me it was my mother holding tight to my hand and struggling to get me, seven years old, moving toward some other flight desk for a ticket back home, while I kept turning around to look at my poor little Pappy beside a duffle bag, waving at me and even making clown-like gestures, miming kisses, hugs. And that look on his face, that last time I would see him for a few years, seeing me change planes out of his life. I never forgot it.

He went to teach in the Southwest, in Albuquerque, and wrote to me often. My father never talked to me like I was a child, so his letters were written as though I could understand the twists and turns his life was taking; they were often obscure, irrational excuses for his prolonged hiatus from my life. Sometimes he just wrote about what was going on, but more often it was long essays about what I should be learning, how I should keep practicing the languages he'd gotten me started on—Latin, Classical Greek, Italian. French, he said was up to my mother, since he fully expected she and I would continue to speak it at home, even though in our little seaside town monolingual fishermen often pretended to be shocked—while others were a little affronted—to witness us converse at a café or waiting in line at the grocery store. They occasionally teased me: "You and your Momma do chat in that there Parleeviewfronchay, don't you, Pardner."

My Dad insisted I memorize long passages from the books he thought I should become familiar with, even if I already knew my career would not be a literary one. He'd say in his letters, "I know you're not going into the family business, but even painters need to build their art on a wide swath of culture, so this week I want you to memorize the first thirty lines of Virgil's *Aeneid*—and as written, in his Latin. Don't try to wicker out of it with some phony 'modrin' version either; make your own translation so you know what you're learning."

I guess it's a tribute to the force of his personality and a sign of our mutual commitment to my education, and a sign of my love for him, that I did in fact memorize the lines he demanded—*Arma Virumque cano*...and all that—and did make my own unartful translations, although it took several letters from him for each passage he assigned to get me to complete the tasks. Still, I didn't learn much from his letters about his life in New Mexico. I saw him once or twice on television being interviewed by the *McNeil-Lehar Report* because his nasty criticism had become controversial. He looked good, though a little grayer, more long-haired than ever, wore a tie—a thing I never saw him in before. After it was over it wasn't like I could run outside and tell my friends my Dad was on TV. They wouldn't get at all, of course, that he was on television performing his autopsy of very much alive contemporaries and accusing them of writing without conviction or heart and of making empty cerebral corpses rather than images of "their life and times and of the real world—the world beyond academia." There he was on the TV screen repeating such things, which was ironic considering he'd been a tenured professor his entire adult life, as the interviewer rightly pointed out. Asked if he saw himself as writing "dead poems," or ones that could suffer improvement by autopsy, he said, "No, no longer—mine have resurrected." His play on the word 'erect' went on for a few minutes before they cut the interview short and went off into commentary by way of some nemesis poet delivering the counterpunch, citing a few of his 'dicta' such as his rules to determine: "cause of death," "DNA or identity analysis," "stomach contents."

Although it's long past his death now, I've made it my business to find out what he was doing in those years. I wrote back to Moses. A brief description of an afternoon when they were in school did whet my appetite, but I wanted to know more. Needed more from him. So, we began a correspondence. Letters. Nobody does that anymore. And Moses who I don't believe used email or PM's or any other electronic means of communication, was an excellent letter-writer. I was terrible at it, responding with trivial notes to his lengthy descriptive stories. He finally got around to telling me how they left New England and how they eventually would lose touch with each other. I think it wasn't really until that summer, the only summer I got to spend with Mac, that Moses and he finally reconciled.

7.

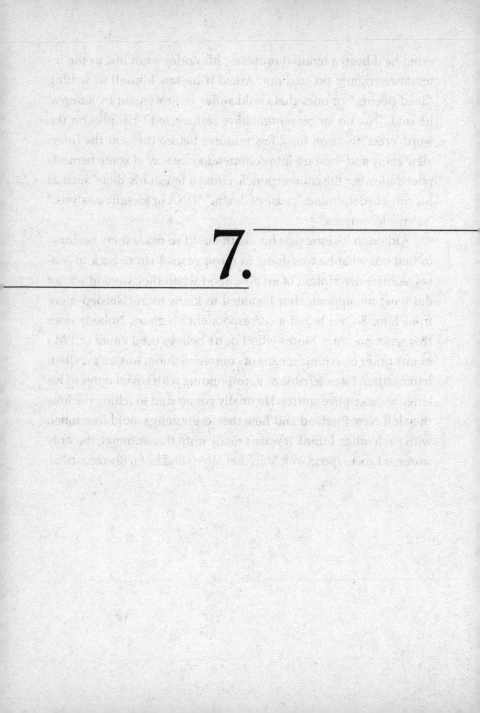

Dear Bobby,

I'M SORRY I haven't written back before this, but I've been reassessing somewhat my own history with Mac, and how that all brought me to where I am today. Also, I must admit, my friend, I was a little taken aback by your calling me 'Mentor.' That's a good one, Bobby! I don't know what I did or said back in the day to earn such a title, but I thank you for bestowing it. You're a gentleman and a scholar, as we used to say. But it ain't true! To my way of thinking, from the little you've told me and what Mac told me, you've made your own way, and you didn't need help or advice. So, let's not exaggerate. I'm happy to be called your old friend (well, maybe not "old" all the time!). Besides, if you ever do want my opinion on anything that's pertinent, that I'm familiar with, I'm more than happy to let you know what I think. But you know that already. I must admit, though, I do like the sound of that—"Mentor." Of course, it comes up a lot in the University. Luckily, I was never asked to mentor any colleagues (hate how classic forms melt into verbs). What a pain in the ass that would have been.

Also, you asked if I could fill you in on certain parts of Mac's life. Well, there again, I'm no expert. In fact, we were not in such close contact after high school for a few years. We went to different colleges in Boston, and we'd hang out when we could. One day close to the end of senior year, we were sitting around, and probably—my guess because it was a daily practice—smoking dope, and the mail arrived with a letter from the Creative Writing department at the University of Iowa. Mac had earlier pitched it as the place to be, among all the avid writing circles and "poets strong" as he called those one or two he admired and others he could tolerate. He praised the University library program, so I found the application, and soon we were both headed for post-graduate bliss among the cornfields.

Of course, we hitchhiked. I'll spare you the details. It's enough that he learned a skinny white guy like Mac should never stand next to a six-foot-four black man and hope for a ride. One morning we woke up in the dewy grass at a rest stop and I lifted one eye past the edge of the sleeping bag; I saw a KKK tattoo on the back of the hand of what turned out to be the local groundskeeper reaching down for a discarded coffee cup. I stayed as deep in the bag as I could until I thought he moved along to cleaning toilets. When we arrived, the librarian did all she could do to suppress her shock to learn *I* was the new Library Sciences fellow. Your Dad quickly settled in right away and started making enemies.

He was, of course, his critical—or, as he said—his "universally honest" self during any and every workshop session. I heard about those "discussions" later; I wasn't in the writing program. Another thing he did which seemed to infuriate all but the visiting, i.e., "temporary poets," as he referred to them, was to graffiti walls and sidewalks with "MASSIMO!!!" in bright blue chalk. When his name dripped down the walls after the first rain or got hosed off the sidewalk, he made little cards and bookmarks (which I strongly refused to distribute in the library) that read "Who Is M.M. Bacca?"

I managed to score a financial aid package that included working several hours a week at the library. Stacking, sorting, and manning the checkout desk where I happily got to read. That's where I met Eileen, the Assistant Librarian. Your Dad didn't know anything about her, and you won't learn much about him from my telling you Eileen's tale of woe, but I'll tell it anyway. In fact, I suppose you *could* learn something about him just by the fact I instinctively kept knowledge of Eileen hidden from him. I didn't want him sneering, for instance, if I were to tell him that before she came to Iowa, she was a nun.

She started in the nunnery at a pretty young age—I don't think they call it a "nunnery" anymore. Must be my Medieval inclinations coming out. So, when she left the Convent, she was still young and had a degree in Botany. She had a little teaching experience, so the first place she went looking for a job was in the science department at the nearest high school in Iowa City. She met a guy who turned out to have been an ex-priest. Well, wait a minute: he had stopped being, if you can do that, a priest before they met, so I guess he was an ex-priest for quite some time. But I digress. I'll come back to him. Let me tell you a little about her short teaching career, what she told me about it, anyway. Which really only amounted to the main event, the thing that brought her to the point of getting out of that life.

Eileen and I would take coffee breaks and occasionally we'd have a beer after work. She told me all this stuff about her life, but you know what, Bobby? She was a little like your Poppa in that she never once asked about my own damn self. I guess that was okay because I really don't like the whole idea of having to talk about yours truly, but now I look back on it, it feels rude that somebody you sat with and heard various accounts of her personal history, didn't seem to have the slightest interest in your own life. I guess she was maybe taking advantage of the chance to debrief finally after years of discipline in the "nunnery" followed by enforcing discipline in the high school hallways and classrooms.

She was a first-year teacher but she wanted to transform the standard plant-life class into a writing-about-the-natural-world sort of a class. I know from experience she couldn't have had approval from whatever admin powers there were in her District. Not back then. Everything then was straight by the book, literally: stick with the textbook and keep your blinders on as you traverse the fauna and flora right in front of you. She decided she was going to make the land itself her lesson plan. So, she devised this lengthy reading list by writers of natural history who wrote about walking. Thoreau has an essay on the subject, Hazlitt does, Montaigne. She worked in Rachel Carson, and she brought in poems too. Of course, the Romantics were great walkers, and back then there were lots of poets writing about the natural world. To hear Mac complain about the classes and reading lists he got, you'd think no poet-naturalist ever traipsed through his precious "I-Oh-Way" Writing Program. He sure *did* like to complain, your Dad. Mostly he kept saying the poetry he and the "Vanishing Class" of poets were exposed to was written by a phalanx of academics, each of whom kept a personal chamois in a briefcase, ready at any moment to polish intrusive mud off a smudged wingtip.

I want you to know a bit about Eileen's efforts to have a life after the nun thing. At least I think that's what she had in mind when she told me the story of how she left her teaching career and decided assistant librarian was as close as she wanted to get to completing her academic aspirations.

To be honest, I called her Sister Joan half in jest. Eileen was her given name and Joan was the name she took on with the vows. Joan of Arc, in fact, was her model, she said. "What was it?" I had to ask, needling, "The hallucinations? Hey, Sister Joan, you wanna buy some Acid?" I think I got to know her over time because we both had a pretty good sense of humor. We, neither one of us had any difficulty laughing at ourselves. Now, Mac, on the other hand, at least back in the day, back in Iowa, had extraordinarily little sense of humor regarding the notorious Mr. B. and his inchoate reputation. He was all about...well, the metaphor of "making the team" comes to mind, but it wasn't like that exactly. More like he wanted to found his team, or his own personal school, be the coach and an expert at every position on the field.

Your Dad. Now that I'm telling you all this about him, it occurs to me you may not have known anything about his career-building and the solidity with which he entered the race as a heavy-weight poet and critic. Sorry, Bobby, if I'm unloading too much, but when I think of those days mostly, I'm remembering Eileen and what happened to her, and Mac was always off somewhere else drinking in the power juices of a startup celebrity.

So, Sister Joan made a long-range lesson plan for her Botany writing class. By long range I mean a plan that she concocted to lead them bit by bit toward making their own written record of the plant life, the terrain, the water supply, and soil types, weather, wind, and abundance, or lack of, sunlight as it all appeared right in front of them when she took them on the culminating field trip to observe just such things in the wild. The field trip, she said, involved oodles of permission forms all in quadruplicate which meant messing up the forms a few times and starting over. She hated all that, all that paperwork just for the sake of the Admin and for the appeasement of the insurance companies, and quite possibly she admitted too for the sense of security a few of the parents would feel when they signed off on the permission slips. She didn't know many parents. In fact, she flat out avoided meeting a parent should one have even approached her, or had she been called into the Counselor's office for an early morning session with one or sometimes both parents who were at the end of their ropes as to how to deal with kids in her first period who couldn't get out of bed in the morning. She failed them despite encouraging them to get more sleep at night because she knew that's what the Admin folk expected her to do. But she was certain this long-range assignment was getting to kids who never had responded to schoolwork and who didn't think they were learning anything that had to do with their lives. One day, she took them out of the school in a bus and plopped them down on a wild trail along a lake where they could hear nothing but October leaves falling and drifting into the water, and the mournful call from a V of geese skating the treetops.

So, anyway, she made those kids walk the trails in pairs which each had an old-school tape recorder. They were to talk into it about what they were seeing all around them, as she'd trained them to do when they had to observe the fauna and flora around the school building and as they already had examples of in Dorothy Wordsworth and people like that. After about half an hour of her walking around on the trail and checking how they were doing, she heard a loud splash. She looked across the lake, through the branches thick with trees, toward a flat vertical rock face and one boy splashing around, yelping like a football hero and another boy up top on the rock ledge. She yelled, "Hey! You! You stay right there!" And I guess he did. The boy in the water started to climb out and she yelled at the top of her lungs, "All right, Everybody, back in the bus! Field Trip's over!" Apparently, it was about two hours ahead of the planned return trip. Some of the kids started to grouse about that, but she just referred them to the big wet kid shivering at the back of the bus.

Of course, now she had all kinds of more paperwork to fill out in the form of discipline referrals. She turned all this into the vice principal who was the main disciplinarian. The next day she got called into the Principal's office. She was a first-year teacher and everything she did was scrutinized. Well, it didn't have to be, but it was. She said it might have been different if she was a man, or a more imposing Science teacher, or Coached football. Of course, nothing like this would have happened if she had been one of those. No such field trip, no reading, writing, or talk about the natural world would have taken place. There was also a meeting with the Vice and the boy-who-jumped-in-the-lake's Dad. Her impression was this was a Dad who gave a lot of money to the athletic department. The VP, she said, was pretty palsy with the Dad and the long and short of it was the kid just had to say he was sorry—which he did without being prodded even. He just couldn't resist the impulse to jump into the water. His Dad was like "Boys will be boys," and VP just grinned along with Dad while she sat there, she said, a little stone-faced and flabbergasted they didn't throw the book at this kid. She couldn't believe they let him get away with endangering himself not to mention destroying the whole field trip, tossing her beautiful lesson plan into some unrecoverable flummox. Basically, she felt the undermining of her authority let alone professionalism was thoroughly confirmed in that meeting and decided to talk to the Principal about a stricter punishment. What she got out of the Principal, though, was like "lemme see this big lesson plan, and I'll let you know what I think...." As if she *were* somehow to blame for taking these kids to a lake where they could have injured themselves instead of having them sit at those beautiful desks and pretend they knew about the real world. (I did mention to her she was lucky they didn't flat out fire her.) She kept waiting for the Principal to talk to her. Meanwhile, classes went on, the kid who jumped in the lake never got more than a hand slap, and she got weary of teaching by rote. She didn't hear a thing until one day in a

Faculty meeting, the kind of thing that takes place after school, and teachers listen to the crankiest of them complain about stuff they could just take care of on their own if they bothered to try. She sat there and took the remarks by the Principal with a grain of salt until he said, "I'd like to acknowledge someone sitting here who lately showed me a plan for learning I think we all can benefit from. I'd like her to stand and take a bow. Miss Bowdoin? Would you please stand?" She said she raised her hand to wave at the other teachers and half-stood, then sat down quickly, as the Principal went on and on about the plan she left on his desk. He praised it and her to the skies but didn't say a word about the fiasco at the bus and the field trip, or about the kid in the meeting with a parent who thought she should just let it slide because boys will be boys. She told me that while the Principal praised her in front of her coworkers for doing what she considered to be her job, she felt embarrassed to be singled out and belittled and patronized, to have been ignored as a professional and decided during that meeting to quit teaching at the earliest possible occasion. She also told me she knew she was lucky they tried to praise her instead of firing her. In fact, she finally had to admit that her ideas of teaching kids were incompatible with institutional education, that she really had placed those kids in a dangerous situation without her realizing it, that it was dangerous because they had impulses, those teenage boys, that she just wasn't prepared for.

At the end of Spring Break, she didn't come back. Got lots of calls she didn't answer, and one or two nasty letters from the Principal and Union people. She took a job with the County. They needed someone to identify plants that fell under the axe when construction projects require an EIS. Do you know what that is, Bobby? I call it Obfuscation Palaver. In this case, it means Environmental Impact Statement, which is just more obfuscating for "how much can we fuck it up before we can't afford the fine?" Her new job required her to ride around the county and determine where endangered plants were. Needless to say, it was a losing proposition—for the plants. But at least she didn't have to put up with the kind of "Boys Will be Boys" mentality the schools showed her. A different kind, but still, she got to work on her own most of the time.

On one of these jobs, she met the man who had once been a priest in Florida, so this was a big deal. He wanted to have certain plants on his property protected from a developer who was crushing everything in sight and brought heavy-duty machinery right up to his property line. The upshot is they got along pretty well, and she married him.

I guess it's not too uncommon, these marriages between ex-nuns and ex-priests. Sister Joan told me she had dated for a couple of years and found she didn't have much to say to people who didn't know a thing about what she had been through. Both, in fact, left their various vows and orders when they were still young adults, but they started in on the religious training when they were teenagers. She said the thing is, about that kind of life, you give up your will. So, when you start complaining about one of your "superiors" who maybe is an asshole, it's a lot harder to remember that you gave up your will, willingly, when you took this thing called the Vow of Obedience. I guess they all do that. Give up the will. Give up money. And, of course, the big one—give up sex. She told me she was over blushing about it, and she was glad to get enough of a will she *could* have sex, and that for the both of them, it was their first time. First time! Having sex with a nun for him, and with a priest for her. Jesus! I don't know how they did it all those years without it.

Anyway, she did say the hard part was learning that they now *did* have a Will. That for the both of them, they fell too easily under somebody else's power of command. That they had to learn to...

well...disobey, I guess. She said they became politically active. Did a lot of marches, that sort of thing, but that they still went to church together, still followed the rules. AND—her husband was our philosophy teacher, Mac's and mine. We took the class he offered, which was basically a spinoff of Aquinian theology; Sister Joan told me he was offering it, so I told Mac and I think he treated it more like a joke than anything else. He called the prof the Pope of the Plains and the Vicar of Iowa, and sometimes the Holly Roller from Minneola.

Mac, as you know, was always quite confrontational. Even when it was smarter not to be. Once, back in Boston, after we got those acceptance letters from the University of Iowa, we went to a bar where his Mom worked as a cocktail waitress. She seemed a little unnerved to see us sitting at her table. She didn't know me, and it was highly unusual for a black man and a white man to walk into a place like that, together, in that neighborhood, at all. But she tried to treat the whole situation as if it was almost normal.

"Penny. Okay? Just like it says on the name tag. A name, not a tip suggestion," was the first thing she said to me after we sat at one of her tables. I didn't quite know what to think. Mac didn't prepare me for meeting his Mom. Not only was she as straightforward as she sounds, but she was beautiful. I mean a really striking beauty! And standing in the middle of this crackpot cocktail lounge, dark and gloomy, with a legitimate Lounge Lizard half-heartedly crooning some morose lyrics through what sounded like rug fibers in his throat, she held a tray and wore a short sequined skirt with legs I refused to look at (—wait a minute, I'm talking about your grandmother. Sorry, but those were my thoughts meeting her that one and only time. She died before you were born, Bobby. So, I'm not interfering with any memory you have of a sweet white-haired old lady).

"Okay, okay. I'm Moses," and I held out my hand.

"You're with this bum you can't be all bad," a thumb towards Mac. "Okay, boys, I ain't got all night here. Tell me what you want. Drinks on me."

"No, Ma, I got money. I can pay."

"Fuck that. You're my kid."

And like that for a while, back and forth. Eventually, she brought us two beers.

"I gotta make the rounds. I'll be back."

We were at a table beside a pretty filthy window that looked out on the Neponset River, the streetlights on its other bank distant and cold, the current more a presence than a movement we could actually see down there, where I assumed some more-or-less healthy pilings were holding us and the whole place up off its drift and silt.

"Cheers," says your Dad and lifts a bottle of Knickerbocker.

"That's really your Mom? Wow. You ever see your Dad?"

"He's off in some war somewhere. Gone for years. See those guys over there? Wait! Don't look like you're looking. Just be casual."

"Yeah, I saw them when we came in. Guy with the thin hair looks like the boss. The other two are porkers. I hope they're not eating here. It looks like they throw their food."

"Well, no. They won't eat. He won't let them. Maybe they can have a Coke or something while they're here, but that's about it. Tight leash."

"How do you know these guys?"

"We grew up in the same neighborhood. In fact, my street connected to the boulevard which it didn't take me too long to figure out led to the bus system that took me to the subway and into the big city. I hopped on any time I wanted. Those guys, on the other hand, lived about two blocks over, on a street parallel to mine, but dead-end. They never came up my way to get on a bus to go downtown. They had too much going on I think on their block. Well, on several blocks for about five square miles. I used to see them roaming around dragging chains and swinging baseball bats. They didn't make a good impression, I can tell you that. They used to patrol the Projects. You know where the Projects are? Right down the street from my old house. It used to be a school. In fact, the Old Lady went there."

"What? What old lady you talking about?"

"Penny. She went there. Dropped out by Third Grade, but she went there. And then they turned it into this monster Housing Development, The Projects. So, anyway, they patrolled it. The street it was on connected to my street, so I had to walk through there when I came home from school, you know? Also, when she sent me to the *dry* cleaners."

He gave me this look, like for emphasis across the table. His eyebrows rose up, a little smirk. You know the way he could look at you? When you were supposed to guess what he was thinking? I couldn't for the life of me guess right then, but his face, against that dark neon background, and his shrimpy little voice trying to not shout over the croaking guy on stage, made me think he had something going on that, to him, was meant to increase, or widen and deepen, the legend of the soon-to-be-great Mac Bacca.

"Yeah. I get it. The dry cleaners. So?"

"The *Dry* Cleaners, man? You know, behind the curtain? Man with a hat on? Sits at a card table and keeps a little radio going for the races? Not a single fucking thing ever got dry cleaned in that place. Except money. He just took numbers. You know, back in the day—before the government took numbers for the Lottery. The Dry Cleaner guy was her Bookie—Peter the Bookie."

"Oh. I see."

"So, anyway, I always had to come walking through on that

street that opened onto The Projects and they had to patrol the area, so to speak. They stopped me a few times and wanted to know what was in the paper bag I was carrying. Well, usually she gave me some extra money for candy and shit like that. So, that's where that went. The Conrad Street Kids. Sounds like a stupid TV show now. But there they are, all growed up, or at least pretending to be. I remember one time watching them hassle a kid who was on roller skates and older and bigger than any of us. They kept pushing and rattling him till he fell over in the broken glass and cried like a little bitch because they wouldn't stop kicking him."

He looked over at the table now and made it perfectly obvious that he was looking at them. They were only two tables away and they were talking to his Mom, to Penny. The way the three meatballs were talking to her was loud, although we couldn't tell exactly what they wanted. Then we heard, "Oh, come on, Honey. Pretty please? Sit on my face?" That's when the Boss seemed to get a little testy. Told whichever one it was to tone it down, and looked up at Penny and apologized, slipping a twenty into her apron and put his icy-looking hand up her short skirt.

"Come on, let's go over and say 'Hi,'" Mac said.

That's when Penny shuffled away from them and held up a hand. "I'll be right there, Maxie. I got a question for ya. Oh, oh, hey, will you look at this?"

She stopped at the empty table next to ours and began picking up some loose change.

"I'll be lucky if I find thirty-five cents in this mess. Look at this! Story of my life. Screwed again and didn't feel a thing!"

"Whad'ya wanna ask me, Ma?"

"Just a minute, just a minute. Look at this shit. Yeah. Hey, I *do* have a question for you, Maxie, and I want you to be honest with me now, okay, Honey?"

She was standing beside our table, one hand holding the cocktail tray and balancing the empties she'd scooped off that thirty-five-cent table.

"Yeah?"

"You got a girlfriend, right?"

"Ma. *What* do you want to know? Why are you asking me a question like that? Come on."

"If you have a kid somewhere, you'd tell me, wouldn't you?"

"I don't have any children, Gramma. Don't worry about it."

I think he wasn't even anticipating you at that time. His life was all about poetry, if you know what I mean, and turning it into a full-fledged career.

"I don't have a girlfriend, okay? But, hey, that barfly over there in the black dress is startin' to look pretty good now that you mention it, Penny. What do you think? Pretty cute, no?"

She turns her head, and looks across the room, still balancing the tray, not even clinking a glass, then turns back and glares down at Mac.

"Yeah. Cute as a bucketful of Assholes. Are you two leaving soon? I think that might be wise, okay, Hon?"

I STARTED THIS letter a few days ago, then believe it or not I got a call from someone asking me to look at a decrepit manuscript the University library was receiving through a donor. That's all I do nowadays, bounce around from one old document to another. Keeps me off the streets, anyway. So, here I go again. Let me see, I wanted to tell you more about Eileen. The weird thing about talking to her was I knew things about our philosophy professor he never would have wanted me to know. That he was a priest, for one, but also that Eileen was telling me that his doubts—in the Faith department—were really driving him crazy. Really crazy, sometimes, she said. Like throwing things around the house in the middle of the night trying to scare off demons. So, when we sat in his class, I would often understand what he was saying about the philosophy of religion, for instance, in two different ways: the way he wanted, which was basic information regarding the historical proofs for the existence of The Deity, and the other way, that this was a struggle he was having with himself and God, if he thought anyone was listening to what was going on inside his mind. I guess I wished I didn't know these things Eileen was telling me about him and his doubts.

Mac got nasty with the Pope of the Plains just because he could, or because he thought the Pope was being pompous by the very act of *teaching* philosophy and relying on old theology class notes to teach what should otherwise have been a method for free expression and interpretation of the universe. Mac told me he had a trick to get on the professor's nerves. He'd interrupt any discussion, and particularly liked it when the professor was excited about something or was thinking out loud about any one of the various philosophical problems he wanted us to analyze. Mac would interrupt him with a question that was preceded by, "I don't understand..." or "Can you help me with this?" or "I'm having a little trouble with..." He loved the way the professor would drop his own line of reasoning and quite earnestly try to boil down the concept that Mac was pretending to puzzle over. This was really a ploy to begin a debate with the professor usually about the existence of a divine being or about the necessity of evil in the world or about fate versus free will. Topics he knew he could get the Pope of the Plains hopped up about, maybe even get him a little riled and downright angry.

Sometimes he just needled him, even if he didn't much care about the topic. Early on, for instance, when the Prof went through Aquinas on the Problem of Evil, your Dad went off:

"So, you're saying one of the defining qualities of God is

Goodness?"

"Yes, it seems to be."

"I see, but then what do you say, or I'm sorry, what does old *Aquino* say about how the Great One can be so Good when there's so much downright evil in the world? I mean, did he even know what evil was? He lived in a cloister or something, right?"

"Thomas Aquinas had an imagination as well as a sharply tuned critical intelligence, and I'm certain he knew what he meant by Evil, Mr. Bacca."

"Okay, professor. By the way, I know you don't mean to call me Evil Mr. Bacca, or anything. When you think about such things as the powers that be, especially as it is in the present, the kind of power even his sharply tuned critical intelligence could most likely never have imagined, throughout human history power has done little but wage war, create famine, sponsor murder, devastation, due to greed, and, back in his day, the horror of something called Divine Right—not to mention The Inquisition, and that was his Order, wasn't it, that held all those *auto da fa's*?—well my question is how can he say—or you, Professor—how can you say that God has to be Good? I mean don't you have to say there is no Good other than basically good people. You know, human decency, not just Good defined by Commandment. How it seems to me, anyway."

That's how it went pretty often, and the strange thing was I knew a bit too much about the Professor already having doubts of his own in contradiction to all that training, all that, well, I can't think of another word for it but "brainwashing." Must have been hard to conduct those classes with a brute like Mac in there.

But this is what I wanted to tell you—one day there was something different, something I'd never seen in Mac before. What may have started as him trying to get a rise out of the professor turned into him, Mac, opening up. That's the only way I know how to put it, really. It might have been the first time I witnessed your Dad in a public situation being really sincere, even passionate about something he believed in.

The Pope told us he'd been reading more and more Buddhist philosophy and could see a connection between some of the ideas and principles there and some of the Greeks, as well as Augustine and Duns Scotus among the early Christian philosophers. After he began explaining what he considered the basic tenets of Buddhist thought, Mac rolled out his tactical ploy: "I'm having a little trouble with...the ambiguity of it all..." or something of that ilk.

"Well, it *is* fairly simple. What's not to understand?"

"What I don't understand is the part about impermanence you mentioned."

"Yes, that seems to be a pretty basic concept for the Buddhists. I don't really see any difference between that and the famous Heraclitan line, but I'm still thinking it through. You know, the one about the wading or drifting away, into the same river twice?"

"Yeah, I get that, but what I don't understand, Professor, is how you can say there's a universe of impermanence."

"What do you mean?"

"A universe of—you know, the concept itself is surrounded by other ideas like inconsistency and change, of course, just like you're saying about Heraclitus. I'm sure there are lots of other Greeks and your favorite Christians who think only in terms of change, right?"

"Yes, and? Are you saying the origin of the concept of change as being all there is, is fundamentally a Christian idea?"

"Well, I don't know anything about that. In fact, I would guess it's just the opposite, isn't it? I mean, once you start talking about eternity, afterlife, if you're not talking about rebirth or reincarnation or whatever, you're really only after a belief system that's suggesting Permanence rather than Impermanence."

"I don't understand."

"Look, forget about the Classics and the Christian philosophers for a second. What I don't get about this belief in something that depends upon one word that is derived from its opposite is how you can say one exists and the other doesn't. If there's a principle of Impermanence it must derive from the larger principle of Permanence. Otherwise, how do we come up with the concept? And incidentally, how does one keep the so-called state of Impermanence from vanishing out of mind when, for instance, you're fucking your brains out and don't want it to ever end, or when you're looking at the intensity of sunlight across the water and you're sure it will last, or when you've just become homeless and you know *that'll* never change."

"Wait a minute. Are you trying to argue with the Buddha?"

"No. Sure. If I see him, I'll shoot him. Here, maybe this is another way to say it: if we rely on the concept of Impermanence, we do so because Permanence in this life is a delusion. I think that's true, don't you?"

"Everything changes. Yes. Can't argue with that."

"On the other hand, we have this hope that nothing will change, right? It's like a basic thing with us. Mommy won't go away; life will remain as pleasant as it might be in childhood. Our miseries will never go away. We'll always suffer. I think that's one of the other basic tenets, by the way—all life is suffering. Well, isn't that a belief in some form of Permanence? But if I take to be true that Impermanence is the nature of Being, and Permanence is a delusion, I can rest easy, and when things change, I can flow with it. I can be at peace, in other words, if I know that nothing lasts."

"Well, the notion of Impermanence should make us more compassionate, don't you think? Another Buddhist tenet, if you will."

This is where I couldn't resist mouthing off: "You know who

you're talking to, right, Professor? I mean this guy and compassion?...I don't know what to tell you. Oil and water, right, Mac?"

Met with silence. A little smile from the professor, not too edgy, though, not wanting to push Mac too far. Who looked over at me, appraising kind of. I'll never forget that cold stare. Nodded, then looked back at the Professor, before he said, "Compassion, that's an inferior virtue. It's feeling what somebody else feels, right? Unlike sympathy—which is basically me saying I'm stronger, better, more virtuous than you are, and that does nothing. Just prayers and good wishes. Compassion, though—sorry, Professor—compassion's not justice. *That's* where the strength is."

"I see. Impermanence is kind of there to make us more accepting of our fate? And out of that comes what you call this weakness of compassionate concern for others? Others who might be in agony because change is inevitable? Is that about it? You think of this aspect of the philosophy as a psychological balm of sorts?"

"Oh, that's a good one, Professor. A psychological balm? Where'd you come up with that one? Very good."

"Thanks. I thought you'd like that. So, this is your point, then, Mac? Impermanence is just a way of feeling better?"

"Actually, yeah. If Permanence is a delusion, why isn't Impermanence a delusion? If I'm down on the street trying to stop the bleeding, I'm concerned with one thing only, life or death. I suppose a Zen Buddhist would say don't be concerned with delusion at all—stop the bleeding, motherfucker! I mean, once I accept the fact that everything changes, everything is unreliable. Reality is either untrustworthy or it's not—you stop the bleeding, or you don't, but once I accept that, I can just get on with it. Right? I accepted the fact plain and simple that life will never be permanently one way or the other when I was a child, that things change, always have, and always will. So fucking what? I'm not really very interested in Impermanence as a way of life or easing my damn suffering. I don't care if things are changing all around me—I don't care if I accept it or not. I can be passive and let change happen, but what if I don't want to, what if I believe in change for the absolute sake of something as delusional as Justice? I mean what a concept! Change as right and just. Sure, it's going to change again when nobody does anything, but maybe somebody will. They won't, though, if the only thing they care about is calming themselves down with the sweet reassurance that Impermanence is the number one principle of life. I don't want to be some smirking Buddha. I want change. And my definition of change, frankly, is not 'let it be.' It's Justice. I want to see change happen, make change happen and be around people who think the same way, and want to make it happen again and again for the sake of justice and equality. Not because that's the way things are, and I better accept it or be miserable. I'd rather be miserable trying to bring about change than jubilant watching everything change minute by minute like some bliss-ninny who could care less about this little 'scrap of dirt' floating in a universe of accident and randomness."

(LATER ON, I got back to this way-too-long letter)

So, Sister Joan married the ex-priest and they got along famously. To see the two of them walking along on the campus sometimes they looked like Hester Prynne and Reverend Dimmesdale. Both in black, and in slow meditative steps along the pathway, holding hands ever so lightly. When I talked to her in the library, though, she was always fun. She joked, and very often she made fun of herself, and portrayed the religious background the two of them had come from and in a sense were still involved in due to their mutual enabling, as she put it, as a kind of handicap, an addiction. Regaining their will rarely led them to know when to cast their lot with the revolution. She had to find that out for herself, she said, and that's how she became an activist, by learning the art of disobedience. Her husband less so, I think. But he tried. He tried, she said, to break his habits, to protest when he could. And on campus back then there were plenty of opportunities to march or to protest, to write letters, to speak out. Especially in his philosophy class, especially with someone like Mac sitting right there spurring him on. But he never let that class indulge in political discussion if he thought it could lead to political action that might come back to affect him. Mac was especially aware of this and thought he was a coward. And, of course, I sat in his class and watched him drag himself through a minefield of doubt and second-guessing.

But the sad news about the two of them is, one night there was a fire and he burned to death. She died a week later of smoke inhalation. I remember standing out front when the EMT carried her away on a stretcher. They brought her through the stone archway that led onto the street. Their house didn't burn down completely, but he died in the back room where he apparently had stuffed too many of his own papers into a faulty stove. He was drinking heavily and passed out. She was asleep in a nearby room and barely made it onto the lawn, choking. When I saw them carry him out, the man who was pushing the stretcher said something like, "burned to a crisp..." dark humor like a war vet.

It was when Mac made his comment that I finally decided to leave Iowa for good. Of course, he really didn't know that I cared about Sister Joan, or even that I'd spent almost every lunch hour with her all that winter listening to the story of her life, and the frustrated careers she'd had before this simple brainless library assistant gig. It was a job I liked and when I deserted Mac and Iowa completely, I tried out substitute teaching for a while, until I finally worked my way back into the library and as you know research became my bread and butter.

Maybe it was just my hurt feelings, or just being plain tired of Mac pushing everybody else aside. He said, "Hey the nun and the Pope went up in smoke," and that was a last straw for me, but when I look back on Eileen and the Professor, I don't really believe they took life as seriously, in fact, as Mac did. I think that for them, no matter how they tried to change themselves after leaving religious life, they were embedded in something coming after this, in another world. Maybe that was the permanent effect of their having been programmed by what I think was a cult experience, but it never seemed they felt things, really felt things—neither Eileen who emulated Joan of Arc for heaven's sake, nor the Prairie Pope always shifting to believe something else. Whereas your Dad never doubted. He knew from when we were high school kids what he had to do, and he let emotions guide him through everything. He was the most passionate man about an idea I've ever met. And yet I didn't talk to him for years, and I didn't know you were born for over the first decade of your life. I was doing fine in Albuquerque, then he had a crackup.

BY THE WAY, when we went over to that table, Mac had every intention of getting something started with those boys. Later on, I would see him try the same tactics on poets in Iowa, only not as fiercely as that night.

"Hey Dominic, how you doin'?"—You know? like they're all buddy-buddy?

"Well, look who it is. Little Mackey all grown up. What are you doin' here?"

"Oh, I come in here every once in a while. You know, have a beer. Visit my Mom?"

"Your Mom?"

"Yeah. My Mom. You were just feeling her up. My Mom, Dominic. Penny."

"Oh, Penny's your Mom. Hmm."

"Mackey, you got a beautiful Mom, man," said one of the meatballs.

"Yeah. Right. I saw you noticed, Peewee. Oh, this is Moses. Moses, this is Peewee, my old pal sort of. These guys were all great friends of mine when I grew up. You guys must be about...what... three years older than me, right? I remember that time...Remember that time, Dom? When all you guys locked me in the garbage shed. Remember that? Flies. Rats. Rotten food."

"Hey, you were a tough little kid, Mac. We wanted you to ride with us, that's all," said the other one.

"I was five. Five. When you did that. Five then, when you beat on the walls of that shed with hammers. Remember that now?"

Dominic was staring at me the whole time.

"Nah, that was rocks, Maxi, not hammers."

"Mose, this is Dominic. This guy knows where all the bodies are buried. And I mean that quite literally. Right, Dom? How many down in the mud of old Neponset now?"

The two meatballs start to get up, looking at Dominic for instructions. He holds up a finger.

"And this specimen of unadulterated vulgarity is Edgar."

"How you doin'?" Edgar reaches out a hand to me, but your Dad waves it away, and says, "You know, that little thing you said to Penny, who, let me remind you, is my *Mom*. What you said to her, Edgar—about sitting right there *on your face*?"

"Well, I was only teasing her, Maxi. We joke like that all the time here. She thinks it's funny."

"Yeah. She thinks it's funny? You know what's funny, Eddie, is that studies have shown—and you can look this up—that guys who make that same request in public, actually utter the very same words you did—really, I just read about this in *Scientific American*—always have been shown to have tiny little dicks. Peckers the size of a baby's fingernail. Okay, boys, we'll be on our way. Don't forget to stop by the Can and pick up some *Trojans.* Do us all a favor. Keep up the good work there, Dom." He looked around the whole place, which was very quiet now. Even the singer had given up.

"Bye, Ma!" Mac shouted across the room. She didn't say anything.

The name of the place was The Pony Room; the Neponset's current under the Pony circled around and played off rocks, muck and logs. Penny stood over by the window. She had turned away from the table where she stopped to take an order and watched.

There was a narrow doorway and an even narrower set of stairs that led to the street. When we got onto pavement, we turned to the right and headed toward the bridge that climbed over the river. Mac didn't seem to be in any hurry, but I was fairly certain we would be better off if we could get as far from that place as possible. We got about a block away when I heard Dominic's voice:

"Massimo Bacca! Got your number, Baby. Where you goin'? Come on back and play with us, Maxi"

"Don't turn around, Mose, don't look at them. Just let's keep walking. I think there's a bus stop right up this way somewhere."

"You *think*? So, there might *not* be? Okay, okay. But maybe we ought to run?"

"No. No running from those clowns. This is a public street. And it's a well-lit bridge. We'll be okay. Just keep walking."

"If they don't throw us off. Can we move a little faster then?"

We weren't jogging or anything but with some urgency we headed toward the bus stop up ahead. The bus was already loading a few people. In fact, somebody with crutches was having trouble negotiating the space from the curb to the first step.

"Ma-a-a-xi-i-i. You're a dead man, Max! Max, we're gonna chop you up..." Stuff like that.

"Why do you always have to do that?"

"What? What are you talking about?"

"Why, Mac? Why do you always go out of your way to make people want to hurt you? Why? Can you answer me that? Did you ever think about it? I mean, is it some kind of a psychosis with you?"

"Ha! Come on, Mose. They're sitting ducks. Those fat slobs are never gonna catch up to us. Don't worry about it. I can't just let them pretend they still have some power over me. Do you know what I mean? What that jerk said to my own mother? I guess they could say she asks for it by working in places like that, but still. Can they just sit there like big King Assfucks and nobody ever calls them out?"

We got to the bus, and your Dad, the once and famous Poet and Media Darling, pushes me in first so he can stand out there and wave both hands up and down at those crazy—and still I'm not sure—maybe murderers, shooting birds at them while the bus driver is yelling at him to *get in the bus, Buddy, we're movin'*.

Well, Bobby, I've gone on long enough, and probably gave you much more about your Dad—and your old Gramma—than you would ever want to know. Believe me, I don't know what led him to wander over to that Andrew Station bench, or what might have caused him to lose heart, or stroke out and die. I'd love to tell you he was a wonderful guy, but you know very well he wasn't and didn't have a load of friends he could depend on. Just me, and only later in his life.

Okay. I hope we get together sooner rather than later.

All best wishes to you from your old friend,

and sometimes reluctant,

Mentor

Nausicaä

8.

MOSES SUGGESTED I get in touch with Winston Roblé, who had been a grad student at the University of Albuquerque and Mac's Teaching Assistant. After our sojourn in Paris, and after Mac and Mom split up, Mac took this job teaching literature and writing at, of all places, a Catholic college. I don't know what kind of vetting process such a school made use of, but they got him on their faculty just before some of his nastiest critical writing hit the stands. Winston, a born performer, so much on stage our weird encounter felt like a circus sideshow, was from the hamlet of Lac Ste Joseph, Quebec; he'd worked his way through the academic realm to become assistant to the soon-to-be notorious literary high-roller and besotted ogre, my Dad.

Meeting Winston so long after he worked with Mac was an eerie moment for me because his name recalled the a.k.a. of that rarity in our town, the New Yorker, a man whose real name was unknown to most of us but who had become Wesley Roblé. Both Roblés spoke French—Winston, the Quebecois of his home turf, and Wesley—the garbled Cajun of his parents. When I met them both, twenty years apart, the

Roblés were nearly the same age. Wesley was tolerant and generous. A follower of three-fingered Django Reinhardt, he taught me guitar riffs the summer I turned thirteen. He was there the night Mac rolled up in his road-beaten Citroen and crept into the Little Friend where my Mom was the bartender; he was there for Mac's famous acid trip, whereas Winston had seen Mac abandon teaching in New Mexico, in disgrace, and told me not only why Mac wanted to live in relative anonymity near Mom and me, but why he might have thrown himself into the psychosis of his age through a clear tablet of Windowpane acid.

Winston was living in San Francisco where a small gallery was showing my work.. He'd relocated when the University of Albuquerque shut down; as part of the writing scene in the Bay area, he'd begun to conduct his own writing classes. I wrote to ask him to meet with me. He was eager to talk about Mac and suggested we could meet at the park in North Beach one crisp fall morning. I was slightly fatigued, if not a little hungover from the Opening, which had gone late into the night. Badly in need of coffee, I struggled with a hot cup, prying the lid and slippery cream pittance they tossed me at a booth called Caffiend Crack Ho and had just about settled myself on a crusty park bench.

"I'd recognize you anywhere. Your Father always had a picture of you on the wall of his office back in the big U of A. Don't get up. That coffee looks like a job in itself."

It took me a few seconds to realize someone was talking to me, and when I looked up, I was glad I had on my sunglasses—not only to cover my bloodshot eyeballs, but the glare coming off Winston's white suit jacket and yellow tie almost embarrassed me, country hick that I am. He had mentioned I would know him by the Scottish plaid kilt, but I also recognized his stout boots with yellow laces from Mac's pictures. A trademark of sorts.

I did in fact need to keep sitting on that bench, but Winston strutted back and forth, animated, happy, I suspected, that he could unload some of the backstory—which I might otherwise have presumed was literary twaddle he'd kept to himself for a decade. At one point he turned to look across the grassy stretch of the park. To survey, no doubt, the great cathedral spiked beyond the trees, but instead, he began to point at a gathering. About twenty Chinese women and a few men had taken up places beside and behind one another and performed a slow synchronized choreography. I never noticed what groups like this did. Nor did I care. For me, they blended in with squirrels, trees, and water sprinklers, but this slow meditative dance, I had to admit, didn't seem accidental.

"Oh look! It's Tai Chi. Look at that! Do you know how to do Tai Chi?"

"Um, no. What's that?"

"The ancient art of movement. Look!"

I still hadn't tasted my coffee.

"Oh, I know how to do that one. Here, let me see," and right there, on the pavement next to the bench where he insisted I watch his every move, he began to imitate, in a manner of speaking, the movement of the people on the grass. A bit contorted, I thought, compared to their unified grace. While he stretched, I managed a surreptitious gulp of lukewarm coffee.

"Ah, 'Snake Creeps Down.' I know that one. Watch me now, I'll show you, I'll do it."

Winston had rather large white legs for someone who wore a kilt. Knee socks would have been a brilliant style suggestion for his get-up. He bent down, one hairy leg stretched out, the other crooked at the knee, a hand flailing upward, another swinging down and out, not quite like the group's sweep of legs and arms. Then he rose upward, sprang to a stance on one foot, then the other, and kicked high into the air.

"So, um, Winston."

He looked at me. I was pitiful. A son trying to piece together a few things about his dad. Crumpled, hungover, weak, and lonely. It might have been obvious I saw those few years in the Southwest as gaps in my understanding of the way my father had ended up. Someone once said every man always sees himself as eighteen in a mirror but having only seen Winston in a photo my Dad sent years ago, I realized the corollary might be true: every man's face comes to obscure that first face; the eighteen-year-old is still there, under layers of neighborhoods, marriages, the abuse of years.

"Okay. Okay." He looked at my dripping coffee cup. "Well, you know about some of the things, right?"

"No, not much really. Just that he taught there for a while. All I remember was he was not the same person he was when I was a child by the time he came back up north and lived nearby my Mom and me. We were living in the house he still owned, but they agreed he'd stay downtown in a studio he kept for years."

"Oh. Well, that's news to me, then. I just knew he left and, frankly, I never heard from him again. He didn't answer my letters and I know he didn't have a phone. He never had a phone as far as I knew."

"Yeah, Dad didn't like phones. I couldn't call him when he went down to New Mexico. He called from a phone booth on my birthdays, but that was about it."

"So, I can tell you a few things. I can tell you why he left Albuquerque. Would that help?"

"Yeah, that's what I need to know. Because, as I said, he just wasn't the same Father. He had changed in ways I can only think of as...well, he was less than he ever was. Do you know what I mean? He was not really there anymore. Not as much of him, anyway. He kept to himself, which wasn't his way when I was a kid, and he pretended to be writing though he didn't produce anything of any importance. So, yeah, whatever you can tell me will help, Winston."

"Well, it starts with Sinclair. Do you know who that is? Or was, I should say. He's dead now too."

"Mr. Ames mentioned him once in a letter."

"Um, Sinclair, your Dad and Moses—so you've met Moses, right?" I nodded. "They all went to the same posh boarding school back east somewhere. Procter & Gamble? Something like that, I guess."

"Proctor's. It was in Massachusetts. That's where they were from, Dad and Moses. I don't know about Sinclair."

"Oh, he was from there too. They all went to that school. Sinclair became choirmaster and music instructor at a small high school not far from the University of Albuquerque. I didn't meet Moses until your Dad and I started making trips to that school. Sinclair helped Moses get hired on as a substitute teacher and later on invited Mac to come and talk about poetry to the high school classes. I think it impressed people that Sinclair knew this guy who had been on TV and was widely published. So, when Mac began as a visiting poet, I went with—but I kept telling him, 'I'm pretty sure you're gonna get a big disappointment, Mac. You won't find the kind of raw creative spirit you're expecting there. I don't think so. They just ain't got it at that age, Sir.' But he didn't want to hear it. He went anyway saying, 'There's bound to be more going on in their fresh little minds than I can find in this Factory of

Not-So-Creative Writing.'"

"He sent me a picture of himself with a class and you standing—diffidently?—off to the side."

"Oh?"

"And another with you and a group of college students. You were laughing."

That's what I was seeing in Winston's now more experienced, learned, dignified face, the young man in a photo Mac had captioned "My indispensable Teaching Assistant" had a wide mouth and sat on a tall chair, torso twisted, feet locked around the chair legs, to laugh with someone behind him. As a kid, I pored over those photos and noticed two or three high schoolers among the college students. He wore a red and white striped scarf over one shoulder of his black sports jacket, yellow laces in his black military boots.

"Listen, do you want to walk? We don't have to stay here on a park bench all day, do we?"

I'VE ONLY LIVED in one major city, Paris, and I did so twice: a year as a child and another year as an art student. Thanks to Mac both times. So, coming to San Francisco out of a tiny burg in the Pacific Northwest, I was stunned by the streets, the traffic, the seemingly limitless rolling script of Italian names for café's we were walking past, but striding along so fast in my scuffed shoes, my ordinary jacket and baseball cap beside the immense figure of Winston in his white sports coat and bright kilt, his big boots clomping past pedestrians, I was more surprised nobody noticed us. To my mind we should have made at least an unusual impression that would have turned heads. But nobody's head so much as twitched in our direction.

"Let's cross down there at the light. Watch out for the Barkers at the Sex Shows. They'll want to lure you if you've got any money. We'll head over there." He pointed diagonally across the wide intersection at Broadway and Columbus. As we waited for the light to change, a young woman behind us began playing a harp. She was dressed in white and wore thin white gloves. Beside her was a man all in black, who, as I was turning toward the sound of the harp, swept his wide-brimmed hat off, placed it upturned on the sidewalk in front of them, and began to intone in a deep bass voice an epic poem, he entitled "The New Pilgrim's Progress." The light changed and we walked fast across Broadway.

"I'd suggest we stop in at Vesuvio's and have a drink, but you've still got that coffee, and by the look of you, you probably don't want to start on anything stronger this early in the day, no?"

I took another sip.

"Have you ever been to City Lights? Let's not go inside. I need to tell you the whole story, and we can keep on walking, but I just want to look here at the discount rack."

Outside the City Lights bookstore was a rolling dolly with plenty of tattered copies of poetry, novels, outdated science, all sold at steep discounts, and on the top shelf there it was: *The Autopsy of American Poetry* by M.M. Bacca. I hadn't seen one in several years. This was autographed "For Guido, in hope and despair. MMB." I wished we hadn't stopped here and tried to pry Winston off a volume of Beat poetry. I turned away toward the storefront windows: photographs of Ginsburg, Corso, Kerouac, Burroughs, Ferlinghetti. And I recalled Mac carrying on a love-hate relationship with their work well into his last years.

As I stood there, a disheveled man came up to me. His two hands out and cupped in ripped gloves and his clothing blackened and muddy.

"Hey, Captain, how about a coupla bucks?"

I had brought along a pocketful of quarters and dumped two- or three-dollars' worth into those paws, but I didn't say anything to him. I don't know what he could tell from my look. Maybe just that I was from out of town, some bumpkin, or nothing at all. I grabbed Winston's arm and tilted my head toward an alley that seemed like a good way to get out of there. And soon we were walking along at a good clip up through China Town, turning onto Stockton. We were heading, he said, toward Coit Tower, when Winston started in again on Sinclair. A man named Jeff Fournier had filled Winston in on the events at the beginning of the school year.

"Mr. Sinclair had an awakening. He came back from summer vacation, Jeff said, and many teachers noted small things. For instance, almost out of earshot, faint music from his classroom behind a locked door, and his absence at lunch those first days before students arrived. Though the teachers ate almost furtively, anticipating as yet unscheduled meetings to update them on procedures, they still chatted about books, music, movies, summer travel, that sort of thing. During a lull, the door opening down the hall sent a chord or two from the Ravi Shankar Singers, when someone, a Mr. Terwillant, I believe, did mention that Sinclair had spent the summer in India.

"There was silence for a moment.

"'Oh? What part?' a Mrs. Vinstaad asked."

Did I mention Winston had a flair for the theatrical narrative? I was still huffing along beside him and wished he would cut to the chase, but I also didn't want to interrupt, since I had assumed, however circular his storytelling, he was going to get to the part about Mac pretty soon. But he did go on: "Apparently as a girl she had tramped over Europe. The summer following her first year of teaching she'd taken a walking tour of ancestral burial sites. During the spring of that year, she avidly researched her family tree, authenticated her lineage with slides she presented at a faculty meeting. So, twenty years later, indisputably a world traveler, she was motivated more by curiosity than personal experience. She loved India from a distance, Jeff said, kept a well-worn *Lonely Planet,* but, had anyone asked, would have reluctantly admitted she'd never been there.

"Bill Chambers—I remember meeting him (not impressed)—Jeff mentioned he was known as 'Bill' even to students, always referred to Mrs. Vinstaad as Mrs. V—Bill added the information, despite that everyone seemed privately to have learned it, that Mr. Sinclair spent the summer chanting and meditating at an ashram.

"They were a close group who had lunched together for nearly three years, although this was Jeff's first year as a teacher. He had been Sinclair's student-teacher the previous year. The change in Sinclair's behavior signaled a breach of their habits; perhaps it even made them question the worth of the group's interdependence. At the least, it was disappointing. Mr. Sinclair would be missed; whatever called him to India took him from them and the immersion they enjoyed in one another's banter. Of which Sinclair had been an important part. He told jokes, apparently, and made ironic, irreverent utterances about administration or biased parents from a bottomless cynicism, sometimes at his own expense. It buoyed up their group and they guffawed over yogurt in the lunchroom, or they choked on their ale after work. But from what I understood, no one really thought he held such grim views about teaching as he pretended. His watery eyes, Jeff told me, gave away his inability to deadpan a joke about student 'untelligence,' and his capacity for laughter—at his own comments or at theirs earned him their endearment. That—which they had taken as an assurance of his sincerity—that, and the stutter."

"Well, when was Mac there? Didn't you say Sinclair helped him to relocate and take up the position at that college?"

"Oh. Yes, I'm getting to that, Bobby. Is it okay to call you Bobby? That's how Mac always referred to you, you know. So, yes, Sinclair let your dad know there was an opening at U of A, when he heard Mac was looking for a teaching position. I don't know that he did any more than that, though U of A, by the way, is my Alma Mater. Well, I was his TA, after all, but I was also Jeff's classmate. That is, we had some of our classes together. He was taking degrees in Music and in the Classics. He wanted to be a Latin teacher who could occasionally expound on and sing Gregorian Chant. That's what he told me he decided the day he finished his Student Teaching assignment in Mr. Sinclair's music classes. He applied for the position to replace the retiring Latin teacher down the hall from Sinclair. I know he had a great deal of respect for the man. Jeff didn't know your dad then; he was already out of Grad school when Mac came to town. They didn't meet until Mac's last stint as the Poetry Man, as he called it, to one of Sinclair's classes. And... that's when it happened. But I'm getting to all that. There's more you need to know about the Sinclair situation so you can see how all this played out, how, in fact, all three of their fates—in a sense, came together."

"Alright, alright. I get it. Go on."

We had to wait on another light to recross Broadway. It seemed like a particularly circular route, but I assumed Winston had some kind of map in his head.

"So. It *was* a disappointment that Mr. Sinclair kept apart. There would be no time to visit when the long march began.

They suspected him of disapproving, and in conversations, which did take place in Jeff's vicinity, they wondered if religious conversion would lead Mr. Sinclair toward doctrines best left out of school curricula. A campaign of letter-writing the year before demanded alternative approaches to teaching evolution. Textbooks incorporating *Genesis* were assigned to students, many more than willing to argue that science was a religion, evolution its erroneous tenet. Jeff told me his own students gathered at dawn under the flag, held hands and prayed, cuffs of their jeans and tennis shoes soaked either by dew or their feet numb in frost, light snow, rain. Yet Jeff wondered whether Sinclair's religious bent might appear silly to other students? Would they laugh? At his stutter? Would professed atheists among them feel betrayed? Would past students expect the confident smile, the sardonic glint, not to mention gray suits and ties—his dignity? At the door to Sinclair's choir room, he heard strings of a sitar and voices so loud they seemed manic; he knocked, but the door had been locked. So unnecessary, Jeff thought, taking it personally as he had willed himself not to on three occasions. His protective feeling reasserted itself, he knocked again, more forcefully, but the chanting was loud and shrill."

We stopped for another streetlight and turned up Vallejo only to have to wait again and cross Columbus one more time. I was a little out of breath trying to keep up with Winston who talked incessantly and walked at this brisk pace. My coffee was gone, too. Here I was hiking along with this madman in the streets and for what? I didn't care diddly about these people and still didn't see any connection to my dad. And yet, oh well, maybe something will come out of this, a little explanation. At least the guy knew Mac and knew more about him than I did.

"And then there was the girl. Well, she was a woman by the time Jeff met her. Harley Marlow had been a high school senior when Mac was first invited to talk poetry in her class. She later enrolled in his college course, *How You Shall Write a Poem*. I don't think she ever had any special feeling for Mac—and you should know—he didn't for her either. It was just something in one of his poems and he didn't know anything about the effect of what he said until much later. He didn't develop an antipathy toward her until she was in college. She became a Math teacher at the school the year Jeff was hired to teach Latin. But!! I'm getting to all that..."

"Okay. Hey, what's this place? I think I need an Espresso."

"Oh? You need more coffee? Wow, well, okay. This is probably the best place in town. Café Trieste. You must have heard of it. Hope you don't mind waiting in line for a while."

9.

STREAKS OF SUNLIGHT were careening off the wide windows. Huge espresso machinery hummed and coughed up front as we crept along in line, and Winston continued. More about the opening of the school year, his friend Jeff, good ole Mr. Sinclair. I couldn't hear him very well, but I didn't tell him that. I only hoped he would get to the part about Mac soon.

"School began. The first day was a friendly day, a hectic day. At the end, when Jeff stared out his window, it occurred to him that all day he hadn't given a thought to Mr. Sinclair. His concern for his friend wore against his hurt feelings. Then, there was Sinclair, happy, spry, on his way through the parking lot. Jeff watched as he reached his black 1959 Jaguar. At least that hadn't changed. It wasn't a surprise to see him stride in bright white shirt and pants, beads, cloth bag dangling from his shoulder sporting the odd smile of some Eastern deity. He *had* been surprised to see Sinclair amble down the walk well before any other teacher left for the day, certainly much earlier than he *used* to leave school. Jeff was more surprised by himself. He kept watching and didn't know why. Obviously, things change, but was he waiting for a sign his familiar workplace was back to normal? Was he looking for some chink in his friend's veneer of exotic faith? Sinclair stooped to the latch, placed the shoulder bag in the boot, opened the driver door, and aligned his long legs in their weird pants under the steering column. But there *had* been a change to the little Jag. The license plate was new; it read: B-HA-P. He couldn't imagine the old Sinclair would send a message at all, let alone one so clueless. Yet here it was. The convertible Jag, with the small sputter, pulled out of the parking lot, the white-clad saint's black hair flourishing in sunshine and breeze, his license plate evoking the wide mustache and peaceful smile of Meher Baba like a chord above the entire scene.

"The mayor of what?"

"Oh. Well. Not important, I guess. Anyway, at the first faculty meeting of the year, Jeff headed for the back row, but Mrs. Vinstaad and a teacher he called Ron beckoned him to join them. She asked whether he heard the news about Sinclair. 'There's already a parent complaint. The District wants him out,' Ron said. Jeff couldn't believe it. 'They don't want him leading the band at football games in his white robes.' He didn't think they could dismiss him without suggesting he make changes. Then he said, 'Mrs. V allowed one of her thin smiles,' and he threw an English accent in for this one: 'My dear, he *made* changes. Nobody likes them.'"

"He's a joker, this guy Jeff. He's a friend of yours, right?"

"Was."

"What?"

"Jeff was a bit of a joker, yes. And my friend. So, that's part of Mac's story, I'm afraid, Bobby. Jeff died."

We moved up in the line. I was next.

"Oh, I'm sorry. He does sound like a good guy."

"Yes. But this faculty meeting, this, he told me, is when he first met Harley Marlowe and thought she had 'the eyes of an Amazon queen; her voice awakened something unfamiliar.' Again, he *was* a jokester, Jeff."

I had to give Winston a look; certainly, he had lost someone very close to him. He cared about his friendship, I thought. But—I didn't want him to stop talking. There was something lurking here about Mac, and I could also tell he wasn't ready to let me know yet what that was. He kept going. As the coffee assembly lines cranked away double time and the line slipped forward a bit, Winston had to speak louder.

"He described her to me as, 'incandescent,' and imagined how it might feel to be one of his freshman boys sitting in the front row of her Geometry Class. She said to Ms. Hedstrom a bit too loudly, he thought, 'Oh, my hands are so full, I have nowhere to put today's agenda. Guess I'll have to squeeze it in my cleavage again,' and glanced across the aisle at Jeff, patting his chest, stage-whispering, 'Ah, be still, my heart.' simultaneously delighted and deflated when he thought he'd enjoy—and then knew he couldn't enjoy—retelling as a vignette this nearly naughty exchange to Sinclair, impossible if not inappropriate at this point in Sinclair's awakening.

"As the Vice Principal was asking, 'Does everyone have an agenda?.. I know you don't want to stay late....' that sort of thing—a few heads turned, he said, to take note of the garb; Sinclair walked directly to an empty seat in the front row. And then, you know, all the questions at the beginning of any meeting... The VP says, 'the first item on the agenda'... and so forth. Then: 'I want to talk about that fight in the cafeteria,' and 'We must address how rude the kids are,' and 'Make them stop chewing gum,' 'no more baseball hats in class,' stuff like that went on for a while until Sinclair, slowly raises his hand and slowly rises and turns to face the staff."

"Next?"

"Yeah, I'd like a triple, two-thirds decaf. Oh, with room for cream. And I'd like the cream heated and on the side in a cup by itself." Usually, when I give my order, it needs further explanation, or I must repeat it several times before the barista gets it. This guy was an expert—his blank expression didn't flicker.

"Five Bucks. Wait over there. Next?"

The Espresso Machine was raucously loud, and voices of morning coffee-drinkers at the tables were louder. Someone was reading a poem. There was violin music, soothing, passing over everyone, filling the caffeinated air, and Winston had to shout a bit more.

"Sinclair turned to address the faculty. Jeff noticed two new PE coaches exchange smirks. Vinstaad whispered to Ron.

"'I'..., he said..."

Another loud blast from the Espresso engine. Someone standing at a table gave a bow, finished reading his poem to friends who were sitting down. They clapped. A shout, "Khorosho!' said the poet with long gray hair and a deep rasping voice... Russian, I think, at the corner table.

"Fidgeting stopped in the squeaky seats. 'I...teach...the same...K-Kids as you.'"

I really didn't see how Winston could become any more theatrical than he was now, imitating the stutter of the man. He got even louder, though, to overcome the café tumult.

"'But I don't have any pr...' he stopped. *Oh, oh,* Jeff thought, *come on, don't give in.* 'Pr..pr..pr...

Prrob...bl..blem,' he said. Jeff noticed the strain got his lips to purse and creased his chin. The room began to fidget again, teachers whispered."

"Here's your two-thirds decaf with cream on the side,

Dude!"

At that instant, there was a lull in the voices at all the tables, the espresso machines went quiet simultaneously for no reason and over it all Winston's loud voice was the only sound:

"'...d..discipline pro...oblems are NOT the f..f..fault of the k..k..KIDS.'" And he smiled, half-heartedly at a few of the poets at the tables. And ended with a whisper: "And then he sat down."

OUTSIDE, WE STARTED uphill, and Winston got right back into it. I had my shot of Caffeine and now I was ready. When we waited at the corner to cross he told me that Sinclair became known as "stuttering holy man." And that some teachers openly joked about him. They discussed the disruption his choking platitudes caused. Some did impressions, for other teachers, for parents even. There were phone calls. Children's religious views undermined. They demanded equal time. Calls to school board members, to the Superintendent herself. Had he suffered a psychosis?

"Okay," I said. "I get it. But, come on—Sinclair, Sinclair, Sinclair. I thought you were going to tell me something about Mac, for Christ's sake."

We stopped dead in our tracks. Winston looked up at the house across the street, a blue clapboard triple-decker. He looked a little hurt. I didn't know what else to say. Maybe it was the caffeine, but my frustration had worn through the morning, and now here we were. What's next? I thought. He's too geared up not to have to tell me everything—he won't just walk away and leave me here, will he? Then he looked down at the sidewalk and started to shake his head back and forth.

"No, no, no, no, no, Bobby—you've got to hear the whole thing or forget about it. Your Dad was a piece of work, and you really ought to know that. I think, frankly, you might have a bit of hero worship left over from your own childhood, if you don't mind my saying so. I have to tell you about these other people because they have such a bearing on his life. He changed, Bobby. He really did. You knew that, right? I mean that's the reason you wanted to know something about what went on in Albuquerque, right? Well, you're going to have to listen to the story of these few other people to understand him and why he changed. Okay?"

He was staring at me now, waiting for an answer. A turquoise convertible—"Galaxy" I thought—floated past us, the light changed, and we could cross. I went first. I looked up that hill as we started to walk along Grant Avenue.

"Where are we going anyway?"

"We stay on this street for several blocks more. We'll turn off when we get to Lombard and go up to the Tower. Are you ready?"

"Okay. I'm ready for the walk, yeah. But wait a minute. So, you're telling me there's something about Sinclair having had a religious conversion or whatever that brought this guy Jeff under Mac's radar, am I right? And when you say he was a 'piece of work,' I guess you mean Mac wasn't the kind man I knew as my father. Is that your point?"

"Well, yeah, I..."

"I'm not delusional, Winston. I know quite a bit about who he really was besides being my jovial old Dad. Okay? Okay, let's go on. But get to the Mac part pretty soon, please."

"Alright," he said and picked right up where he left off when I interrupted him.

"One day after school, Jeff told me, he turned a corner too quickly and crashed into Ms. Marlowe. Nearly a ream of dogeared student assignments fanned across the floor.

"'Oh, no. I'm sorry. Oh, shoot, what have I done...I'm...'

"'Shit, will you help me pick this up!'

"'Oh, yeah. Sorry.'

"'They're just papers to grade. Not in any order or anything. It's okay, it's okay.'

"Jeff squatted to pick up the assignments scattered under tables, chairs, and stools. They were crawling around the floor, picking everything up, and, from what he told me, they had a conversation somewhat like this:

"'Hey. What's with the guru? He's a friend of yours, right?'

"'Ah. Yeah. We've shared a few beers together.'

"'Not much for the beer department lately, I'll bet, right?'

"'No. He doesn't go out with us after school.'

"'My students love him, the kids in chorus.'

"'What do you mean?' Jeff had thought students found Sinclair incomprehensible, making jokes about him, or worse.

"'They adore Mr. S. Most of my fourth period come directly from Music and rave about him, literally saying he's a Great Man! They say like he's so fair, and like treats them with such respect.'

"'I do that too, but I don't think kids rave about me. Do you?'

"'Do I what?'

"'Think they're raving about, you know...other teachers? Me?'

"'Oh, all the time. Fournier this, Fournier that. On and on all day.'

She was smiling down at him as he handed the last papers up from the floor.

"'So, did he have a nervous breakdown? Some religious conversions take time to kick in, from what I hear, and a person can become deranged before, you know, settling down to normal behavior. Not to mention start to dress normal."

"Jeff didn't know how to respond.

"'Hey. You wanna hang out? Go have a beer? I don't want to grade these tonight. Not really. Sometimes I take papers for a ride and bring them back the next morning.'

"SEVERAL HOURS LATER, 'Mr. Fournier' was impetuously removing the underthings of Ms. Marlowe in the dark and meeting little resistance; she was unbuttoning his shirt, kissing him, pulling at his belt buckle.

"Wait." She stood up and started dressing.

He stopped and sat up on his own bed and turned on the light.

"'I can't go to bed with you.'

"'Why? Wait, you're not married, are you? You have a boyfriend? You seemed to like me.'

"'No, it's just that...You're the Latin teacher, aren't you?... Um.... I don't want to sleep with you, then go home. You know? In the middle of the night? I don't want that. Do you?'

"'No,' he said, 'I want you to stay, and...'

"'Well, I can't go to school tomorrow in these clothes! The kids know. They'll say something. The walk of shame, you know? *OH HO! Looks like Miss didn't go home last night!* They notice what we wear, you know? They'll put two and two together. Maybe another time? Is that okay? I'll bring a change of clothes. Or we could go to my place? Wanna do that?'

"He recognized her heart wasn't in the invitation, and he didn't feel like leaving home.

"'No, I'll stay here. See you tomorrow. Thanks for explaining.'

"So, from what Jeff told me, he was left to stare at the ceiling. Soon he picked up his guitar and played something new—he didn't know quite what. It reminded him of Sinclair's Sitar, what little drifted in the hall. Was Sinclair immune to attractions of the opposite sex now? Did spirituality eliminate lust?

"Jeff strummed out two lines of a song:

'Oh, Sinclair was a c-c-c-celibate,

'but he ate only h-h-h-halibut.'

"'Jesus, what am I doing?' he said out loud and stopped strumming. And laughed at himself because there were more lyrics. He wanted to go on and on because he suddenly thought Sinclair was a fool who abandoned friendships, not to mention collegiality. 'This religious idiot only gaga students, for Christ's sake, respect. They adore him. She couldn't be exaggerating, could she?'

"It was then Jeff saw what remained of a link with Sinclair was gone. He no longer saw him as his old friend, could no longer defend him if anyone criticized him, or mimicked his stutter. No, he *would* draw the line there. But wait, that's part of the song, that's what helps it, the stutter. So, he was already there—Sinclair gets no special treatment...but maybe that was his way, special treatment like an invalid who everyone treats with kid gloves.

"AND? SO? ARE we there yet, grampa? Is Mac even in this story?"

"Here's the point. You might have noticed I said Jeff turned *on* the light. They had been making out *in the dark*, okay? Then she was putting on her clothes? Huh? And she had to find out if he taught *Latin*, right?"

"Again, my friend—So? So what the fuck!"

"She didn't want him to see the tattoo, okay? That tatoo is *the* link between Harley Marlow, M.M.Bacca and, I'm sorry, the death of my friend Jeff Fournier."

"I don't understand. What tattoo for fuck's sake?"

"Well, let me go on, okay? In high school, she was a slightly troubled girl, she'd been abused at home from what Mac told me, and he knew this from her poems. But by her second year of college, taking his writing course, she wrote about suicide, which she had attempted once. She loved one of his poems quite a bit, he said. That is, she loved the Latin epigraph he dropped under the poem title. She was a fourth-year Latin student when he visited the school. Well, maybe she loved his *translation* of the epigraph even more—from Cicero, I believe. Maybe that's the cleverer way to understand what she did. What she did was have a tattoo made from the phrase. He recounted all this to me later and said the girl's English teacher told him this. The teacher thought he'd find it flattering. But the following year the girl entered college and asked him to waive the prerequisites to join his writing class. But it seemed odd to me—he told me all this as if without any sympathy at all, almost with a sneer—at her, a victim, for heaven's sake. I didn't understand that about him. I don't know if anyone really did. His almost universal lack of empathy. It shows up in his criticism constantly, which is how he got that reputation. A reputation, I might add, that he seemed to relish. Oh...I'm sorry, you probably don't want to hear all this...Here's the rest of what I recall about the events that led him back up to your little town, up there in...where is it? Oregon? Idaho? Just before he left, or about six months before you saw him again, that is, after he resigned as a full professor in Albuquerque.

"This is what happened the day after she left his apartment and Jeff realized he'd had enough of Sinclair taking his best students on field trips. At lunch many teachers brought up their frustration with the effects student absences for Choral Field Trips were having on courses. They had to repeat far too many lessons, and many had the impression students, in Choral groups or not, thought Math, English, Social Studies,

Science classes, were less valuable, even burdensome by comparison. Jeff agreed with every objection, saying, 'Yeah, that sounds like Sinclair, all right. We're just babysitting when he's not with them.'

"At the end of the school day, Jeff went to the dragon's lair as the bell dismissed students. He said he was sure, 'Sinclair would be in his room long enough to pack up his begging bowl and scuttle off to the Jaguar.' Theirs was one of the old school buildings of solid walls and marble hallway floors that echoed the sound of Jeff's boots as he hurried towards Mr. Sinclair's door. The door itself was made of heavy wood, and when Jeff turned the knob to enter without knocking—as had always been their habit in bygone days—and pushed the door inward slowly, even before it opened enough to enter, he perceived late afternoon sunlight pouring in across the room through windows that, like his own classroom, filled the entire wall. To his surprise, the person standing with his back to him was a tall black man in a white shirt and tie, fastening clasps on a briefcase, and who turned to see Jeff enter, and smiled at him.

"'Hello. I'm Moses. I'm the Sub. Are you looking for Mr. Sinclair?'

"So, here we are, Bobby. The connections, you see?"

"Well, at least it's someone I know. Did you know Mose in Albuquerque?"

"That was the first day I met him, right there in the classroom. And I also met Ms. Marlow there. Mac insisted she show me the tattoo, which he knew about. So, I was leaning over, looking at her tattoo when Jeff walked in. Now, when he met Moses, you should take into account how he was raised; he had few brushes with a world outside the suburbs. This was an all-white school, or mostly white students and no full-time Black teacher on staff. Jeff Fournier, who spent his life in a small farm community, never had contact with a single person who was not Caucasian. So, saying that Moses' glowing smile took Jeff by surprise is as much an understatement as saying people in front row theater seats are complacent when someone yells 'fire.' He kept approaching Moses, then turned his gaze toward the desk in the corner where he still expected to see Sinclair, only to witness Ms. Marlowe, her back to him, holding up the bottom half of her blouse, pulling down the waistband of her skirt, exposing her hips, willingly apparently, to a small fellow—your Dad—with long scraggly hair, his face inches away from her bare waist, his own battered briefcase on the floor where he knelt, and to a big man in a kilt, me, standing there and I guess leering at Ms. Marlowe's belly when I looked up and noticed who entered, 'Oh, it's Jeff! Hi, Jeff!' and I waved at him."

We were at the corner of Grant and Lombard, waiting for yet another light. A person dressed as a mime was also waiting there. He didn't seem interested in us at all, thank God. The last thing I wanted was to make a new friend again here in the street. Winston continued on and on and I was just as glad that his droning voice kept anyone else at bay, had they even taken notice of two people wandering the streets with this seemingly endless perhaps even shaggy dog story.

"Meanwhile Jeff was unable to turn away from looking—*oh my God, I'm gawking, he said to himself*—at the three of us across the room. After a few seconds, he said to Moses, 'Um, yeah. Isn't he in today? Where's Sin?' He felt embarrassed by his awkwardness but didn't know how to talk. But this Moses, even his handshake was different from anyone Jeff ever met.

"'Sick day, I guess. Or wait,' Moses smiled again—his teeth are so white, Jeff thought—'Is today Buddha's birthday?' Jeff continued to stare. 'Nah, I guess that's April. Or is it May? Do you know?'

"Jeff—nothing.

"'Somebody's birthday, I guess. Anyway, all good for me. I get a working day and with nice kids. Hardly any work at all, though, because The Poet was here for most of the classes. Do you know him?' Moses waved his thumb in the direction of the threesome in the corner. 'Um. No, I don't think I do.' 'Well, come on, Man, I'll introduce you.'"

The light changed and the Mime looked at me. He then began to mime walking downstairs. I think I gave him a queasy look, and he changed into two people shaking one another's hands, which he performed all the while we were crossing onto Lombard together. Winston hardly noticed this guy's antics, but he did slow down his tale slightly. I had the thought he was the victim of a chronic logorrhea, and he began a hip gyration, swinging his kilt, as he spoke: "They had... to work their . . way around the desks... strewn around the room... in no particular order; scraping a few of the chair legs... along the floor made a sharp hollow noise... ." as the mime too scurried along the sidewalk ahead of us, moving invisible furniture and showing an ache in his head as if the hollow sound emanated from there. I gave him a handful of quarters and waved goodbye. He mimed money falling from heaven.

"Well, that was something, anyway. So, there was the little scruffy man, Mac, who looked up, stood slowly from where he'd been on his knees. Both of us smiled and took in how strange this scene must have felt walking into for him, and how awkward Harley might have felt. She turned sharply to see, for the first time, that Jeff was in the room, and immediately rearranged her clothing and said goodbye. She walked quickly keeping several desks between herself and Jeff who was having no little difficulty negotiating while looking at her; she gave him an inscrutable glare and hurried out the door.

"'Hi! Mac Bacca,' said your dad, holding out his hand. His handshake was often particularly thin, cold, and sweaty.

"I stepped in. 'Mac, this is Jeff Fournier. He works here.'"

"'Well, she was in a hurry to get out of here, Jeff. Something you said?' He grinned. 'You know Winston, then? He's my bodyguard...oh there I go again, I'm not supposed to say that, like I do all the time... Teaching Assistant. What do you teach?'

"'Oh. Um, some Freshman Language Arts classes, stuff like that. Latin.'

"'Good for you. They must like having you around.'

"'What are you doing here?'

"'Oh, Sinclair invited me. He wanted me to talk to music classes about Librettos. So, I talked a little about Auden's *Rake's Progress.* Do you know it?'

"'No. I don't know a thing about opera.'

"'Nobody does. Wish he'd been here. The geezer's always got sumpin' to s-s-s-say-ay-ay-ay,...know what I mean?'

"'Hey, Dude. Come on, now.' said Moses, smiling, not as if to protect Sinclair from Mac. They all went to school together, after all. Then he invited Jeff to have a beer with us.

"'We're off to the Brewery, Tra La! How 'bout chew? You wanna have a few, shoot a little pool wid us?"

10.

"WE STOOD IN the school's parking lot between our two cars and Mac told me the whole thing from the beginning starting with her tattoo. She was auditing the class as a freshman at the college, reading poems aloud, even though he made a rule she couldn't speak, and breaking it, which made him angry; she came up to him after class to ask a question about one of the poems he taught that day. It was then, he said, he told her he knew about the tattoo she got in high school and asked to see it. She seemed to squirm a little he told me, but she did lift up her blouse enough—'modest as a queen,' he said—for him to read the gothic script that, as he put it, 'undulated from just past and along the roll of her hip in a curve that stopped beneath her navel.' He said it was an erotic vision—the ink tones graceful against her olive waist—but he simultaneously experienced a queasy revulsion because the tattoo was not Cicero's *Dum spiro spero,* but longer, more awkward: *Dum ego sum spirans, habeo spem.* His rising lust dispelled by nausea, he realized she misremembered the quote, and her tattoo was her own Latin from notes when he loosely translated an epigraph to his own poem as, 'As long as I am breathing, I have hope,' and that she rushed his paraphrase into her own Latin for the tattoo artist instead of bothering to look up, as he said slamming his fist down onto the hood of his car, 'the actual five fucking syllables, or even my own translation: 'while I breathe, I hope.'

"'He said he had been too sickened by her own pretended intelligence to say anything in the lecture hall that day. 'Oh, but what an emotional mess she'll become after she fucks an actual Latin scholar who recognizes what a cretin she is to have painted that inept script permanently onto her lovely body and starts to laugh at her in bed all naked and stupid. Ha! White trash that she is deep down. Wait a minute, wait a minute. That will be the trick, a nasty trick, but I could manage it, something pretty sneaky's going on here, Winston,' tapping his skull with his forefinger... Oh *Ho!* wait a moment, Heathcliff! He said he teaches Latin, didn't he?'

"Which is when I told him Jeff had a double major, the Gregorian Chanting and all that. Certainly, she had irritated him in class and had committed the 'sin' of mistranslating a quote which she had tattooed on the intimacy of her person. Was he disappointed in his former idealization of her and wanted to punish her for his own disillusionment? Even knowing of Mac's mean streak—and he *was* mean, Bobby, you must have known that—and his purist tendencies regarding the elevation of language and his defense of truth and literary standards—all that—his behavior seemed inordinately over-the-top behavior, almost unhinged. I mean what was it more than snobbery? Did he really feel so proprietary toward the dead languages and toward poetry that he found what she'd done was such an offense that he had to try to wreck even her love life? Why didn't he just *tell* her that the Latin was wrong and be done with it? I don't know, Bobby, what was aching inside your Dad at that time, but I know for certain that he didn't intend what happened to happen. From that brittle conversation, I took my time meandering through side streets, instead of following his Citroen like he wanted me to, down to the Brew Pub where we were to meet Moses and Jeff. He was already in full swing when I got there. He sat at a round table with Jeff and a student I recognized named Alton.

"SO, WHAT DO you look for in somebody else's stuff? You know, like, their poem's gotta have...what? Rhyme? Meter? all that? Or do you want something more about what's the meaning of life sort of thing?...Or..."

It was apparent that Mac had already arranged to be interviewed by the student paper. I had seen him do this before, but I sat at the table after ordering a beer. I was somewhat used to The Poet going public. The student reporter was holding a thin microphone toward Mac who sat at the table, a dark beer in front of him.

Behind them, Moses was racking pool balls. Some jarring music came from the bar, this young man asking a question that finally reached its conclusion.

"'So? What do you look for?'

"'I look for deceit, Alton. Trickery. Lies. Complete abandon, and utter foolishness. I hope to be bamboozled by the poet, or at least by his or her own poem since an author can be hair-brained and still create something so unparalleled it defies my best efforts toward *finding the truthiness* of the poem. I hope that helps. Now I must talk to Jeffrey here. Goodbye now.'

"Alton, who while half-listening appeared to be phrasing his next question, sank into a look of chagrin, his shoulders slumped. No further attempt would be greeted with as much energy as Mac's last perplexing bit.

"'Poor excuse for an answer,' Alton muttered into his shoulder bag as he put away his equipment. That and, 'Jesus!' He stood up, hoisted the bag onto his shoulder, nodded to Mac, but ignored Jeff and sauntered up the three steps where he faltered but regained composure quickly enough, only to sit at an empty table and take out a notebook.

"'He'll get over it,' said Mac. 'Marlowe's here, you know,' he told Jeff, 'That's her coat.'

"He pointed toward one of the chairs around the table, a woman's jacket draped over it.

"'Oh.'

"'Don't pretend you're not into her, my friend. She's in there. Behind that thin little door. That's where she is. You could almost hear. If this music wasn't so loud, you could almost hear people talk to you. Anyway, she's right behind that door. You can almost hear.'

"'Oh. Hear what?'

"'Yeah. Hear what, that's what I'm saying, Pal.' And then his perplexing stare.

"'Right behind that *leetle* bathroom door.'

"He took a sip of his beer. Behind him the knock of pool balls, the soft drop of one into the side pocket, and Moses' 'Ah ha!' filled a moment Jeff thought a little awkward, not quite seeing Mac's need to repeat this reference to the door.

"'Don't you know that story about Joyce?'

"'Joyce? Are you talking about something in *Portrait of the Artist*? Or...'

"'No. In his life. You must have heard this. The tinkle?'

"'What?'

"'The tinkle story.'

"Jeff sipped from his own beer glass, and smiled at me, unhappily, possibly thinking he might find a way to change the subject.

"'A young woman came to Joyce's studio—he didn't always have a studio, but he was working as a language teacher—and while she was there, she needed to pee.'

"'Uh, no. I don't think I know this story, but that's okay, you can...'

"'So, she goes behind the screen he had set up there and uses the chamber pot. It wasn't like Joyce saw her bloomers or anything, but he declared later that listening—the sound itself—was the most erotic experience he'd ever had up until that moment. It was a singular epiphany! Anyway, she's in there, and we can't hear a thing because of how damn loud it is out here.'

"'Oh. Thanks.'

"Jeff looked down at his glass.

"'I'm sorry. Are you offended? Well, gee whiz, gosh and golly. So sorry, my good friend. You must think me a big A-hole.'

"'Yeah, kinda.'

"'Okay, okay, Jeff. Just yanking your chain. Won't do it again. I really am sorry. It's a funny story, though.'

"I saw Mac's dark urchin smile float over the rim of the glass as he sipped his beer.

"'You should have seen the look on your face.'

"The 'thin little door' opened just then, and Harley Marlowe emerged and had to stand against the wall, wedged rather indelicately between it and Moses, whose very large posterior was toward her as he bent over the table; he wasn't aware of her standing there, and directed his pool cue back and forth, its butt end preventing her from stepping away. She waved her right hand at Jeff very quickly side to side and gave a brave painful smile to all of us, to indicate it might take her some time to cross this treacherous terrain. Telling you this now, I realize it had been only an hour earlier that he'd seen her and maybe frightened her in Mr. Sinclair's classroom and that he'd seen her only the night before at his place. Now here she was again, and it was apparent he felt the same rush of attraction. In hindsight, he would only see her once... Well, there's more to tell, let's put it that way.

"'So, did she show you the tat?' Mac was leaning across the table and asking Jeff with an expression of concern.

"'Tat? What are you talking about?'

"'Oh. I thought you knew. That's what we were looking at when you barged into Sinclair's room. She got a tattoo she was showing Winston over here.'

"'Oh. Why?'

"'Why what?'

"'Why was she showing you a tattoo that she had to...you know...uncover...remove some clothing to get at?'

When Moses completed his stroke on the seven ball and missed sinking it into the corner pocket, he straightened up and noticed for the first time Marlowe standing quietly behind him.

"'Oh, I'm sorry, Ms. Marlowe. Here, I'll make room. Sorry about that."

"'That's okay. No trouble."

"She walked rather gingerly around the big pool table until she reached the empty seat beside Jeff. And then she was sitting with them.

"'Hi, Mr. Fournier," she said with a bow, and a smile, a little sarcasm, I thought, in her formality.

"'Ms. Marlowe.' He nodded.

"He stared at her a moment, but without returning the smile, and I remembered a conversation I had with him once when he said any less-than-cheery look would betray how giddily happy he was—in this case, happy to simply have found her here; his straight face never seemed to suit what he thought were funny if inappropriate, things to say.

"'So. Would you like me to get you a beer or something?'

"'No. Thanks. I have to get back to the school to set up for the performance for the Parents tonight. Sinclair's students are singing. You're coming, right?'

"'Of course.'

"'Great. I'll save you a seat. Mac, you get there at seven, so I can go over the details, okay?'

"'Yes, Ma'am.'

"'He's going to read a poem. And you better keep it clean, too, there, Bacca. It's for the parents and the students. And the damn school board. So, mind your language, too. No swearing! I mean it. Okay?'

"'Uh hunh. Yup. Gotcha.'

"'Okay. I gotta go.'

"She looked at Jeff, this time without smiling, and gave his cheek a quick kiss. Then she got up and left. It stunned Jeff that she'd thought to kiss him, and he realized that most of the occasions he'd been near her she burst away suddenly. He hadn't realized she was so involved in events at the school.

"'So, I guess Sinclair took the day off today so he could be well rested for the performance tonight. Does that sound about right to you, Jeffrey?'

"'Well, I don't really know. I haven't talked to him since last June. We haven't had a conversation of any kind since school began. I don't have any idea what's up with him. How do you know him?'

"'Know him? Oh, yeah. We were crib-mates!'

"'What does that mean? You're old friends?'

"'No. It means a lot more than that, actually in our case. Our dads worked in the Post Office together and so our mothers got together and pushed the baby carriages around the streets of South Boston. There are pictures of the two of us in snowsuits building a snowman.'

"'I get it. What...well, what do you think of this religious conversion...? He's totally changed from the person I've been friends with. Do you know anything about that?'

"'No. I don't know. He doesn't talk to me about it. In fact, now that you mention it, he hasn't talked to me at all, since I moved here. I got here just before school started and we communicated by mail. He set up this day I would talk to his classes, but that was all done in writing. I don't use phones. So, I can't tell you. But...that's Sinclair. He's always been a little odd, a little 'out there,' you know? He'll get over it, and on to the next thing. Now, about her tat...'

"'Hey, Mac,' said Moses behind him. 'You're up. Were you going to play the winner?'

"'Okay. Jeff, I gotta talk to you about her. You were a Classics Major, correct?'"

11.

WE STOPPED FOR a breather. I pretended I wanted to look in the window of a store with the bright pink sign, "Haberdashery!" Nice hats were in the window. Overcoats, and leather gloves. All sorts of men's clothing appeared to be in there, and there was our reflection, two geeks standing in the street.

"Oh, I go in here all time. Do you need anything? This is where I got this great suit jacket."

His white sports coat. Who would have guessed?

"No, I don't think they'll have anything in there for me." No beat-up baseball hats, flannel shirts, or worn-out t-shirts. I definitely didn't need any new clothes to cart home, though maybe one of those nifty brims would look cool, I thought, and then I again saw Winston's dapper reflection.

"Nah, I don't want anything. So, what happened? It sounds like they met, they got along. What was it that...? I mean, you're suggesting Mac had some big life change, right? So far I can't tell what could have caused it."

"The accident..."

"Accident? I never heard anything about an accident..."

This disconcerted Winston. The way he looked at me was

a cross between sympathy and disbelief—as if I was pretending—maybe for my own sake, to protect myself—to not know anything about an event in my father's life that both Winston and Mac had marked as a "before and after," a way of reckoning the calendar, of knowing all dates in relation to that day. Before that day life had been innocent, whereas all anniversaries and calendar days thereafter became tinged, to some extent, by knowledge he could never escape.

"He didn't tell you about the accident? I guess he wanted to leave the whole thing in the past, or just didn't want you to know. I guess that's what he had in mind when he relocated—to escape the troublesome experience—and perhaps even responsibility. I don't know. No, wait, he did stay on until he was told no charges were brought, but he had to pay a substantial fine for negligent driving."

"What happened?"

"That's what I mean. This is what he did, okay? He knew Marlowe wanted to start seeing Jeff more seriously, so, after this big Open House night, his plan was to take Jeff for a ride under the pretense he only wanted to show off his exotic antique Citroen. He also knew Jeff hadn't seen the tattoo, and he wanted to tell him the story about the fake translation. He really did just want to mess things up for Marlowe. He thought of her as trailer-trash who should never have tried her hand at poetry to begin with and who completely broke his rules about how to treat poets and the Classics. He sincerely believed she had cynically appropriated the epigraph in the poem he read and was incensed. He did manage to keep his wrath hidden from her until he thought he could dig in and get revenge in a truly nasty way—upending her potential love match with a real Latin scholar, which he believed Jeff to be. On the other hand, as far as I knew, Jeff had only taken a few courses in Latin and was hired because the school thought continuing their Classics program, even in a small way, would be a feather in their cap, so to speak: to offer something arcane. Yet Mac wouldn't stop talking about it. I didn't understand why he wanted to do that, but days later, he seemed terribly regretful. It was something he had initiated, a movement in his own life and in hers that he himself was responsible for. So, of course, guilt was appropriate. But you know—he was so—I'm sorry, Bobby, but he was so self-obsessed...that guilt never did quite make sense.

"MAC TOLD ME much of this soon after the accident at a bar one night, and he was very drunk. And, I think, filled with grief. I'd never seen him blame himself for anything before, but he was blaming himself, telling me he was yelling to Jeff over the growl of his old car's engine trying to get across all the details of Marlowe's tattoo and of course adding his hints and innuendos in his own brand of sarcasm, which, as you know, laser sliced to the bone—and laughing at her and at Jeff, sitting in the front seat across from him: 'This is who you want? She's a complete fake, a joke.' In the bar that night he told me, 'Oh, I was good, Winston, I was very good. And I was pleased with myself too, let me tell ya,' he said, to be able to tell Jeff that now he could escape having this white trash lovefest—thanks to me,' he said, very, very bitterly there slurring his speech while we sat in that dark room, that night—those very words he kept repeating, his head hanging down, looking into his whiskey glass—the words which were also the last thing he said to Jeff before he swerved for an oncoming semi, drove headfirst into a tree and Jeff, beside him, was killed.

"Oh, my God!" I said.

Just then, on the street in front of us, a man was on his

knees, in knee pads, and surrounded by cardboard signs he had set up, bearing the faces of famous people who were to stand in for an audience. And one other sign with the words: "Police get out of my brain!" He was giving a speech from that kneeling position on the sidewalk and didn't appear to see anyone who might be walking past him. He had on black, empty, sunglasses, his head was bald and shining with sunlight. He was waving his hands as he spoke:

"It ain't sun. You see that big beam up there? That's what it is that's melting my mind. Sure it is! My mind and yours. Melting MELTing the MINDS like Butter, my babies. You just keep your eyes staring right there into that thing and you will see like nobody else ever has like I have many many times the great EYE that can't do NOTHING else but keep a firm watch on YOU And Don't You Dare Try Hidin' in Them shadows, you mutherfuckers. Where you gonna hide? The shadows ain't shadows of nothing. Not a thing exists that's a shadow. You get me? There ain't nothing there. You try looking at one and it moves, it creeps, it slimes along, onto the next tic in the clock. Believe me they are the blocked-out sunlight. They block that beam and drop death smears onto the ground, call 'em shadows and make yourself feel better but who do you think can be dripping those twigs off the nothing tree? You Do. You Do You Do..."

We could hear his voice even after we were a block past him. Finally, though, when he was out of earshot, I felt I could say something to Winston.

"I didn't know that. But I have to admit, he had a way with trying to ruin other people when he got a chance to. I'm very sorry. He was your friend. I guess it's a great loss when you lose someone in a freaky way like that. I think you're right that Mac didn't intend anything as bad as that to happen. He couldn't have known. Of course. Yet, he's still responsible. He's gone now. So, I can tell you, knowing him the way I did, which wasn't the same Mac you knew, I'm truly ashamed for the actions my Dad set into motion that led to your friend Jeff's death."

12.

WE WERE APPROACHING Coit Tower. We were at one of the highest points in San Francisco, and I wanted to take one more moment to examine the 360-degree view, to look all the way down to Telegraph Hill and toward the Embarcadero and turn around to face Stinson Beach well beyond the downtown area. I wished I could have been up here all morning painting instead of listening to all this. Why did I pursue Winston if not to find out what Mac's life was worth? What he did that mattered so much he couldn't have spent those years with me when I needed a Dad. Why did I think knowing this was so important I had to track people down who knew him, if I only found he went out of his way to hurt people for the sake of hurting them, telling himself it was all about truth and beauty? Truth and Beauty. What bullshit is that?

We sat down on the grass, and he told me the rest of that story.

"Thanks for saying that, Bobby. Of course, I only knew about the way Jeff died the day after we all went to the Open House at the school. It was there I overheard Mac's somewhat jive talk to him and Marlowe, hinting—he was forever hinting—at some deep mystery regarding her and her tattoo he wanted to talk over with Jeff. Jeff, who he seemed to want to show he had great respect for, although as he kept talking, well, whispering in that crowded audience as we all were, I realized he wasn't really doing anything but trying to manipulate the lives of two people. I didn't know why, and I still don't know why, Bobby. He was your dad, though, and you deserve to hear the whole tale. He knew Sinclair's chorus would perform and what that entailed he couldn't predict. No one could tell from the crowd in the cafeteria, where parents and teachers gathered, if rumors were true that a vocal minority demanded Sinclair's resignation. Bright colors, a flood of fluorescent bulbs, the dark October evening, wayward burnt orange leaves at the windows, bright neon green chairs flamed out in rows for parents to meet the faculty. Jeff chose his only tie with a gray tweed jacket and faded jeans and tennis shoes. He was passing a small group of three parents, as a woman he didn't recognize looked away from the conversation and directly at him. She seemed to wonder if he was a single parent or a teacher, her face lined about the eyes and forehead, her hair a swept-back tint of faintly reddish-purple-brown like crinkled paper, her jaw moving as to a metronome while she chewed gum.

"There was no way to know what could happen, and when I waved at him and pointed at the chair to the right of Marlowe, I did feel a bit protective of Jeff. He's my friend, I thought, so is Mac. And I liked Marlowe, I really did. I had no idea what Mac could do. I only thought he wanted to play a joke somehow. That side of Mac I was used to, the prankster. He sat to the left of Marlowe, and I was in the row behind them. To get to their seats, Jeff had to pass a couple who were whispering, the woman whispering and the man—I noticed Jeff staring as his bald skull nodded rhythmically while her lips moved, her teeth clenched. Her left hand under her right elbow, she extended her right hand toward the man's shoulder, occasionally touching him, two fingers, fitted for an invisible cigarette. Her eyes were not focused on the bald man, but ahead on the school administrators near the makeshift stage. One of whom, Mr. Leads, tapped on a microphone as Jeff reached his chair. Next to Jeff, Marlowe both smiled and sort of frowned at him, teasing him, I think, for being late. I thought of the look she gave him while she danced out of Sinclair's room. To her left and leaning forward to smile toward Jeff was Mac Bacca's head, *or is that a leer no one should take seriously,* I thought.

"Mac whispered across Ms. Marlowe, 'Jeff, after this shindig, I want to take you for a ride in my car. Have you ever been inside an antique Citroen? Smooth as a butterfly. I've got something I want to talk over with you. Okay, Buddy?' I really thought, Bobby, that he had some joke up his sleeve he wanted to play on Marlowe. I guess I was naïve, but it felt like Mac had a present he wanted to give her that involved Jeff, somehow.

"Jeff whispered his answer, 'Okay...maybe...' as the Vice Principal began to speak quite softly into the mic asking for everyone's attention. I couldn't help but think, naïve as I was, what did Jeff think the poet had in store for him. After all, he had just met the man this afternoon. I wondered if he had any hesitation; it was only because of my own connection to Mac that he might have thought he could trust him, even though all he saw was a strange greasy man with an urchin's face. Jeff might have seen how his own suburban world was expanding, though, and thought a ride with the poet was a chance to see through those unusual eyes, eyes which, nevertheless, seemed chipped out of shale.

"'Jeff...Jeff,' Mac this time leaned over Ms. Marlowe so closely his wispy beard brushed her blouse, and he seemed eager to tell Jeff something. 'Jeff. Listen. You know she was my student, right?'

"Jeff looked at Marlowe, who rolled her eyes.

"'Yeah. That's why she was showing me the tat...' He rolled his own eyes toward Ms. Marlowe '...on her voluptuous body.'

"With both hands, she pretended to cover his mouth.

"'Yeah. My student and, no, we never did it—in case you're curious.'

"He said all this in a whisper. I could see a chilled look come over Jeff; he may have decided not to take the ride—antique poet car or not. Ms. Marlowe's brown eyes were now quite alert to what Mac would whisper next.

"'But you probably want to fuck her, am I right?'

"Jeff gave him a pained smile to show disapproval and sat upright in his chair.

"'Jeff, Jeff,' he whispered again, placing his right elbow and forearm across Ms. Marlowe's lap.

"'Jeff, one more thing. One more thing,' and he motioned with his left hand for Jeff to come in closer. Jeff gave another annoyed look but did lean closer. That was the first time I saw it: Mac's smile was that of a thief who had lain in wait for an innocent, someone like Jeff, farm boy with a degree in Classics, teacher of Language Arts but not English Literature—'Jeff. Jeff. What about me? You and me. We can be *friends* like that, yeah?'

"Questions, I thought immediately, I wished I hadn't leaned in to overhear, which so easily could have been, but wouldn't be, drowned out—out of my memory, or out of Jeff's or Marlowe's consciousness—by the loud scrape of the door at the end of the room, wind fidgeting through the courtyard, footfalls, parents' shushing noises to whisperers like Mac who said, "Hey, isn't that Sin?" The chorus of eight enrobed boys and six girls entered, and the audience hushed while they briskly—and rather proudly for this far too fleeting escape from the good of the order—filed through the door letting in cool night wind and a few orange leaves. They walked flapping their long magenta garbs, and then I finally saw the elusive Mr. Sinclair, who stood only after they came to a halt. His starched white figure against the students' colorful gowns floated from one to another for a moment, smiling, tapping chins upward, patting a shoulder or an arm. And then after three taps of his baton, parents came to attention. Utter momentary silence, and his sweeping right arm, while the chorus's eyes followed, slowly rose, then fell and rose and a first shower of high notes poured over the room, raced along the stucco walls, the low ceiling. "All We Like Sheep," brisk concentration of every sound, their mouths in unison, in rapt attention to the meaning of the words; *allegro moderato* up and down to Mr. Sinclair's right hand, and at "have gone astray" the sopranos and tenors themselves took delirious flight, their crisp chords mounting above the figurative path where music rushed away with them, with his students—their ecstatic voices all astray together."

The Telemachia

13.

A MONTH AFTER meeting Winston, my little world was shredding itself. Mac was not Mac, and I was, well, who was I? When I was on the cusp of teenagerhood, he came back to town, and I didn't recognize him. He could have been some old goatherd with mangy hair; the way he dressed then was pretty much in rags—or unwashed clothes, which I found out later he'd been living in his car for the six months prior to landing in town. Now, when I look back on it, I could have made an effort. That is, I could have seen him, have found him, somewhere buried inside that ragman, but I didn't. I didn't know that having killed someone could have brought about such a drastic change, and of course, I was no longer the eight-year-old who worshipped his daddy. Besides that, Winston's overwrought revelations aside, I needed to get back to work, and back to hermit life with canvas and brush strokes day in day out, so my girlfriend left me. I thought self-medicating was a good solution and kept at it for a week or two.

When I awoke—but I wasn't dreaming, and I hadn't really slept; when I came to—even that's not right because I wasn't knocked out—it was something different where all memory and recognition was a blot; like a guy called onto the hypnotist's stage in Vegas, I emerged from my trance, let's call it, sitting on one of the unprotected toilet seats, headache you couldn't imagine—the kind that begins as a wave under your left eye and snakes back behind the ear to pop upward through the cap of your cranium. And there it was, right in front of me in my own handwriting on the wall-sized chalkboard the bar owners had salvaged from the high school remodel, along with hardwood floors that sailed under my shoes and out the open Men's Room door to the loud halfway-to-a-drunk-Happy-Hour—there it was: my writing in a hand adopted from the old master himself, my *Papá,* Massimo Monroe Bacca, the famous poet. I didn't recall standing up at that chalkboard, let alone writing so much that I covered it in blue script. But I did recognize the lines my father had me memorize the summer I was thirteen, excerpted from *La Divina Comedia;* they, he had drummed into me, were the best lines in *Il Purgatorio.* I must have stood at that chalkboard writing a long time to get it all down, not that anyone had the slightest idea about the Italian; I could barely remember writing it, what with the ache unpacking its briefcase to serve a writ on my frontal lobe.

When I went back into the bar, there were two of my old high school buddies; I couldn't remember their names. But I climbed back onto the barstool between them anyway.

"You didn't see me, man. You didn't hear anything," said the stool to the left of me.

"You couldn't look around, you were writing, totally writing on the board, Dude. Nothing else going on," said the right.

"I went walking past that door and there you were. Your back to the urinals and shitters, writing on the old-school slate. Blue chalk, too, and I thought all they ever had was yellow. Where'd you get blue, man? You brought that in with you? You had it in your pocket or something?" Left.

"Yeah, scribbling so fast, your hair bounced off your shoulders. Man! You never heard a thing, and I shouted at you." Right.

That was at least a week after the night my girlfriend decided my life was too boring and wanted out. I took what I was feeling to be "heartbreak," but I also thought how could someone like me feel that? My life wasn't a soap opera, but I guessed I was feeling something, and that's what should have mattered to me. A novelty, in a way, to feel *some*thing, even though I couldn't put a name on whatever this was. Maybe I didn't think of soap opera, but I saw how pathetic my wallowing was. Or I do now. For an hour before I found this very nice chalk, I wallowed on the barstool with those guys, dredging up old high school pathos. Before that week, I hadn't been anywhere near that bar since the night I was thirteen and my dad swallowed Windowpane acid and thought he was going to stab my mother.

Now here I was. She was bored, my flighty photojournalist, and going out dancing in some other seaside town, going back on coke, her mood enhancer of choice, and it would stay that way till the money was gone and her new friend kicked her out. I was unknotting my unfamiliar emotions repeating lines my father had me memorize: *Purgatorio,* Canto 31, Beatrice reprimands him for love itself. When I stopped and woke up on the broken-down toilet seat, and looked up at what I had wrought, there it was, my own perfection:

> *"...Che pense?*
> *Rispondi a me: che le memorie triste*
> *In te non sono ancor da l'acqua offense."*
> *Confusione e paura insitem miste*

Mi pinsero un tal "si" fuor de la bocca,
al quale intender fuor mestier le viste.
Come balestro frange, quando scocca
da troppa tesa, la sua corda e l'arco,
si scoppia' io sottesso grave carco,
fuori sgorgando lagrime e sospiri,
e la voce allento per lo suo varco.
Ond' ella a me: "Per entro I mie' disiri,
Che ti menavano ad amar lo bene
Di la dal qual non e a che s'aspiri,
Quai fossi attraversati o quai catene
Trovasti, per che del passare innanzi
Dovessiti cosi spogliar le spene?
E quali agevolezze o quali avanzi
Ne la fronte de li altri si mostraro,
Per che dovessi lor possaggieare anze?"[1]

---

[1] *"What are you thinking?*
Answer me. You haven't purged bitterness
In this memory stream."
Confused, an impoverished spirit made
Me utter in my misery, "yes"
Only her ears could know my inward life.
If you draw a bow with too much force
The string and bow snap together and the shaft
Strikes weak, like me, shattered
By intense emotion: tears, sighs, burst
And my voice failed.
She said: "You journey desiring me
Leading toward a Good beyond which
The heart wants nothing.
What did you find? What chains snared you?
That you thought you had to abandon hope?
What desires appeared so promising
you wasted your time Courting?"

Despite this childhood remnant of Dante, it was my John Proctor Period. Even drunk, I could think that's how I wanted to look to anyone entering The John and looking for recent graffiti, which, like an obsessed Puritan, I wiped out so I could inscribe the Dante. I had no respect for drunken repetitive political opinions and unfortunate sex adventures. The "cunts" and "twats" and the jizz-spurt members cartooned on the board or the "moon in Scorpio" and, "you can't pick your friends or your ass in this place" "for a good blowjob (or any other kind) call..." and numbers, numbers, endless numbers.

From the evidence, I had erased the board with my black sleeve—and why? I was boring. The woman I was more-or-less happy to spend nights and days with for now went off on a cocaine binge and told me I was. I never realized just how boring life with me had been. I'd been painting Italian landscape miniatures for ten years, those images I carried in my head since grade school. Three little houses I saw on a hill where I thought, "I could live there." But she found me boring and here I was—bemoaning her loss, and in my best John Proctor outfit. I had recently read Arthur Miller's play and refused to see the movie version or performances anywhere, my long black hair stringy and greasy down to my shoulders, all dressed in black dour. That Proctor who was burned alive for a witch, seduced by a bored Salem teenager. Proctor is the only honest man in Miller's version, the only non-heretic. A True Believer, he never questioned his due, unlike me, scribbling Dante with my supposedly broken heart; it was *her* fault, I told myself like who knows how many others who consider themselves jilted cry out? Now I think of it as pathetic hopelessness and judge myself overly romantic, though there I was, in the piss of men, thinking of Proctor, a trunk filled with whose confiscated possessions were tucked below a huge circular staircase of the mansion in the private school where my old man once was an innocent high school scholar. The Proctor Estate was originally owned by a family of profiteers judging by his pictures of vast acreage and ornate buildings; he talked about before the Great Depression when they released the property into the hands of debtors who turned it into the private school that took him away from city life and set him on the road to poetry. Even the Dante was *his* choice. Like his version of my John Proctor array. Dark Italian, dark Puritan, Heavy Metal in black, my only light I created in quaint Italian pastoral miniatures. Scratching away at the chalkboard, away from the bling band and my few friends on the barstools, because my latest Beatrice descended to earth and found me a waste of her precious time.

We did talk about it, just before she left since that was the adult thing. As if both she and I *did* have something at stake yet were always ready to end it.

"Yeah, you should...Why spend your time waiting for me to finish a painting?"

"Right? There's only this life! Let's be smart. You don't want to have me around. I'm a distraction, aren't I?"

"What do you mean...I..."

"Oh, come on. You could never...you don't think I can see what's going on in your... *land*scapes...your own little swampland?"

"That's not true. Of course, you can..."

"Oh, I know I can, but you don't really see that, do you. You think I'm not smart enough to appreciate your creepy attitude in these utopias of yours. You ooze sarcasm in every brushstroke, but you're talking to yourself, aren't you? Like there's no one there, except maybe Daddy, who can understand what you really think. Isn't that true!"

"What the fuck are you talking about?"

"That I'm a dope and you're...well...you're You! You don't need me...or anybody."

It was that talk I didn't want to remember now at the actual breaking up part, talk that comes back often, one of those memories you don't shake no matter how much replaying them in different ways seems to help, ways in which you get to say the things you wish you really *did* say, until you're back in it, steeped in the regrettable solidity of the past.

"So. I'm going off to do what I do, Hon'. Okay?"

She made quotation marks with her fingers as she said, "*We can still be friends,* okay? Don't be mad. You don't need me, and I'm just not having any fun, ya know?"

Her eyebrow going upward at this, her face seemed to redden with the thrill of some meaning she'd hidden in every nuance of gesture and flex of her voice.

"So, I don't want you to pout. Or be sad or anything."

She tilted her head to the side and pouted her own lower lip, "but don't you fucking *ever* come looking for me!"

14.

I WAS STILL sitting on my bench in the sunlit studio, and I heard the door behind her as she hit the street, triumphantly I thought. That is, even sitting there immersed in self-concocted hurt, I could imagine she must feel great, maybe for the first time in at least the last two of our four years, as she stepped into the street—off to look for fun. I sat on that stool while sunlight shimmered the harbor, dwindled and transferred its effects to a puddle of streetlight glow, and then I went out myself, to The Pocket, my dad's own bar, and found his cloak of true gloom fit me quite well. The hood I place over my emotional life was perhaps the same as the emptiness my father succumbed to after his accident. In that tiny office "slash" apartment above a street full of tourists all that summer, he was the hermit staring at a television, drinking by day, and writing, he said, his nightmare poetry, which he showed only me, his urchin, thirteen years old and wild in the streets. That was the summer after what was for me and my mother our worst winter; not only due to the relentless rain our part of the world depends on, but the arrival in our lives of the creature who I still refer to only as Deputy Dave.

Sitting in that moody afternoon barroom, I forced myself to recognize how I had already fabricated the ways I blamed my erstwhile girlfriend—she was shallow, she was out to make money, she left me alone months at a time, she was crazy—but it was my own strategy to force her out, to become passive so she would have no choice but seek relief somewhere else and I could prove a diminished self *is* a valid mode of art. People break up all the time. Women accuse men of being boring, many ruin their lives after the breakup. Not necessarily the fault of the boring boyfriend, although I still do feel guilty, and I *can* still blame my father. He gave me the model for the reclusive artist, the detached creator. I wrote on the wall in a foreign language a poem no one would read to declare my loss without talking, without anyone knowing. Much like Mac, I found that in my own John Proctor avatar I could burn at the stake of self-loathing and suffer myself into a work of art worth crying over. Neither father nor son could have directly expressed emotion. Adult males. No big deal. Who can? Without being laughed out of the bar, I mean.

No adult I knew when I was thirteen talked things over with me. Mac was this giant piece of cheese who every now and then spoke. He was destroyed, I know now thanks to Winston, by an accident that took someone's life whose future—even whose love life—he'd made it his business to attempt to manipulate. I don't know if he cared about this guy Jeff. He was like that, before the cheese persona. He could find someone and act like his best friend, but he didn't have much feeling one way or the other about anyone, as a person I mean. He could become anyone's friend, he had a way of getting inside people's skins, of appearing to want to hear "all the sunny trifles" as he was fond of saying, quoting some book. I think Moses made him pay attention and keep at least one friendship alive. Yet he learned the trick of appearing to be everybody's friend. That's like being nobody's friend. He's why I'm the way I am. A whole lifetime and I still don't know myself. But I look back at my little breakdown in the bathroom and wonder did I feel anything. I'm like a doctor testing a paralytic with a stick: "Anything?" I can say I thought about John Proctor every time he got dressed. And painting minimalist landscapes, brush tip under magnifying glass, I might have deserved to be called boring by her, whose portrait I never tried to paint—would she have found that less boring? Was I so far into my mind I didn't recognize feelings when they spat in my face? (More about spit later). Well, I got that from him. Expunge the feeling part. Shun cliché; I learned from his behavior up until that accident and he turned into a lump of cheese, that emotion is excessive, broad strokes are best expressed ironically. So, I look back on John Proctor scribbling Dante for Christ's sake on a wall, and all I can see is irony; I couldn't have a feeling. Where did four years go? We gave them over to the tyranny of the couple, a life I embraced, and John Proctor gave me the model when he goes to his pyre, renounces the authority of God, not God-fearing, but God likened.

15.

UNSURPRISINGLY, I TOOK a regular seat at Happy Hour after the night I wrote out my Dante in chalk. I enjoyed the hubbub in The Pocket, the steady drone of morose voices, and that surrender I witnessed all around me, and began to acquiesce to a life devoid of optimism, became one for whom the lives of others if not compelling were at least worth listening to, worthy of feigning concern. Idealism was foreign, and life was scraping by on piecemeal enjoyments. Little by little, I backed away from the actual drinking part and learned to nurse a glass for hours. They weren't all drunk either, and I found I liked to listen to people's stories. Grim stories about failure—in love, in money, in their own sad efforts to be halfway meaningful parents. On and on, but if somebody spouted an opinion about art or the art world, I'd call it a night. Only stories kept me on my barstool. Especially those edging near my own memories of this place, Mac's very own bar, the sharpest among my memories of him, and those I sometimes—now more and more late at night—tried to paint.

People came up to where I sat to strike up a conversation or ask a question to do with art because, in fact, most of us lived along the beach, tucked away in studios off the tourist path, artists of one art form or another. Practical questions I could tolerate—opinions, no. Quentin, for instance, a well-known sculptor, was a different story. His studio out in the woods, far from the heavily trafficked areas, allowed him the isolation art demanded. In my case, distraction was pleasant, which could have explained why my work sold only enough to pay rent and buy some beer. Quentin was too high-strung to bother with a barstool—to sit still. He was right beside me, waving the glass of beer he'd brought over from the other end of the bar to describe the immense sculpture he'd been working on for months. An unusual-looking person, he always wore a baseball hat stained with clay-dust or soot or maybe mud, and his eyes were a brightly lit heterochromia if you will—they were each a different color. He had one eye on me and the other on the bartender. His head bobbing side to side, he uttered profundities about his "process," the richness of his sources, that is, his dreams.

"Bobby, do you paint from dream images? I work that way. I'm always scribbling in the night. Anything and everything that arises in a dream. Jung says..."

"Jung?"

"Yeah. You know who Jung was, right? I've studied his work for years now and the way the clay feels or the depth and even the solidity of marble takes me to places in the dream..."

I stopped listening, turned away, and made it appear I needed to commune some more with my glass. My own Italian landscapes occasionally represented a familiarity I had with a mythic life. Houses appeared to me as adaptations of the storied castles I grew up with, maybe castles we visited when I was a child in Europe, even though what I was painting were middle-class farmhouses. They carried me back, always without fail, to some place I touched, or were in my vivid dreamlife which I believed I should barricade off from art. Now, annoyingly, here was Quentin, trying to illumine the grand style that imbued his artistic enterprise, a financial success that I'll admit made me envious. Yet he believed, and I'm sure he had his followers or cohorts believe, he drew his art from the "Collective Unconscious," which he could elucidate as eloquently as any professor. Although in fact, I saw him as a total primitive, he was an autodidact and a leading West Coast sculptor.

"Jung," I said, tilting my head back toward him, a "close-talker" who made even looking at him a chore, "Jung, now..."

"Yeah, when I discovered him, my life just..."

"He was a Nazi, right?"

With certain people, you just know. He rolled his head, so I almost thought he was exercising a stiff neck; either that or he was about to hit me. His eyes popped wildly and fiercely large out of their trembling lids, and something was happening to his mouth that I knew was an inarticulate shaping of words to confront what must have been a familiar observation regarding the Master. Even I knew that Jung had signed documents which may or may not have condemned some German subjects to persecution, documents that described diagnoses which he later found the Nazi government used to stock the work camps. I knew Jung was no Nazi. Still, this could be fun.

"Oh. Oh. Oh. I've heard this before. I know all about this. That's just, I don't know, that's just...just stupid!"

Luckily, he didn't say this directly to me since he was spitting beer with almost every syllable and wiping drool off his lips and chin.

"Look, I've got documents at my house that will prove

to you...and...and...I want you to take it back when you see them...I'm going home right now to get some of these papers, and I want to show...show you that you're absolutely fucking wrong. You're off base, here, sir."

He banged his beer stein like a longshoreman onto the solid oak bar some enterprising seaman had lugged around Cape Horn for an early Northwest capitalist who commissioned a clipper to sail it from New York and around Tierra del Fuego.

"I'll be right back," and he rushed away, slamming the gigantic glass door behind him.

16.

THE MIRROR IN The Pocket—have I mentioned it was my father's favorite place?—was pure. It reflected all faces, mine included—shaggy, half-surprised to be found there—and the light, every light, splashed off Sea Street where I could see Quentin in a diminishing perspective—humping across the pavement, waving angrily at oncoming cars, shaking his head and most likely grunting about accusations against his hero. He hobbled toward a ratty pickup. Along the bar, as the sun burst off the mirror, all our faces lit up for the voluptuous barkeep at the till, her back to us. In the mirror I spotted a hand down the bar, waving back and forth, a little wave. To me? Oh, yes, to me. and then I recognized the face. Pure in this purest of mirrors, but distorted, backwards, there he was, who used to be a kid I knew, possibly a decade ago, Tristan who was, unluckily for him, the son of that fucker, Deputy Dave.

He was five years older, and everybody my age looked up to him when we were kids, but he went away. Nobody knew why or where he went. One day he just wasn't there. As it turned out, Tristan went off to a private school near the Canadian border.

"MAYBE 'I WAS sent away' is a little harsh. I did ask for it myself."

He wanted to be by a river and have lots of territory to get away from the school and roam around in the wilderness. Tree-hugger, that was Tristan.

"My Dad felt pretty good about it, you know. He really wanted me to go. And even though I told myself that was the reason, I just wanted to get away from them."

"You did?"

He looked down at his hands. "A lot of bitching each other out all the time. I mean they hated each other. I remember this one time...I must have been like a toddler or something... and I guess she had enough because she was smacking him. He fell back down onto the bed holding his head with both hands, you know? Because she was whacking him, and then the damn bed collapsed, legs broke or something, the mattress fell to the floor."

The Pocket's high ceilings and brick walls I discovered long ago and re-examined them now. Excellent place to show some paintings, the less pricey ones. My early efforts attracted tourists who wandered in for a keepsake from the beach. One of my small landscapes, with a cottage sinking into a healthy bog, hung at the end of the bar, a little out of our line of sight. He rambled on about his terrible childhood. The painting was in too large and ornate a frame. Maybe I'd take it home and reframe it after a beer or two. He did seem to repeat himself a lot for someone who thought he'd become a scholar. So, anyway, he wanted to get away from them (yeah, yeah, yeah, who wouldn't, I thought). He was surprised his dad wanted him to go away, pushed him to go.

"See, when he came back from Vietnam, he needed some counseling like a lot of Vets, but he didn't look for help. He refused to consider his temper problematic; he refused to think he was weak enough to go to a shrink. That's how he looked at things. He wasn't weak. He was Deputy Dave. Even I called him Deputy Dave. Sometimes Pop."

Maybe they had an agreement. Tristan goes off to private school was the best thing that happened to both. He didn't see his family more than once a month, and the mother mostly showed up alone. He was in this remote part of the state and later went to college even farther away. He stayed away from home until he was twenty-five. I bought us both another round.

"When I was about twenty my mother said things were unbearable with Deputy Dave. She was going to leave. I didn't get many details until later, and that was from my sister. She's your age, right? You must have known her at school. I know, I know—always a grim expression on *her* face. I guess she's what you'd call a Stoic. She grew up in Dave's house, what would you expect? She wasn't like me—she witnessed bizarre paranoia firsthand. It got to where Dave was doing a lot more than shouting and arguing. Throwing things—dinner platters and dishes when everyone was eating. Whenever he didn't like the spaghetti or whatever, he threw the whole thing against the wall, then went out and sat on the porch with his Vodka. Some people, I guess could understand that what they were witnessing, if they weren't a part of the family, was a typical response to being in a war, but my mother didn't have any patience with Dave, and sometimes she fought back. Mostly, she not only yelled and screamed while my overweight sister sat there trying to be invisible, but she picked up those plates and the food and threw the shattered bits in the sink."

After these sessions, his mother told him, Deputy Dave went into the bedroom to smoke in the dark. When she started to work the night shift at the hospital, which is when the dishes started flying, he spent every night lying in there and all sister ever saw was the glowing tip of the lit cigarette. She did whatever she wanted. Tristan by then was in college and became a good scholar (of what I wasn't sure, maybe physics) and could easily forget that back home the women were terrorized. Certainly, Dave whacked her plenty of times, and then the place was explosive. Tristan couldn't sleep after that visit from his mother, imagining what it was like back home. He had such head pain and stomach problems he went to a doctor to be tested; they referred to it back then as a nervous breakdown, although there are more clinical names now—severe anxiety attacks seemed the prevalent symptom for the next year or more. He had little interest in creating a future for himself in some academic arena and finally had to confess he was in school primarily to get away from that shitty family.

"Even when I was fourteen and the fighting had been going on a few years, I knew this was not the way people behaved around one another, not in front of their kids. Why do you want to know all this, anyway?"

It was so long ago now I assumed he already knew what happened after his parents split up, but it was only at that instant, sitting on a barstool with Tristan that it came to me that no one else in town knew because we could never tell. Not back then.

At one end of the bar were the tall windows, almost floor-to-ceiling looking onto the street. Not a busy street as far as traffic goes, but there were lots of tourist families, grandmothers licking ice creams in front of giftshop display windows, and little kids crying for more. All this made me ill mostly, and it hadn't changed since I used to fly wild around these streets barefoot on my bike. I nodded toward the dark end of the bar, the short leg of its L-shape in shadows, room for only two barstools.

"See those guys down at the end?"

"Yeah. So?"

"It's almost like they could have been our dads, yours and mine, except yours probably never even came in here except to roust drunks, and mine usually sat over there, at the other end, at that round table beside the window. Everybody left him alone. Those guys could have been our dads—if, and only if, we had a normal life growing up in this town. You know what I mean?"

"Yeah, I know exactly what you mean. And in a few years, that could be me and you, plunked down there with a pitcher of beer in front of us, baseball hats on, staring into space like furniture."

"I could have called either one of them 'Dad.' "

I held up my glass toward the two geezers for a blasé cheer. Down the old wood bar, sunlight along its surface rushed in. It had been raining when I came in. The bartender, the blond woman in tight jeans, worked her way toward us with a white bar rag for beer spillage and wet rings where fishermen and out-of-work carpenters used none of the coasters she tossed in their directions. When she reached us, she gave me a coy smile, or I thought it was coy, if only because I was certain she knew and everyone in town must have known my former girlfriend was shacked up with a drugged-out freak at the edge of the Marina. Was I at least "interesting" now?

"How are you gentlemen doing? Can I get you another beer?"

Back then I took my delusions seriously. What she said I translated as, "Why don't you wait around till I get off work?"

"I think back on everything nowadays," he hadn't even

noticed her, his head down, fingers shredding the label off the green bottle, "and I sort of blame myself, you know? Of course, we all knew later he had PTSD, but a lot of good that did our family—or anybody's families, or the people he busted for that matter. Hindsight, you know? I guess it's useful when you want to forgive somebody twenty years later. Anyway, if I just didn't want so bad to get out of the house, or to get a different education, if I didn't want more than I had, I guess, I probably could have stopped him from what he did to my mom and sister."

"What do you mean? Weren't you only a kid then too?" I nodded to the bartender, held up two fingers, and took out some bills, then pointed at the two old guys at the dark end of the bar and bought them a refill.

"Yeah, he sent me away...no, wait, I have to admit to myself that I was actively trying to find a way out of our house...but, yeah, I was fourteen. When I went off to the school, I mean. And it was cool, I admit. It was the coolest place, and I really wanted to learn things there. I mean it was a private school, you know? I was very aware nobody I knew had a chance to get that kind of education and I didn't want to blow it. So, I guess part of that was not thinking about what was going on at the old homestead. But I think about it now, and I know he wanted me out of the house because he never would have gotten away with half the shit he pulled if there was another male in that place. I'm certain of it. He might have kept on being a dick, but he wouldn't have gotten to carry on with his tantrums and roughing people up like he did. Not that I would have been able to fight him or anything, but I think just having someone who could look at him from a man's point of view instead of the way he thought the women ought to see him. You know—servile handmaidens or something? No, if I was there, my father might not have been on his best behavior, he might be insulting, but he wouldn't have been all that violent. Not to them, anyway. Hell, whenever I was around, he wouldn't even shout unless I purposely said something to get him upset. Always a possibility, too, so I usually was on my best behavior when I came home like for holidays or something.

"But what I've been thinking through lately is...well, it's a 'what if' kind of thing which I'm sure everybody goes through, looking back at things they didn't do when they did something else that later seemed like a personal failure...I keep thinking what if I went to the high school like everybody else, like you and my sister, and not been so fucking ambitious? What if I never left home until I *was* old enough? I would have sat right there every night at that damn table and he wouldn't throw a dish."

If he'd been there, he would have stood up for them, he would have. At least in hindsight, that's what he was sure of when he talked to me. At age thirty-nine, many years after all that happened, when he finally knew what was going on. Then it occurred to him that even if he wasn't quite brave enough to stand up to Deputy Dave beating on the family, he knew that Dave wouldn't have known that.

"On the other hand, what kind of parent lets his kids make big life choices at fourteen? I guess a lot do, but why? Don't they think *they* should be the adult? Why is it always 'what the kid wants the kid should have?' I don't think it used to be that way in the good ole US of A. I think kids just did whatever they were told and going to work was most of it."

Just then the pretty blond woman gave the geezers their beer and brought us bottles of our rank German pilsners, set fresh glasses on two new coasters, and took the five and the twenty I'd laid on the bar. She gave me a glance, and maybe half a smile, by which I figured there'd be no change and turned away.

"Anyway, my dad he knew what he wanted, and he saw this as a chance to get me out of the picture. Hell, he jumped at the chance; he wanted to be the only male in the house, rule the roost. He sent me to live in an institution to study, become a scientist maybe, and he never even tried to teach his own son how to be a real man; he would be the one to show his wife, train his daughter, to see what a real man was, someone who's the boss, lord, and master of his house. He gets what he wants and doesn't care about the screaming old lady, screaming daughter, barking dogs. He had a hard day at work, was all he needed to say—if anyone asked, he was Deputy Dave."

17.

ALTHOUGH NOBODY AT first knew where Tristan had gone, it was easy to predict, back in our school days, that he'd end up a drunk. Maybe because of growing up anywhere near Dave or just because he started to drink and smoke dope before he came to school. But the guy everyone knew right away would have a hard time with alcohol was Chet Dyer, who occasionally would leave town in the hope of a self-induced recovery and then come back and fall right off the wagon. As we sat at the bar, in fact, Chet came in through the big glass front doors, a wide, toothy smile at everyone, dressed as a Hari Krishna disciple. Maybe he'd been trying to dry out in their community in Seattle, but at the moment the shaved head and the saffron gown were the latest costumes of Chet the Drunk. He immediately jumped onto a table waving his arms to the rock music coming over the tavern's sound system, then leapt over to the pool table where he danced around the rolling striped pool balls in his bare feet.

The music stopped. The beautiful bartender grimaced and motioned with her hands to the two geezers who sat, their arms crossed, before the two beers I'd bought for them. They both got off their barstools. One of whom was carrying a pole, too short to be a cane, and they hobbled quickly over to the pool table, grabbed Chet by the arms, and tossed him onto the barroom floor. The one with the pole poked Chet in the legs with it. It turned out to be an electric cattle prod. Chet jumped to his feet. The two burly geezers each grabbed one arm and hustled him to the front door, opened it, and threw Chet onto the sidewalk. Then the music came back on, and people started laughing.

Tristan was rocking back and forth, twisting the swivel seat of the barstool and he chugged his beer bottle as if he hadn't seen what just happened, his left hand flailing for the sleeve of a denim jacket draped over the back of the seat. Out of the jacket pocket, a white glove fell to the floor beside his boot.

"Well, I gotta get outa here, my friend. Good to see you, and thanks for buying the beer."

"What happened? Are you in a hurry? I have to get out of here pretty soon too, I've got an appointment with a landlord down the street, but...what's wrong?"

"Look! Wait, don't turn around. I just noticed that's my ex at that table behind us. Maybe you can see her if you look straight ahead in the mirror. See that table with all those women? The red-head? That's my ex, and I don't want to talk to her."

"Oh. Yeah."

"Do you know her?"

"Know her?... Um...No, should I?"

"Yeah, right." He drank the last of the beer. "I think she's fucked just about everybody in town."

I started to stand too. I didn't have a jacket draped over the chair like he did, so I thought, if I kept my face toward the mirror, I'll make a quick getaway. Took another sip of beer and one last look at the bartender who stood at the cash register. Along the curve of her bare shoulder was the tattoo of a harp.

"Okay, I found it. Here, Bobby. Look!" It was Quentin.

"This oughta prove what I was talking about. Jung was a respectable humanitarian. Here. Look!"

He was holding out a large, padded envelope, a bulky one, and I didn't want to touch it. His screwball eyes pointedly fixed on me, this "proof" some bone he had buried in the yard.

"Well, you know, Quentin, I'm late for an appointment down the street."

I was trying not to talk too loudly. I'd suddenly become self-conscious of the sound of my own voice, and I managed to get him to shuffle along with me toward the door and talked in a voice quiet enough only he could hear.

"You know, Quentin, the other day I was thinking about how Jung defines synchronicity, his word. It helps me see the power I have in shaping what I become aware of. He was defining coincidence as the occurrence of two events that are related but have no causal connection. I don't know. I have great respect for what he wrote, for the work he did. I just thought, well, everyone's flawed, you know? Sorry if I caused you any trouble. But I'm especially interested in what he has to say about time."

I had this sense of urgency, now that I knew Tristan's ex-wife was there, and hopefully, hadn't spotted either Tristan or, God forbid, me. I kept talking until we reached the big double doors where bright daylight poured in and made those of us who watched its effect on an amber beer glass so sad that we had no reason to go outside.

"Like very often when I look at the clock, I see eleven-eleven, one-eleven or seven-eleven and variations on that. I was in room two-twenty-two on February twenty-second, the day I turned twenty-two. So, all that has a significance to me because I'm noticing or maybe even witnessing what I think of as recurrences, but he has a chapter on numbers connecting them with the *I-Ching* which, I know you remember he wrote an Introduction for. So apparently, he was a believer in Astrology, ESP, telekinesis, and other forms of...do you believe in those things, Quentin?"

"Well, yeah, I..."

We were nearly at the door now, and I couldn't let him drone on and keep me there, so I just rolled along, opened the door, and with some relief stood on the street corner. Quentin, holding the dirty padded envelope, stood in the open doorway. He looked a little frightened. I knew he would go back inside any minute now but wanted to do him the courtesy of saying something about the Master he claimed stimulated his own sculpture, and I needed to make it seem I was just getting started. I knew as soon as I was finished, he'd find another clutch of doofuses who would pretend they too thought he had some deep insight into the world and into art itself. That he'd hoist his glass in the middle of two or three boat-builders or carpenters and spew opinion after opinion, looking up at them with a craving for a bit of respect if not the admiration of the working man he thought was his due, a craving that can never be quenched.

"Jung lets the interpretation of coincidences be up to one who searches for archetypes which can be found in the Collective Unconscious," I began my lecture loudly because a log truck was passing behind me, down Sea Street.

"Hard for me to come back to Jung because I was for so many years pretty skeptical but to explain my thing with numbers I have to think each occurs twice a day at eleven minutes after eleven or eleven after one or seven, both morning and night, each hour has an eleven and variations on eleven are everywhere just as variations of other numbers and the number one is omnipresent so the frequency with which I see elevens and variations isn't a recurrence of the number, but of my focus and recognition."

I was surprised he kept standing in the open doorway of The Pocket attentive to my shout in the street, his one hand on the latch, the other half-heartedly extending every now and then the filthy envelope, a Jungian image I thought, a synchronistic one as it popped into my head, even while I jabbered on and on, that this was the very corner where my Dad stopped mid-lurch down the street beckoned by another man at the door, "Donnie the Unplugged" Mac had named him, who called him back one night, into his own Dark Night of the Soul, a soul on acid. But I couldn't stop myself now, and quacked on, even though I was already turning away to step off the curb and walk down Sea Street toward my appointment.

"To say there must be an explanation," I shouted over my shoulder as I walked away, my voice louder and louder, "Psychic, spiritual or otherwise, seems pretty egotistical to me. You take away ego-superiority and nothing in the objective world needs explaining. Recognizing elevens is like noticing goldfinches, or spotting eagles, and not seeing elevens is like dropping a habit, forgetting you used to like oatmeal every morning, or marshmallow as a kid in hot chocolate. You don't intentionally let go—you move to twelves without noticing."

18.

THREE MEN IN a bar, one is me. The other two sit side-by-side almost finished with their beer. Happy Hour's over, and they're a little more affected than I am. We're all sitting in high stools with swivel seats on the backs of which each has draped a jacket. Theirs more rugged for the weather than my thin black thing with blue paint sprinkled here and there. I don't wear it to paint, but I'm not very careful lately flinging the chartreuse, mauve, and praline.

"Let me help you guys with your jackets," I said.

"Oh, no. I got it..."

But I was already up, and helped Jim get his arm into his right sleeve and helped Gary with his left sleeve. Then, I slipped Jim's left arm into Gary's right sleeve at the back of Gary's stool and Gary's right arm into Jim's left sleeve.

"Okay, then. There you guys go..."

The two pulling on the same jacket in opposite directions, the swivel chairs did the rest. Each pull swiveling the other's bar stool, and they kept yanking, while I sat beside them, a smirking prankster. I think it was Buddy Glass who said, "If a Chinese or Japanese verse composer doesn't know whose coat is whose, on sight, his poetry stands a remarkably slim chance of ever ripening." As the son and only heir of a poet who could have matched coats and hats with respective guests and whose ripened poetry in one way or another led him, years earlier, to this very bar, I was the one witless enough to intentionally mismatch arms and sleeves on two grown men, so they could question whether their trust in me made them ridiculous, but they were not drunk enough to miss the humor, or my own childishness, as they twisted back and forth, my prisoners on two swiveling bar stools. It took minutes to untangle the coats, each gave me a hard fist to the shoulder and vanished into cold night. And when they got up, their places empty, there she sat, alone on the next barstool, Tristan's red-headed wife. I didn't know she was his or anybody's wife then, not until the moment he made me find her in the mirror. Looking at me as if she wished she'd played that prank herself, and admired my getting away with it, she lifted her glass of wine, a salute. And I suppose that's all it took. It would be a year before I ran into Tristan.

"Lie to me," she said.

"What?"

"Start with your name."

I DIDN'T UNDERSTAND what could lead a woman, especially one so young, to start talking that way, and no ring to give away she was married, let alone to whom.

"Where's your car?"

"How do you know I have a car?"

"I didn't, but now I do. Aren't you going to take me somewhere?"

My girlfriend, the famed photojournalist, was on a tour of Central America. It would still be more than a year before she found me too boring or said so. When she later learned about the redhead, she screamed at me, as if I was lying.

"What did you do? You just met and went off and fucked?"

"Well. Yeah."

That was almost how it happened, an hour later, we were at my studio, finger painting each other. The lie, "I live alone." I've been asking myself about the point where I could have just driven her home, dropped her off at the foot of her driveway, along deep woods where driveways are indentations in the broadleaf by the highway. I could have brought her there, maybe delivered her to the door where, inside would have been Tristan, and we could have renewed our friendship then, while I told him I knew I had to give her a ride home when she told me her married name. But she never told. Instead, I learned from the man himself and intended never to speak to him again, although I didn't expect to see him only hours later. That it was his driveway where I dropped her off just as first light penetrated the hard shade under his trees strikes me now as an accusation. I did have options, after all, and several moments to back out before I committed to joining her in this—the word puts me back in Proctor tradition, even Reverend Dimmesdale accuses—adultery.

I could have stopped even before she got in the car, and even when she sat in my passenger seat, pretty as a picture. Even when we ran out of gas a mile from the tavern where we met, I could have just said, "We'll go fill this gallon can, and then I'll take you home. I guess this is a sign." But harder to stop after the long walk to the gas station with her holding my hand. And I admit she did dissolve my last shred of resistance, and I couldn't turn back. She seemed so delicate and friendless. The empty gas can in my other hand, we passed by a circle of parked cars, teenage boys laughing, to my mind, at my obvious predicament. Anybody could read the scene: no gas, walking with the little redhead not much older than they were, the kind disturbed husband in some far-off wood. And hardest of all to stop when I parked a block away from my own house to ask, "Are you sure about this?"

IT WAS AN OBSESSION. Of ten days. Less, maybe eight. When I had to meet or find her somewhere, it would be in an obscure place so someone whose name went unspoken couldn't locate her. But why was I so attracted? She was not in any sense a good-looking or beautiful young woman. And sex itself was not especially compelling with her. So, what was it but the simple notion that she could speak frankly from the next barstool? Her age, too—that she was younger than me; unlike my girlfriend who was frequently and conveniently out of town, and saw in me an inexperienced child-man, Isabel thought me capable and wise, though I was certain I was not. She had a second-floor two-room apartment next to the high school, in a rank blue triple-decker where I had to sneak in. We only just climbed the stairs one night, when I was surprised by the care she took with the three locks on the front door. I heard a pounding, and someone was yelling in the street, hammering fists on the front door; it might give, or crack and I would have to confront whoever this was.

"Isabel, let me in!"

"Who's that?" I asked.

"Don't worry about it."

"But who is that?"

"Don't worry, I said. They'll give up and go away any minute now. It's just a drunk."

She hadn't turned on the lights. But pounding her door meant "they" knew she was home. Maybe saw me come in with her, had been waiting in a car on the street.

"Hey, don't go near that window—he'll see you!"

"Who is it?"

"It's nobody. Just don't worry about it."

Across the street from her building under the streetlamp by the schoolyard fence was a dingy green Dodge van, front door ajar so the light inside showed ripped upholstery, street maps, and clutter in front.

More banging, but weaker. Almost as if the dog in the cellar got tired of scratching and ramming to get out. I didn't have a dog and none of my friends did, so I had to wonder, while I looked at the dented front end of that van and heard its owner's fist get sore and probably swollen on my new illicit girlfriend's locked door, how did an image like that pop into my head. I watched him lumber back to the van and slam the driver-side door, which needed several slams before it stopped falling open. Then I remembered. My father grew up in a house at least a hundred years old when he was a child. He brought me there once. I think he was having it appraised. I roamed all over the place and found the basement the most interesting. Masts and rigging left over from someone's excursions on the sea, were tucked into corners, hung from the basement ceiling, the cement floor bare. A heavy oak door at the top of the stairs led back into the house, but it had several locks and a place for a chain. What caught my eye were deep vertical grooves alongside the door, down the length of trim boards, grooves so uniform and evenly spaced they could only have been cut by claws. Grooves sliced into repeatedly—imprisoned animal was all I could think. A memory I'd forgotten about for so long, but it came to mind now that this man pounded and pounded on her door and was going to wreck my little tryst here in her apartment. I never asked Mac what made those scars. All along the bottom of the door too, as if the animal tried to gnaw underneath. I was afraid to ask. Afraid his grandparents could have been more than capable of locking him in that basement with or without a dog to claw its way to freedom.

19.

I WAS ON TIME for my appointment. That morning I had called the number posted on the "For Rent" sign in the window of his former office, the rooms Mac rented when I was a kid. I did need to expand past my home studio, but to be honest, I rarely set foot downtown other than recent forays to The Pocket, a few blocks away. One day I happened to pass Mac's old place in his creaking Citroen, my inheritance, and looked up, a little nostalgic for the dust and grime in his old windows. The sidewalks were filled with tourists shuffling past. People whose parents had once strolled them through the shops and gawked at kids like me in my Zorro mask cranking bikes down Sea Street. The street hadn't changed, but shops were gaudier back in the day. The face of the building was the same: second story up to the gutter pipes of the flat metal roof was faded brickwork, pigeon shit sprinkled on the wide window ledges. Those tall windows had been his, above the pedestrians who now stopped in the middle of crossing the street to take in the Bay with binoculars. Its blue glaze bright today, rare as the Aegean without a ripple. It seems to me now my childhood must have been idyllic, although back then I envied other kids, thought their lives more "regular," that somehow things came to them I would never deserve; still, mine was an endless summer where no one was watching.

The main difference was the new security system, a bright metal door with tinted glass, but I could see an elevator beside the creepy stairs Mac used to limp up after Happy Hour. Though I hoped to have a look at his office, I felt I had to pretend I wanted to rent it. I would have never dishonored Mac by spilling paint and scattering half-finished canvases around his stark room, but I very badly wanted another visit.

The Landlord wheezed down in the elevator, and looked me over through the tinted glass, then welcomed me as if he remembered who I was, but I knew he didn't. He was the same old guy; more rot had set in, but the same glasses, the same magnifying lenses enlarged his head like a foraging grub. He took off the glasses to clean the lenses with fingers like soft dough and rub his eyes; his head was not much bigger than a rhododendron blossom. At first, I thought he was going to say he didn't really want to rent the place anymore by the way he sized up my black clothes and the turquoise paint sprinkled on my boots. I took out my billfold where I kept a frayed and faded business card and held it out, ostentatiously displaying a wad of cash.

As we entered the building, I heard behind me, down the street coming from the direction of The Pocket, the whine of a cracked muffler; when I turned, the same dented and rusty green Dodge van honked, a big, gloved hand waving over the steering wheel—the van that I'd seen in front of Isabel's place at least a year ago. It *was* Tristan. Most likely drunk that night, he needed a street map to locate his wife's apartment and beat on her locked door. Not the first time he pounded on her door. Now the green van rumbled in pathetic complacency. Well out of his marriage, I hoped he didn't have a heart-to-heart with his ex at the Pocket after I made my escape.

"NICE DAY OUT, i'n it? What's all that honking anyways? You know that guy? I think more people here today than yesterday—sure do draw some crowds to the shops these days, though. You know I get tired of lots and lots of sun all the time, so I just pritnear always keep to mahself during daylight even at night anymore; meandthemissus roll over to the window and look at sunsets...now that's why I live here youbetcha. I ain't never left, my whole life spent in this town; lots and lots of folks comin', goin' but crowds just get bigger 'n bigger every year. Well, guess we won't be moving on none too soon though, by golly; meandthemissus we're pritnear used to this ole place by now ha ha. What do you think do you think you want to rent it? I don't like to keep places empty long; fella here a few years back found dead right on that kitchen table, you know what? Erection big as a banana, can you believe that?—ain't that somethin'? Years ago, why prolly before your time. I wonder what you're gonna do when you do rent it?"

"Paint."

20.

AS SOON AS we were upstairs, I was a kid again. I didn't expect that. The building itself locked into my thirteenth summer. It wasn't Mac I thought about first as I ascended those creaking stairs so near his old office, but Tommy. Tommy was Mom's boyfriend when Mac moved back to town and into this building. Back then I wanted to talk with the confidence I found in one of Tommy's smiles. He was buoyant, like he belonged, even though he had only just arrived when we first met him and was far from Chicago, where, as the story went, he was on the run. But that was what everybody thought, and we may all have been wrong about Tommy's past. People had the impression he was a gangster, maybe because of that smile, or was it a smirk that betrayed he had no front teeth? I thought he just might have been part of some criminal organization because he did seem dangerous to me, and to most everyone except my mother, who never found him to be much of a scary person. He made an impression on me, enough that he's the subject of a painting. There's a memory I've never been able to shake and don't want to. Time passing made it a good memory, though back then I didn't want to be in the room.

With either of them.

I was coming into our house, the house with the round oak table—which is the house where I live now, 777 Mangan Hill. Sand was always on my bare feet back then. I walked up three steps and tried to brush it off, as I was harangued to do again and again. The house was blue; I was leaning with a shoulder against the door frame to brush away sand. A blue pale as the beach on good days. From the vase in the window that looked onto the harbor, three thin dried flowers speared the sun streams, dust-coated a chipped molding over the door. For me, not for my mother who lived somewhat gracefully amid her clutter, the beach was my escape. I couldn't run right inside now, though I was hungry, and the refrigerator was just beyond that door, sunlight flooding the gray painted kitchen because I heard her and Tommy inside. But that wasn't it. I knew Tommy. It wasn't like he didn't eat with us night after night. This was different. Inside I could hear him laughing, and her laughing, and him calling her those lover names I've always found embarrassing: "babe," "darlin'," "sweetie pie..." Words only, but they still made me uncomfortable. My parents never uttered such *inanities,* as Mac would have called them, and he shunned the use of anything but my mother's real name, Natalie, though he often called her his Beatrice, his only Beatrice.

"R-r-rob*air*? Is that you?"

With her thick Parisian accent and her "Mother" voice, she called shrilly from the living room. How did she know it was me? Was brushing sand off a foot so loud? I didn't know what to say. She couldn't see me, and besides, she was giggling, and Tommy calling her those names. I liked Tommy, as I've said. I suppose I idolized him, and I found myself on occasion comparing him to Mac. I didn't want him in there with my mother. That summer I toyed with the idea of becoming an Oceanographer and Tommy laughed at me, although he thought it was a respectable profession. Of course, Mac overwhelmed me with brochures from universities—the best places to study science, he told me, and went on to describe various American poets, long dead, who embraced the sea as metaphor, wrote from experience on the ocean, and good old Hart Crane, he said, embraced it with finality. It bothered me only a little, perhaps because I was under his spell at that time, that he took my interest as an occasion to lecture. Now I see it was in his DNA, the lecture, the academic outlook on his universe, that a "real dad" might have just let me find what I needed without interference.

Deputy Dave, who had not just then begun to damage my aunt Cecile, only grunted when I spoke of Oceanography, while she refilled his coffee by the window at the empty diner; he didn't quite smile although she did, a little too shyly, I thought, even for Cecile, until I explained it in French, and he went back to eating lemon pie.

Tommy didn't laugh at the profession or my interest, but at me, which he always did, joking that at thirteen maybe I shouldn't start taking a career quite so seriously. He did, however, rent a boat and take me out on the bay. A thing Mac never did, but I knew a little something about boats anyhow, just from hanging out with kids whose dads had them on the water most of their lives. I had to show Tommy how to get the motor started, and how to get that skiff past the jetty.

HIS SMILE APPEARED to be one a dangerous person shows you before trouble. In that rented boat, after I got the engine started, he told me about the Bermuda Triangle, and how many lost ships, how many people supposedly disappeared, and so on, and I pretended to be interested. I may have wanted to show him even a kid who memorizes Dante could think what he had to say was important; if I thought the whole thing had been debunked long ago, it was only polite to listen. I leaned in to pretend to hear better over the roar of the motor. He was talking more to the chop alongside the boat than to me, and then he twisted his head toward me and said, with one of those toothless smiles, "Yeah, it's a pretty good story, Bobby, but it's only a story, you know?"

He said that sort of thing often, especially about grizzly things happening in his childhood, and smiled deadly—top front teeth missing, a black hole in the middle of his handsome face. Crime gave him the smile, gave him confidence, I imagined. I envied that. He was scary. To me, he looked like a movie hitman who would chew glass to get your attention. He might have been an extortionist, for all we knew, or a petty thief, or only some pathetic habitual traffic offender, but his smile let you think he was your friend and protector for life.

EVENTUALLY, I DID open the kitchen door, and out of character bypassed the refrigerator and headed for the living room where their voices wafted like the awful music at a roller-skating rink. It's the image I've tried to paint. Unsuccessfully, I think still. I can't quite get it right, even though their two faces engraved themselves into my memory. I can see my mother's back in her ivory blouse as Tommy in his usual black t-shirt has a muscular arm wrapped around her, her face and its tentative smile turn to find me, his black eyes looking at me over her shoulder. That black unmistakable smile. Something has happened. No words. He extends, with his big right hand, my mother's bare left arm, his thumb, and forefinger pushing her fingers toward me with a large, and I thought, gaudy turquoise ring. That was when, her eyes shifting in my direction, she found me, her lightning turned-up corners of the mouth almost in a smile, her eyes like a deer on guard burned my cheek to a hot blush.

21.

IT USED TO be the kind of town you could leave your car unlocked with the keys in the ignition almost anywhere while you went off and did errands, or leave your house unlocked and go away for days. Nobody would bother anything. Neighbors watered the plants, fed pets, brought in the paper or your mail. That kind of place. Deputy Dave who didn't really have all that much work to do came often into Café Noblesse Oblige where Cecile poured the coffee. She was reserved, so much so she might have become a shut-in if Mom hadn't found her this job to get her out of the house and around other people. She surprised us one night when she came home and said she really liked the place and the people she worked with, even being around crowds of tourists who came evenings and didn't judge her or make her uncomfortable or tease her for her French accent. I don't know if this was before or after Deputy Dave became a regular. Deputy Dave started dating Cecile, and within a few months, they were living together. Mom didn't think that was such a good idea, but she couldn't put a stop to it, and Cecile who I had until then thought was exactly like a clam shut up inside a shell, was all of a sudden smiling and effervescent, determined she could be happy with Deputy Dave. Maybe she was in love with him or maybe she just wanted to get out of our house, get out from under my mother's thumb, her older sister, her sponsor. Tristan's mom had long ago moved out, or as I later learned, was thrown out. Literally. Belongings tossed off the porch, she landed on the lawn. Lots of screaming. I knew even as a little kid that Dave had a temper, long before Tristan described what it was like in his house. I probably knew much more about his life than he would have wanted, and of course, now I'm talking about not only how he grew up, but who he married.

When Cecile went to the hospital, the doctor in the ER kept telling her she had to press charges. *So, who did this?* the doctor and nurses asked us. She wouldn't say. My mother was extremely upset. Tommy came by our house once with a dinner he himself had cooked—spaghetti with Wonder Bread, which she wouldn't let me touch and pronounced inedible; he only wanted to spare her the trouble of preparing a meal. She was on the phone for a long time another evening when he showed up with a bouquet of purple irises. She was talking in French.

"Who's she talking to?"

"Uncle Auguste."

"Oh. In Paris? Where's he at?"

"Oregon. Forest fire."

"Wow. Expensive call, huh?"

I didn't say anything. I was heartbroken to be honest. I'd seen Cecile in the hospital and now she was back here in our house. I was back on the couch, and she was recuperating in my room. Her left eye looked exploded to me, her collar bone broken, and she'd been kicked so hard her spleen burst. She was on a medication that helped her sleep and when I looked in at her, if my mother wasn't in there keeping a cold cloth to her forehead, she was groaning painfully or having a very bad dream. I'd had nightmares and I thought I knew exactly what she was going through, but of course I didn't.

"Probably telling your uncle all about what happened, huh? Yeah, that's not a good thing," his thumb jutting back over his shoulder toward my bedroom. "I wonder what he'll have to say about it."

"Uncle Auguste?"

Tommy looked back toward me sitting there, all glum. He gave me a quick half-smile as if to say, "Buck up, kid. I got this," but he didn't say anything.

I didn't say anything.

THE FEW TIMES I'd gone over to Deputy Dave's house while Cecile lived there, I had to wash the dishes, and the last pot was always the one without a handle, dented on its rim so that it was out of round. The lid didn't fit tight anymore, but they still used it. I'm not sure why it hadn't been thrown out. I think it's because it had been my mother's favorite and she'd given it to Cecile to bring with her to Deputy Dave's. That time the pot became dented wasn't the first time they'd gotten into a fight, but it was the first time I'd ever seen Cecile screech at another human being. The night she was hurt was worse; she held a steak knife in her left hand, told him in English just above a whisper she was leaving, and with her right hand she squeezed my arm and made me walk backwards toward the door. Deputy Dave came toward her, and she was waving the knife at him. He was laughing at her while he kept coming forward. She took one wide sweep with the knife, and he grabbed her wrist, both of her wrists, pulling her hand off me, even though she'd held so tightly. Then he shook the knife out of her hand, slammed her with his fist, and threw her onto the wood floor. He began kicking her then, even though I yelled for him to stop, and tried to get in between them. He flung me against the wall and kept kicking her. I ran out of the house and got my mom. She came quickly, but it was too late. Dave was finished with her, and he was gone. Cecile was so small my mother and I carried her to the car and brought her to the emergency room. And no one told who did it.

WHEN TOMMY EMERGED from what had been my room and from talking to my mother, he wasn't smiling. He didn't seem to notice me, but I saw, as he came into the kitchen, that turquoise ring in his hand. With it pinched between his thumb and forefinger, he walked to the little fridge, the kind barely out of that era when you would have called it an "Icebox," when it would have been "modern." A modern-day device the little lady of the house stood beside, kept a sheen on, a larder she kept full for centuries. But this one, as far as Tommy went, kept beer cold. Icy green bottles with a cap he would have to lift, slowly—it's almost in slow motion as I recall now—up to the metal Coca Cola pry, screwed years ago by Mac with two screws against an old, splintered cedar post, upright beside the harsh, chipped sink, white porcelain scrubbed spotless by my ruthless mother. Tommy undid his bottle cap and sauntered through the screen door, which he let bang against the door frame, and stood on the back porch, hand in pocket, beer bottle dangling, and faced the green hill of fern that shot up right behind our house, a wild wall of green and overhanging cedar. Maybe he was watching birds, but Tommy, he was the kind that would have whistled to a bird through that big hole where his two front teeth were missing. I don't know because I wasn't around when any of his friends were, but I got the feeling you never mentioned that gap, the dark hole where his sentences, full and well-thought-out, complex in the human sense, would emerge within his amicable smile. I watched him contemplating, or meditating, memorizing maybe the peace of my mother's house. It *was* peaceful, even though her sister was suffering in the little bedroom I could hardly think of as my own anymore, and instead, I had to go in and out quickly if I needed clean underwear or a book.

So, I decided no one would miss me, and they would certainly know where I could be found (if they ever wanted to)—at Mac's. And I slipped out through the front door, barefoot, scuffing sand down along the wooden steps to the open carport where I kept my bike. It was a beater as bikes go. Years later I had a beauty of a ten-speed the girl I sold it to called a "Cadillac." I had no idea. I thought they were all the same, some harder to pedal than others. This one was just my bike, and I was already outgrowing it; my legs stretched on either side to the ground, so I put on the flip-flops I had left in the dirt beside it and sailed away.

The house is on a hill, and you can see the harbor from those big picture windows, but down by the carport you only see out toward the neighbors and their smooth lawns and dented cars. I rolled onto our street, bumping along the curb and a hole or two. The street curved along another neighborhood where I knew some kids, but rarely spoke to them. Instead, I was bathing in that anticipation like on long car rides to the beach. The feeling you can only have in the back seat where at each hill you think you're going to be the first in the family to catch a glimpse of blue or the sparkle off the horizon, but instead there's only another hill of sand, a dune, and maybe a string of white cottages behind hedgerows. And your stomach flips into your throat as the family car descends those hills, or everybody feels themselves swirl together and sings out, "O-o-O-o!" But you know you'll see the ocean after just *one more* hill, and when finally you do, you all utter gasps at its beauty and admire it so and feel even hotter than you were a few moments before and the sun beats through the window down on you, on each arm and bare knee. This is how I felt, a little bit, coming down our street before entering the next street, a bigger thoroughfare that led downtown where the bay glistened and where I could see my dad, and tell him how it felt coming over those hills before catching the first glimpse of the beach.

Years before this, I came out of the house to sit on the curb and study some shards of amber glass. Mac came along and found me. He didn't know what to say, he never did. So, it was just, "Hey, your mother wants to talk to you." And pointed with his thumb back at the house and ruffled my hair and kept walking toward his office where he did his writing. He had it even then, for the office space, but now that he was living in it, I thought of it as a sanctuary—at least for the time, Cecile recovered in my room from the beat-up by her so-called beloved. A sanctuary because he left me alone, and I didn't bother him. But that day as he patted my hair and strode off, I was sitting on the curb a little confused by what I saw. My parents, who I hadn't been so sure even loved one another any longer, were in bed with their clothes off. I knew what people did in bed, of course, but I'd never seen them doing it. I don't know if this would be classified as early trauma, but I wasn't going to get up off that curb and let my mother talk to me about them having sex.

When I rounded the corner onto Aurora Avenue, I remembered that after my first bike accident was when I stopped pedaling to my friends' houses. I rode one time to a birthday party I wasn't invited to at Richie Anastos's house and saw the bunting and everyone inside playing their stupid games. Then I came back home, probably in a hurry, and took this corner fast, right into the front end of a woman's Buick. Luckily, she saw me and stopped instead of plowing right over me. But I flipped off my bike and landed on the big ugly hood ornament, a naked silver man in mid-stride, then rolled off onto the sidewalk holding my groin. Some kid on the street ran to our house and yelled for my mother, and now two adult women were in a panic, and my mother took me to the hospital. A doctor had to examine me and wait with me until I could pee. He assured my mother I wouldn't have any trouble "later on in life," but this was before I saw them fucking, so I had absolutely no idea what "later on in life" meant. It was only now, rolling down Aurora with my flip-flops in the air, legs stretched out on either side, my arms out wide above my head, that I realized I'd known for some time the kind of trouble *I* could have wasn't what most people had "later on in life" and cruised towards Mac's dump of an office downhill, squirming above my giant handlebars, jiggling arms and legs like a big white 'X' way too fast on my banana seat.

Sirens

22.

HE LIVED BEHIND a smoked glass door with the banner of a previous enterprise: *Alfie's Hair.* I could make out shadowy movements inside: his big-headed slouch, sunlight through one of two high windows. Then, the slide of the deadbolt, the hinge creak better now that he oiled it, and there he was, My Old Man. Didn't say a thing. He knew something was going on, so he stared me down. But I flopped across his stuffed couch pillows scaring up a stream of fluff and dust where the evening light flooded in from neighboring brick buildings. He sat at his desk and pretended he had worked all day. Whenever I dropped in he did this but without evidence of writing. A stack of paper, like a manuscript, sat beside the typewriter. I didn't say anything. I was in no mood just then to suggest a hint of adulation. He would have grumbled how people look up to others and don't expect it to crush their own freedom. He said things like that. I was thirteen and stood in for audiences he most assuredly missed. Disinclined to mull psychology and certain I didn't want to be like him, I thought how different Tommy was from my dad. Both had principles, and I hadn't known many adult males who did. Tommy, who didn't care much one way or the other about the law, seemed like the happiest guy I knew, whereas Mac, who "wouldn't break a law—except for smoking dope," was fairly miserable.

The remnant on his smoked glass door he kept, but the old-fashioned rusted barbershop chairs were long ago hauled away. He and a few of his doper crew lowered them with greasy come-along pulleys. That day was all angles, elbows, shirt sleeves, and ass-cracks, the three stoutest, certainly no poets, cranking the come-along handle to keep the cable taut. I wondered why those chairs were so heavy, and for that matter who lugged them upstairs in the first place. Alfie? Behind Mac was his old blackboard. Chalk dusted its surface, the floor, even his pants, and fingers. A chalkboard kept his projects on track, he said. I thought he was like Einstein when I was little, spreading versions of Relativity in drafts across the board till he hit on genius. After he worked something out on the board, he got going in longhand, then typed, over and over. I was fascinated by this process as I understood it. He never succumbed to a computer. That evening the by-now-familiar words, *An Autopsy on American Poetry, Par Deux* were on the board. Unlike other ideas, this had only the title, and one sentence: "First, let's prove we have a corpse."

"SO, WHAT'S UP, CHAMP?"

Long pause. Sitting there behind that stack of paper, he began sharpening a pencil with a tiny German device. I made a face.

"What's wrong? Tell me."

I waited for him to stop looking at how pencil shavings curl on blank paper, waited for his eyes, which when he looked my way, caused me to study the dust floats along the evening sunlight before I spoke.

"Can't sleep in my room and I want to spend the night here, maybe a few nights. Okay?"

The pencil sharpener not quite silent, I could hear it twist on an already sharp tip, the soft click as the pencil went into a white mug where duller pencils waited, then that hollow sound he could produce rubbing his palms and fingers together.

"Why can't you sleep in your room? Insomnia again?"

"Cecile was in the hospital." The sound stopped.

"Oh? I didn't know that. Is she okay? Is your mom okay?"

"Cecile, Dad. Mom's fine. Cecile was in the Emergency Room. Mom had to take her, now she's at our house. Sometimes Tommy's there, just so you know. Anyways, she's in my room and I can only go in if I need like a shirt or something."

"Well, why was she in the ER? Was she sick? I mean, I know she's always been frail, even genteel you could say, but I never thought she was sickly as such..."

"She was beat up. Pretty bad, I think."

"Beat up? What? Well, who would beat up someone like her? She's as shy as a bird, and...and...so unassuming. Who did that, Bobby? How could somebody...? I hope the hell someone filed a police report."

I kept looking out the window. Shadows began to sweep away the last light of day and blend nicely with the slate sky. I was pretty sure it would rain.

"I said..."

"Can't file a police report, Dad."

"What? Why not?"

"It was Deputy Dave."

"What?"

"Deputy Dave, Dad, kicked the shit out of Cecile. I saw it. He put her in the hospital. Now she's in my room and I can't get in there except to change my fucking socks."

"Oh."

He stood. He was wearing his own black socks, as it happened, chalk dusted and getting more so as he shuffled across the room to the bureau and a cracked coffee mug, a twin to his pencil cup, beside his Hoppy lunch box, and a bottle of something amber.

"Deputy Dave."

He took the cup over to the window and stood there. No sun now. I had no idea what he could be thinking, but I wanted him to concoct a plan to make Deputy Dave pay for this. I wanted him to think about breaking a nose or, at least, "bending the bow," as he used to say about his poetry enemies. He stood there in silence for a long time, and I kept waiting for him to say something. It was still early enough no voices from the street rose to this ethereal zone where he lived, just enough above it all quite literally to think he could eke his "autopsy" out far away from blood and cracked bones.

He stared out the window and said, "I'm sorry to hear that."

Then he turned to look at my scrunched sullen lump of a being soaking up the dust of his couch.

"She'll be okay. You'll have your room back soon."

He held that mug up like he was toasting one of us, maybe just to put an upbeat spin on the tale for both of our sakes, to so subtly change the subject.

"Hey! It's Happy Hour. Wanna go to the Tavern?"

THE STREET WAS already bathed in neon flicker from two or three bars and restaurants, favorites of the tourists; blue haze under the street lamps, metal cylinders, they tilt and whistle in a good breeze off the Bay. Most of the cars were parked—

the early customers easing toward The Pocket up ahead. We stopped half a dozen times to stare into space, the Bay unusually calm, a stream of stores, and The Little Friend, where my mom worked, a few blocks behind us.

He mumbled something I couldn't understand. I almost didn't want to disturb this near state of meditation we could sometimes conjure together, but I didn't want to give in, maybe from a perverse need to refrain from the "mind-meld" he'd bred into me. So, instead of sustaining him in the silence, I said, "What's that, Dad?"

He was surprised I spoke, but he looked down with that raised left eyebrow of his and complied anyway.

"Oh, you know. Your mother's name. I *did* use to call her Beatrice, for whatever reason, probably my own inside joke, though I'm pretty sure she knew what I meant, how I meant it, anyway, to show her the devotion I felt, I've always felt, you know. That hasn't really changed over the years even though, well, here we are, you and I on our own on a downtown street where no one knows either of our names and your mother apparently couldn't care less. But her name is definitely not Sabrina, nor is it Marie Antoinette I've heard people yell in her bar. I think they use some name they think is outlandishly French-*ish* to get her attention. I've never been in there, though, I was just walking by and heard that once. Have you been in there, Roberto?"

"Yeah, Dad, I'm old enough to drink."

He looked down at me, his elbows against the two-by-four, a temporary railing but a solid enough affair it kept us off the rotted dock where the oyster truck caved in a year before. He just smiled when I said that, already lost in some other thought.

"She used to be a weaver, you know. Or did you know that?"

"A weaver? No, I didn't know that, Dad."

"Doesn't she still have a spinning wheel in the basement back home?"

"Um, I don't know. I don't go down there much."

"Hm."

I had no idea why he spoke about my mother like that, but I didn't want to pursue it. I assumed the way his room hovered above the vicinity of The Little Friend, he may have thought about her often, maybe worried about her, but I refused just then to get him going on the nature of marriage, former marriage, the problems of parenting a child whose parents' dwelling places can neither one be considered a home. And so on. He'd riffed on such topics sufficiently for me and without any, not the slightest, change in my so-called "situation." I was just as happy to have made it this far in life without having to follow the strict guidelines laid down for those who, like my classmates, purportedly emerged unscathed from blessed normalcy. So, we kept ambling toward The Pocket, a big building; several stories above the bar were rooms for the "family," a group of bar-jockeys, waitstaff and maintenance workers, all close friends it seemed, who lived there and ran the place. One of the oldest buildings around, its cracked bricks needed the masons who, along with boat-builders and carpenters and lay-about hippies, were frequent customers at Happy Hour, which is why we were headed there.

At the door, he gave me one of those eyebrows and went inside. I was assigned to an outside bench where usually the kids sat. I was happy enough to have the bench all to myself, up against the wall of windows where I could peer inside as I wished at the old-world bar and ancient Happy Hour customers on full view. Long ago he convinced me we had a little European tradition in our part of downtown America just as when he was a kid waiting at the corner barroom beside the swinging saloon doors for his own dad, who, if involved in a heated discussion, could delay dinner for hours.

Mac got his glass of beer and sat at the table facing the street and me, a tall window between us, which by law, he could not open. He pulled out some paper and started writing, indicating—by eyebrow—and a held-up hand, I was to leave him alone, as most people did. No one sat at his table unless he had a pitcher, but now with a glass and a few pieces of paper, he went to work. I turned and faced away from him as two cars eased along Sea Street in opposite directions and right in front of me, stopped side by side so the drivers could shout and laugh above the roar of their engines. They were close enough one driver reached across and patted the arm of the other.

"Sorry to hear about your dad, man. What a way to go. I think about him every time I jack up my rig and get under it. I'm sorry. I'm real sorry. He was one helluva character, that man! Well, I better get off this street, Hombre. Catch you later."

And each drove off continuing to cruise in opposite and aimless directions, radios thrumming and undulating. Their music for a moment filled the evening air, and I looked back inside the tavern. There was the Old Man, there he was, and I felt relieved, perhaps for my first time ever, that he would never jack up a car or crawl under one. He was at his barroom table and alone, which was also a relief. Scribbling on his "Pocket Papers." He didn't like to walk around with a notebook or backpack, so he took to folding up at least ten pieces of typewriter paper to hide in shirt pockets, pants pockets, or in his jacket; at the table, he would smooth out each sheet, stacked them atop one another, and began to write. He said he used his Pocket Papers long before The Pocket hung up the sign with the scrawled Mae West quotation across the bottom, "Is that a pistol in your pocket, or are you just glad to see me?" That was his way. Often, he read me a passage or a poem he just wrote. I didn't know why he thought I listened or could understand that pure gibberish, but I recognized at least for the moment there on my all too public bench that I was a part of that voice, and I could trust that it wouldn't go away now, not for a good long time, that he too was a "helluva character" but one whose risk-taking remained confined to chalk dust and words on crinkled paper.

He looked up, sort of made a face—big eyes, eyebrows again, then a strange leer. I turned around to face the street. Was I distracting him by looking in at the tavern window? Along the street, the full moon just risen, glittered over ripples on the Bay. What did people see there they thought so beautiful? To my mind, the adult tendency to gawk at and muse on the variegated stages of the moon had always seemed boring, or if anything a desperate distraction from true, bone-deep, ennui. If anybody back then sought my opinion, I'd have had to ask "Who cares about the aesthetics of a thirteen-year-old? How old are you supposed to be before you even know the first thing about reality?" Right then I really was wishing I could have wised-off and hoped some adult might come along and ask me what I thought of the sparkle in that moon.

"So... You look a little bit troubled, my Man. What's going on?"

I hadn't noticed he slipped out of the tavern and sat alongside me on the bench.

"Nothing. Just a little bored, I guess."

"Oh, that's good. I thought maybe something was troubling you. You looked a might pensive if you don't mind my saying so."

"Pensive, Dad?"

"You know what that means. Overly thoughtful. Preoccupied, let's say."

"Yeah, yeah. I get it. No, I'm not. Just sitting here, thinking about stuff."

"Oh. Well, glad you're not getting too serious about all this..."

"About what?"

"You know. Your aunt Cecile. And, by the way, I'm glad you're going to stick around with the Old Man for a while. I'm sure we'll have a grand time together."

I wanted to go back to studying the lipstick smirch on a chewed cigarette butt in the sidewalk crack assuming he would go on and on. He looked down the street toward The Little Friend where my mother was probably working that night, and I thought for a minute, "Oh shit, he must be thinking about walking down there now, and wants me to wait up at his place and sleep on the couch."

With the street as background, his large, hooked nose reddened a little, I thought maybe he's been out in the sun a lot lately, but more likely he'd been drinking wine before I tapped on his door. A breeze whistled from the Bay and woke us both up, so to speak, lifted his long hair when he turned his face toward it so as to inhale the sea. There was the wider bald spot at the back of his head, the "tonsure" he called it, of the "monk poet," though he was lately as far as I could tell, neither.

"I wonder if your mom is working tonight. Do you know?"

"Yeah, she's down there. I think she's there, anyways, but she might be late because of Cecile. You know she's taking care of Cecile because Deputy Dave beat the shit out of her, but we can't report it, right?"

"Yeah, I know. You told me. Remember?"

"Oh, I remember. I just didn't know if you heard me. You didn't say anything, you know."

"What can I say? 'Well, by God, I'll restore honor to the family name?' How's that? 'I'll teach that ne'er-do-well. Why, I'll beat the living bejesus out of that heathenish lunk, that bastard Deputy Dave?' Which would be sort of like telling everybody he did it and then I'd get tossed into his own clink. Besides, he's a lot bigger than I am, and—by the way—I've never beat the shit out of anybody in my life. Did you know this?"

"Yeah, you told me that before, Dad."

"Oh. Just repeating myself redundantly ad nausem as usual, I guess it's all tautology to you, huh?"

His eyes glistened at me. Blue like mine, and he made that smirk again. He had some duty here to fulfill, almost the knee-jerk aspect of being a good parent that he fell back on to take away the sting of my having been relieved of an already not-so-innocent childhood. Had I known how to be grateful then, I would have said something more appreciative, but I'd become abundantly aware of having abandoned myself to whatever you were when you no longer were *just* a child. Instead, I tried to move things back toward his own expertise.

"So, what were you writing?"

"Oh. Thought you'd never ask."

He tapped the pocket papers he'd been holding, now rolled up in his left hand, against his knee.

"I keep remembering where my father worked. Post Office not far from our house. Used to drop in on him often. Kind of like you dropping in at my quote-unquote office. So, I was trying to describe that street, but not doing well."

"I guess that's why you came out to talk to me, huh?"

"Very funny. No, I came out to talk to you because, as I told you, moi amoeba, you looked troubled?"

"Moi amoeba? Is that even a language, Dad?"

"It's not, but then, everything is, right?"

Eyebrow.

"Okay. French for 'my' you know, but 'amoeba' I'm sure you realize is a pun for 'amigo,' the Spanish word for 'friend.' But you knew all that already."

"Why'd you say 'amoeba' instead of 'amigo' then? And why did you use the French word?"

"You're a harsh critic. Do you want to hear about the Post Office where my father worked, or not?"

"Yeah. I do. But could you just tell it to me, and not give me a *reading*?"

"Jesus. Okay. Well, it was an old building in Dorchester where I grew up. One day I'd like you to go there with me, and maybe we can find the house where I was a kid. Would you like that?"

"Yeah. Yeah, I would, Dad."

As I know now, this was the house where he lived for his last years, and I never did get there in time to see it with him, but I think that, sitting on that bench, I really *did* like the idea of traveling back East with Mac to see his old neighborhood, but most of all I just wanted to get away from what was going on with my mom and her boyfriend. And I liked Tommy, but he scared me. And now this with Cecile. I wished we could get in his beater Citroen and hit the road for anywhere.

"Well, the Post Office where my dad worked was probably made of crumbling plaster, but it had an elegant wood sign like those the government hangs over their edifices. I never crossed at the lights like I should have since after all, I was just a kid. Instead, I j-walked between cars stopped at the light.

And I always recognized at the far end of his building a dark hill with several trees that looked dead and huge granite walls where the foot of the hill met the broken sidewalk in front of the Chinese laundry where my dad had shirts starched, and where Mr. Chang was waving at me, and smiling. I don't recall ever—ever—smiling or waving back at Mr. Chang. I just walked the sidewalk in the direction of that hill, which was bordered at the far end by granite steps leading to a church that was a couple hundred years old. By the way, in sixth grade, I kissed a girl there. She was the girl I loved in first grade, but I knew that because I was the class clown, she would never have anything to do with me. So, it was surprising she stood on those steps and kissed me. First kiss." He finally turned his head to look at me.

"Hey, what about you?"

"Dad."

"Okay, back to the story. On the other side of the street from the Post Office was the graveyard. It took up about five acres and names on those gravestones dated from the early 1600s. I don't know who the founders of that part of Boston were, but they're all there, in hard dirt and rocks."

"Hey, Dad, wait."

"What?"

"What was his name?"

"What? Who's name?"

"Your Dad. What was his name? My grandpa. Wish I met him."

"Yeah, you would have liked him, maybe. He would have liked to know you. His name was Leo, but that was a nickname. His real name was Laerto. Died before you were born, I'm afraid. Did you ever see that big quilt that used to hang on a wall in the upstairs hallway?"

"Um. Oh, the big lavender one with all the clouds? Yeah."

"That was his. Your Mom made that for him about a year before he died. I hope you know that it belongs to you."

"It does? Wow. When did he give me that?"

"He didn't. I did. I just gave it to you, just now. Okay?"

"Oh. I get it. Thanks, Dad."

"So anyway, the memory that keeps coming back is not what I thought I wanted to write about. I used to go in and see my dad in the back of the Post Office. Dark in there. And there were these racks with smelly, long, gray canvas bags to sort the mail. And Dad sitting at a desk eating a fried bologna sandwich. I remember it, but it's the sort of thing I have to work on to bring up the details. I guess I was a little frustrated because I couldn't recall exactly what was so special about that mailroom, with my dad plunked in the middle of it. The memory that keeps interrupting the image I have of where he worked is this: I'm standing on the sidewalk, across from the Post Office and next to the ten-foot wall that protects the graveyard from traffic and the public; a parade's going by, and I can't remember what costumes and marching bands or instruments, or what kinds of cars and trucks were even in the parade or who those people were and whether they were in costumes too. I can't remember what holiday was going on just then, if it even was a holiday, but of course, then I'm wondering why they would have a parade with balloons without a holiday. That's really the only thing I do remember; I was holding a blue balloon, across the street from where my dad worked, and it came loose and floated above every head of every adult in front of me and over the parade, a huge balloon above the float passing just then, maybe a Cadillac even from the local dealership; and over the heads of everybody, I watched it go up and up and up, and nobody else saw. Bobby, what I don't understand, even as old as I am, is I feel like I'm still watching the balloon, like I'm still looking up from that low viewpoint below the pockets and purses of grownups and watching it get away from me. Nobody knew I lost my balloon. And I watched it soar over the Post Office rooftop, over the roof of the hundred-year-old church, over the squalid Chinese Laundry shop building and the dark bar next door with a big Shamrock above its entrance. And then it vanishes into blue sky, and I never told anybody."

"Until now?"

"Until now. Yes. I'm telling you, and don't tell anybody. Okay?"

"Sure, Dad, it's a secret? Why?"

"Oh, it doesn't matter. Let's just not tell. After all, who cares? A little thing that made a big deal impression just because it's one of those memories that never leaves."

"So, why are you writing about that parade? What does that have to do with anything?"

He sat there on the bench beside me, looking off across the street where a white Volkswagen sputtered up the hill. Then he sighed or let out a breath that seemed like a sigh at the time, like he didn't want me asking questions anymore, like I was too self-conscious for my own best interest. A sigh, maybe, or a letting out of air he had pent up while he talked to me who, I already understood, made him a bit uncomfortable, though he did his best to be not so much my dad as my friend, or wanted to. That was who Dad was. He didn't treat me often as his kid, or his little boy, but as a friend, and he'd talk as though I comprehended where he was going with something when in fact, I could follow not a word he said.

"Well, I've been writing about other poets, American poets, you know?"

"Wait, does this have something to do with the Autobiography of American Poetry?"

"What?"

"I saw it on your blackboard. You know, and you had like a manuscript of a book came out? The autobiography of American Poetry."

"Oh. No, it's not Autobiography, Bobby. It's *Autopsy of American Poetry.*"

"Oh. What's that mean?"

"Autopsy?"

"Yeah, I know what autopsies are, I mean what does it have to do with poetry stuff?"

"Oh. Hm. Are you really interested?"

"Yeah. Well, a little anyway, Dad. I just want to know why you need to write about a parade when you're talking about dead poetry people."

"Not dead people so much. As talking about poetry might be dead."

"Oh. Why?"

"Well, the first job of the autopsy is to prove the subject is dead and give a cause of death. But that's not what I was doing, or what I think I was doing with the parade. I think that was just a way to talk about the poetry I've been reading. In fact, it's a way of talking about a poem I've always loved, but then found that even though most of that poet's other work leaves me cold, that one still has beauty. The thing about the parade is I remember it clearly, and especially watching my balloon sail over my neighborhood and the building where my father worked, and where my mother brought him those fried bologna sandwiches. She walked me into back rooms of the Post Office with a sandwich which she bought at Kresge's, across the boulevard from where the parade stopped for a moment, red and blue marchers stamping their feet against the pavement, keeping the rhythm for the marching band. What I think I'm writing about is my first experience of real beauty. Every time I encounter a painting or a poem, or a song, I'm back there—and when everybody I know is out in the street in their brightest colors, happy as could be, over their heads my balloon sails away from me privately, but also, it's sailing away from all of us, and it's not about losing the balloon but about watching it liftoff, a string out of reach when anyone of the five or six people in front of me, if they had seen it, would have grabbed it, and off it went. The whole thing…somehow… an act of beauty. Do you get it?"

"Um…yeah I guess so, Dad."

As I've said, he didn't always care much whether I *did* get it when he talked this artsy way. Keeping me in the loop I guess was one way he thought about it, part of my education, to keep talking above my pay grade.

"So, I've been writing about it because this woman's poetry is a little reminder for me of something beautiful and an act of loss, and the love of her work, or of whatever was the beauty of what I found there slipped away, maybe from everybody's grasp. It's a long way of saying some of her work held up, and can be revisited, is still, I guess, *alive,* even as it disappears."

"Oh. I get it, Dad."

I really didn't anymore and was thinking about the rooms upstairs, above the tavern, where I knew that in the great hallway someone in residence there had hung an immense swing, and which I'd only seen once, and couldn't now stop thinking I'd like to use.

"So, I guess the Autopsy part comes in when I think about trying to find out if the patient is alive or dead, and if dead, what was the cause of death. And if not totally dead, can she be revived? You see?"

Long sigh. Suddenly, I really *did* feel like a kid, and recognized my tactic of constantly changing the subject on him had outlived its usefulness. On the plus side, it frequently led us into territory like this, the near-lecture, and veered away from things like "how you feeling," which when asked, I could have been counted on to fabricate something not too surprising, or alarming, but with enough depth, he wouldn't fire up one of his "why don't you read more?" fits.

"I guess, Dad. Hey, do you mind if I go upstairs for a while and find that old swing?"

The look he gave me then has flashed back for most of my life; it comes on as unexpectedly as a train at some outpost, hauling a kind of freight I'd never care to inspect—regret. Even though I wanted to be alone a while, to get away from his need to be more than my parent, I recognized but would not acknowledge his disappointment, shadows of betrayed trust, not with just anyone, but with the image he'd packed with expectation, with me; for only a few seconds he'd cut away from the role and been just another human being.

"Yeah, okay. You go ahead. Listen, I'm going down the street where your mom is. I'd like to know something more about Cecile. I'll be down there having a beer. You can meet me there in a bit when you're ready and we'll get something to eat. Okay? You must be hungry. It's almost 9 o'clock."

He got up and started across the street, then about halfway across stopped and turned around to give me a wave and one of his goofy looks. A shuffle and a shrug like buster Keaton who he once said made the only great movies. Just at that moment, the tavern door, that huge glass door, swung open:

"Hey—Massimo...Max*ee*...hey, Mac! Come on over here. I got it. Come on, we're all ready, man, come on."

Dad looked at me for a second, then started walking slowly back toward the tavern. He seemed, I can only say "sheepish," weakened in fact by this man's voice. I knew who it was; though he couldn't see me, from where I was sitting, I could see his immense head jutting out past the tavern door, his big mustache, his potbelly, a noticeably big man, much bigger than Mac. Maybe that was why he seemed sheepish as he walked back toward the man and The Pocket's door; other people inside were shouting his name as if they were cheering at a boxing match. Three men and a wiry-looking woman all sat at a round table in the shadows of the bar, far from where he'd been writing at the window. Wolfish smiles. I knew what it was all about, but I wasn't supposed to; he didn't talk about these people. He was going to take LSD, though every time he did, something crazy happened. He didn't take it often and didn't go off alone; he had to be around these wolves, these losers. I don't know why he felt it was a good idea. Maybe he saw it as a way to have a breakthrough. He didn't look at me now but kept his head down. "Sheepish" is the right word, as I recall this one moment when I saw my own father change instantly as if he could by an act of will abandon who I knew him to be; a kind of warrior, I think. On a strange, unforgivable level of his own mind he could flip over into that unfortunate lost set of inadequacies and confusions I wouldn't know about until I discovered his pathetic tale in a letter he wrote me about what really took place that night, the night he duped himself into believing he could commit a violent act against *my* mother. As Mac made his way into the tavern, Donnie the Unplugged held the door and leaned over and "gave me the eyeball,"—a weird, anonymous grin, closing the door behind the two of them, Mac's old Italianate name shouted inside, and shouted again, faded and dissolved into the street silence.

23.

I CLIMBED SOME steep narrow stairs toward where they had hanged the giant swing. I didn't want to think about Mac or even my mother down the street, definitely not about Cecile, Tommy, Deputy Dave, and all those problems. So, I slogged upstairs. It took a long time; climbing those stairs was like ascending a tower, they were so steep. At the entrance, they were cluttered with shoes, coats, some beer bottles where brown cigarettes were doused, crushed milk cartons, candy wrappers, and one wilted stick of celery. Worn steps, their edges rounded where each had borne the weight of a thousand traipses, each footfall pressed down forcefully, the challenge of such steps seeming to run so high and well above the tall ornate tavern ceiling where my father sat—and fidgeted, I was certain—in the strange company of wolves, and where at that moment he made a decision which would unravel a thread he would lose.

Psychedelics, the few times I tried them, brought a memory of him front and center, making the experience the more existential. Not entirely unpleasant, I had to admit, but the confusion and desperation in *his* experience that night would make it difficult to cope in *my* world, which, due to the gap of years in which we each ingested, was not the same world Mac was tripping in. Whereas now an array of legal and illegal substances—psychotropic, psychedelic, and otherwise—seamlessly connect to ideas of freedom, self-discovery, and revelation, in his world the broad swath between legal and illegal generated an allure for some now unimaginable heaven of paranoia. The terror, at least for him and his indisputable renown, of a bright light exposing him as if in a delirium was as compelling as the interior discoveries toward which he thought himself a devout pilgrim and believed he was a chosen pathfinder.

DIVOTS IN ROTTING steps had collected rain, or beer, in small puddles off the boots of those who lived upstairs: the Tavern staff, the workers in the woods and on boats, who also paid for room and board. I was ascending in flip-flops, so my rubber had no trouble what with wearing down anything, but for me, a spry kid ready to run up those steps—carpentered by people a century earlier, who had *had a few* for lunch in the tavern and stumbled upstairs with the working girls, and the deliquescence of whose work may have yielded some inconsistency in the heights of a few of their risers—all of this made my incline sprint an obstacle course. The ceiling in the Tavern trapped a yellow smoke of cigars, but here the second-floor lobby was bright white and wide open. Up above me, on the exposed third floor, some walls had been torn back to reveal ancient, splintered studs and lathe. Flushed from leaping up each irregular step, the flight up there seemed virtually perpendicular; a temporary catwalk was scabbed onto the shattered plaster of formerly whorehouse walls. Inviting light leaked from suspiciously half-opened doors where cobwebs wafted off the doorknobs.

The swing hung down to my level, at the end of thick rope from a set of gigantic hooks screwed I hoped with uncanny force into that far-off ceiling. It hung so loftily I would have to stretch out from the landing to step onto its seat, a four-by-eight plank; more like mounting a trapeze than climbing aboard a kid's safety-inspected yard toy. That's what I was contemplating—leap to the stout ropes and cling to the wide swing seat—where I could escape the messy world of my parents.

But a flickering light, a fizzing sound, got my attention and I turned to where one bulb dangled and a reek of fume coated the pale lobby. An electric band of neon green was at the bottom of a closed door; behind that door, something popped, then I heard loud voices. The door flung open, and a girl flew—she really flew—to my mind like a fully-empowered magical being—and crashed against the wall, slid as if pressed by an invisible gigantic hand slowly, agonizingly slow, down onto the floor. She herself had big hands. The neon flicker out that doorway made her mouth and eyes old. In the room from which she flew, a curtain furled above the windowsill, a television sat like a toad on planks set on bricks, smoking, neon in the TV screen faded the way air leaves a balloon, a baritone voice recited a statistic slower and slower.

The girl, several years older than me but almost an adult, sat with her back against the wall, her legs in blue tights straight out in front of her, rocking her head back and forth in those boney hands. The only word that comes to mind now to describe her is "compact." Meaning everything she was, all she had, all of her, was right there; a being without possession, she could have shifted into dust, and no one would know or call for her. That's how I remember her—no one would search if she disappeared.

Rocking and talking to herself—she didn't realize I was standing right there—her voice in a whisper seemed to recount recent experiences: "...must have been asleep. Why did I go to sleep? I don't know. Why did I take that bad acid? Oh, shit...oh, shit...oh, shit..." and on and on like that, rocking her head in her ugly hands.

She gave me a look, finally, a little horrified. Her eyes glazed blue by the TV glow, its exploded light along with smoke streamed out of the room. She looked like a painting, an image I've *never* tried to capture, that puzzled question on her lips and in her eyes and furrowed brow bathed in the flicker, strobe-like, beginning to dim. Maybe the questioning look was her gradually recognizing that I was a kid, gawking, maybe a tourist who lost his parents at the ice cream parlor. I saw her expression change: my face—I'm certain my mouth hung open—must have betrayed my shock. People told me things. I didn't want to get myself into their kind of difficulties. "Difficulties" may not be the correct word, but as a spectator, all I noticed were states of heightened stress. I didn't think it was attractive to make yourself a fool in places where anybody could see and have the chance to judge you. She spoke to me, though not much different from the conversation she was having with herself, except she no longer kept rocking her head like it wouldn't be still on its own. She told me she needed to relax. She said she closed her eyes for a few minutes lying on her bed. That was hours before the TV exploded because she recalled sun through her window. She heard the TV, the news, names of victims of recent crimes. She heard her own father, a million miles away, but then standing right beside her bed whispering.

"Valery, Valery."

"What, Daddy? What do you want?"

"Clean your room. Then go outside and wash the car!"

His voice was loud, but she wouldn't open her eyes.

"Why are you dead?"

"Who's dead, Val?"

"What are you doing talking to me? Do you like being dead, Daddy?"

"Who's dead?"

"You. You are. This is making me nervous."

"Get up, Valery."

"What?"

"I said 'Get up.' Now get out of that fucking bed, Val!"

He sounded angry, but she laughed at his voice, the sound so familiar, happy to be hearing him again. She didn't care whether he *was* angry. What was he angry for? She was lying on her back, her eyes closed, her dead father screaming at her, shaking her shoulders, she saw his face, brows knitted when he's worried. Then the voice stopped.

"Daddy?"

Nothing. That's when she opened her eyes and sat up. The TV blaring, the picture turned lime green. She smelled smoke and something bluish wafted out the back of it. She heard a funny noise, saw flame, dove through the door, and slammed against this wall.

We stared into the room. The curtain brushing the sash, smoke guttering. She held a tiny white envelope. I was going to say, "What's that?" but then I knew. She was staring straight ahead.

"Windowpane."

"What?"

"You were thinking what this is."

She bounced the little envelope in the palm of her left

hand.

"Oh. Yeah. I've heard of it."

She looked thoughtfully at me, her eyes rolled around the hallway, up toward the broken plaster and the bare light bulb, and back to me, just above my left ear.

"Sorry. I can't give you any. Thanks, though. I can see you're a kid. How...how old are you?"

I didn't say. Up at that broken chunk of plaster, my eyes had latched onto the minuscule husk of a spider probably there since last summer. At least that long. I wondered if these halls were ever wiped clean. Considering such things at a moment when I might have answered a question like "how old are you"—the irregularity of housekeeping or the improbability of ghosts, dead fathers waking you for explosions—was an old habit that now made me stare at dust and spider remains for the next three minutes before I could look back at this person. She was staring at *me* now. I don't know what she could have been doing those minutes other than staring at the dead spider with me. She stood up, then stepped forward, almost toppled dizzily, her back to me, and her long blue arm reached down for sandals beside the door. Her blouse fell as she bent, and from my sitting position, I saw for the first time ever a girl's breast, pale and white, the nipple pointing down like a sign to look. I wanted to keep looking but she stood, closed the door to her room, turned around, toward my hunched-up kid's body, and gave it a smile like you do with someone who has no idea what's going on but trusts them to think you believe they can handle anything, and then she walked down those mismatched steps. A stairway built over a century ago for men and women to wander in and out of these rooms; she didn't look back, her palm faced me, fingers waved. I watched until I heard the latch at the foot of the steps click shut.

24.

AS WE STOOD out on the street below Mac's old studio, I looked down along the road that led out of town. A remarkably familiar view for me. The tavern where my mother used to work, The Little Friend, only a block away from where I stood, was now known as *Lou's Bar & Grille*. Parked across the street from it was the dented green van. Tristan's, I knew now, and he must be inside that bar, even though he said he was going home. I was about to leave when I realized the little landlord was still talking. When he caught his breath for a second, I thanked him for showing me the office. I said I don't really know if I can paint there. It had been my father's office for many years, I told him.

"Oh, I remember that guy. What was it he wrote, some kind of books on something? Wasn't he a painter, too? Was he an art critic, or come to think on it he wrote the news, was always snooping around asking questions like he was writing a book or somethin'—that your dad? Well, I'll be, never thought he had anybody, what do you know? The man had children... how big a family did he have? You must have some brothers and sisters still here... Where the hell did he ever get money to support a big family like that?...Jeez, he must of got hisself some family money inheritance or something... wasn't he independently wealthy if he raised those kids? And do all you live here in town still? Well, let me know when you want to move in, I'm right here in the store down below the apartment most of the time so I could have it rented any time I wanted but I'll hang onto it for ya a few more days while you go ahead and get your finances straighten out, that's just the kind of guy I am; I'll do anything for my tenants so long they don't screw me over, so just you let me know, okay, you have a good day now bye."

STANDING BESIDE TRISTAN'S van, hiding in fact, I looked across the street into *Lou's* windows. I didn't think Tristan might look out and see me, but I saw him. Waving his arms, dancing, or rather jerking his body from side to side alone beside the jukebox, other drunks at the tables shouting happily, laughing at his gyrations. He would be pretty drunk by now. Men and women clapped along to the rhythm of Country Blues goading him on and hoisted him onto the table where he twirled, to the delight of Lou's customers.

Other than our conversation down the street, I didn't know much more than the miserable events with his father, our only shared memory, until it became clear to me I had been one of his ex's "experiences." I had to wonder if seeing her at The Pocket triggered more drinking. Did she tell him she noticed me slink out of there in a hurry? His dance moves, drunk and showing off for the home crowd, led him gingerly from one tabletop to the next, until he flopped into the laps of a few blubbery patrons who laughed louder, spilling beer on the tabletops and work clothes. The irony of Tristan, scion of Deputy Dave, making a fool of himself was that years ago in this same tavern began the downfall of Deputy Dave. And the snapped off ending of my own simple childhood; at The Little Friend was where Mac and my mom switched things around on me; he from the dad I thought an esteemed poet turned into a nerve-addled acid-freak, and she from my own precious mom had become the babe drunken men strutted around the room for and fell over themselves to get her to smile at them.

I almost run down those steps and away from The Pocket, and now I'm sitting on the bench in front of her bar, The Little Friend. Not that she owns it, but she worked there so long most patrons assume it's hers and call her Mademoiselle or ask how she pronounces this French wine they're ordering, just to hear her accent. Every now and then I turn around on the bench to look inside, and if she sees me, she waves—like a mom, not like a beautiful bartender: surreptitious, from her hip pocket, a wave to the kid out the window. After about twenty minutes, she raises one finger in the air to let me know she has a break coming, and she'll be right out. Then, when she does appear, she's bearing a bowl of soup on a tray with a baguette and butter; a glass of milk; she's arranged a saucer with slices of orange for me. An Iris curves from the thin stem of a standard table vase.

Tristan at these same tables, I thought I should make some sort of amends, which I could do if I went in there and helped get him away from a humiliating scene and back to his home. I thought of it as amends, even if he didn't know what I'd done, amends for knowing too much. When I got inside, the jukebox had stopped playing, and the very large guys at the table in the corner were shifting Tristan from one to another of them, and into an empty chair. I didn't want to be there. But I walked over to their tables anyway. There must have been about twelve people in all, several tables pushed haphazardly together so they could all reach the pitchers. They turned their corner of *Lou's* into a kind of mead hall—with their own noises and chaos, wafting any number of glues and gasolines, fiberglass from the boatyard, the strong scent of goat barns, or resins and sawdust from a day at the lumber yard, and bright gold lager, quite a bit of it, puddling the tabletops. I sat down next to Tristan, and he turned toward me, squinted at me as if he didn't recognize me, then he did, and leaned toward me, motioning with his hand as if he had something to say; it was then he spat in my face.

Mom has her own way of pronouncing my name. No one imitating her could do justice to it: the trill on the 'R' *as if her tongue enjoyed saying it, and then she emphasizes the second syllable to rhyme it with 'air' by almost singing it, her voice rising with that happiness she knows I always need to hear:* "R-*r-r-o*BAIR! *Heer you are! Je...I know you must be hungry. Did you see your Papá? I didn't know where you disappeared to." "I saw him, Mom. I didn't want to be in the house just then, so I figured you'd know where I went. He's down the street at The Pocket. He said he wanted to come down here and talk to you. I think he wants to find out about Cecile. But he's still there, I'm pretty sure."*

"Yes. I must go back inside now, Mon fils. Did you see your Uncle Auguste at the counter?" No, I didn't. And there he is, half-turned around on a bar stool, waving at me, his grin somewhat sad, I think. His hickory shirt and his tin pants are cruddy, his boots have soot on them. He has come directly from fighting forest fires down by Leavenworth. He looks tired. "Bon Appetit, Mon Cher," in her singsong voice. "Wait—Mom..." She ruffles my hair, rubs my shoulder, and says, "Stay here. I'll come back, and I think Uncle Auguste wants to take you somewhere when you finish your dinner." "Okay. Hey, what time is it, anyway, Mom?" "Let...me...see." She is

making a show of stretching her neck toward the big clock on the wall above the mirror. A cruiser floats passed, and every now and then blares out from the horn: blip-blip and its red light, blue light, sweep across the building, across our faces.

The best thing you can do when you feel a drunk may have been justified to spit in your face is get as far away as you can without leaving the room if you're still determined, as I was, to attempt to find some way of making amends for having slept with his former wife who was, "Just trying to have a little fun..." So, I moved just out of Tristan's line of fire, and he forgot about me for the moment. I decided, though, that he couldn't get back in that wreck of a van tonight, and I would wait to drive him home.

I kept my distance. Sitting beside Tristan, but deep in his own conversation with someone on the other side of the table, was Quentin, who had turned just in time to see Tristan spit on me. He looked at me with some slight interest but quickly resumed his conversation, nodding to me as I stood up and walked to the bar. From a barstool and without turning around, I could observe Tristan in the mirror that loomed over the cash register. Why is it that bars have mirrors? On a practical level, they make the room bigger. But at the metaphysical stage of imbibing, it could be so drinkers can measure their aging process. Or theatrically examine their consciences. Or could it be to spy, as I was doing, on the rest of the room while seeming to take an unusual interest in one's inner life? Or they could, we could all, keep track of our immediate state of drunkenness, unless one was drinking to get drunk the way Tristan was, who should have been, by all rights, cut off by any judicious bartender.

Lou, the bar owner, had a "swarthy look about him." A

black trim beard and mustache, his slick-backed hair tied in a ponytail, he was short and quick in his moves behind the bar. A shot glass never refilled more abruptly in my experience. Nor had a precise coin count been selected from a drinker's palm more efficiently. Lou had little to say, and I gave up any attempt at conversation. When I looked into the mirror again, I realized I had lost track of Tristan. He was no longer in his seat, and not performing for the collection of friends and roustabouts around the mead table over the throbbing of the jukebox, though, Lou, as well as I, became alert to a rather loud and suspicious thud from the stairwell beyond the Restroom sign, the sound of yelling, or screeching, and banging on the walls. His nod toward me signified he'd long ago recognized it had been because of Tristan I entered his greasy establishment. Maybe he witnessed the spit incident. He placed a glass down, wiped his hands on an apron and, with one quick wave said, "You coming?" and I followed him down the stairs that led toward the Men's Room.

Tristan, moaning, tried to elbow himself off the floor. Once he fell, he slid face-first bumping all the way down about fifteen stairs. His legs and feet were elevated, his boot caught on a loose plank. I followed Lou and we jerked the rubbery body into a feasible enough position to get his legs back in motion. He put a grimy hand against one dank brick wall. We were standing on a clay floor where someplace beyond two swinging doors a ferociously pungent Men's Room might have been discovered in that catacomb, dark and unfathomed as Lou's soul, but I wasn't going any farther. Tristan, who had pissed himself already, was covered in dust and filth, frankly.

"So loaded he didn't feel a thing, but he will tomorrow. Listen, can you get this asshole the fuck outa here before something serious happens to him? Bad enough I'll have cops here if he remembers where he got those bruises. Just get him the fuck gone."

Lou, it seemed, was used to giving orders, and used to Tristan. I didn't know how he was able to read me, but I suppose he didn't have to think about it at all.

Eventually, I did stand with Tristan at his front door, his heavy left arm slung over my shoulders and his head drooping forward. He was awake, though perhaps not completely, and standing, his other hand leaning against the door jamb just above the white glistening button I had already pressed to be let in.

"Oh, she'll be pissed, but only for a minute. She'll forget everything. Don't worry about it."

From my 'child's bench' out front, I hear Tommy's voice, and smell cigarettes and cigars, a stale concoction they all breath, foam on a beer before each face, Tommy's friends. All voices loud enough over a deep blues twang invading the jukebox, clink of glasses where Mom stands somewhat meekly behind a stainless sink in yellow gloves. Tommy holding forth over the racket, saying things about my mother—he has no idea I am listening—saying things that are just vile. I try imagining what makes him so angry with her, though it's obvious he's drunk. My mother doesn't look up at all but keeps washing glasses, and maybe rewashing to keep herself busy, because she isn't going to their table to hint they should buy refills. Tommy so loud and obnoxious his voice dominates the room. "N-n-now, T-T-Tommy, come on. D-don't b-be like that." "Oh, shut up, Victor, fuck you!" I look in because I never hear adults stutter. I always used to when I was little. The man who is talking has long hair and is dressed in white clothes, but I don't recognize him. I don't really recognize anybody in that part of the room, except Tommy. In a little while, he gets up, stands there a minute with a grin at his friends. They don't look at him when he lays a hand down on the table, turns around, and walks across the barroom in his clunky boots to stand at the bar across from my mother who's at the sink still, water running, her head down. He places something on the bar before her, and she turns off the faucet. Then he stands back, arms folded across his barrel chest, staring at her. This time without a smile. It's the ring. She removes the rubber gloves and is drying her hands, but it doesn't look like she's about to touch it; she never believed it was meant for her. "You keep it, Natalie. Hock it. It's worth a lot, believe me." He turns around to look back at the boys lounging behind the big table, and grins at them again when he says, "At least that's what they said when I stole it." Guffaws all across the room, louder than the jukebox. "In fact, Nat, I might go rob somebody right now. Don't wait up, honey!" More guffaws. Then he walks through swinging doors out of the barroom, onto the sidewalk, and glances at me sitting on my bench, eating my late-night dinner. Streetlights making a kind of glare in contrast to his black t-shirt, his face seems whiter, ghastlier when his smile empties where those front teeth used to be. He points at me with his index and middle finger, thumb up, which he pulls back like cocking a gun, pretends to pop me, blows fake smoke off his fingertip, opens the door to his turquoise Galaxy convertible parked at the curb, and streaks away, his rear wheels a bit wobbly down the street.

At the door to Tristan's place, I saw it in her eyes immediately—that look, the way the whole family glares. It was a face I hadn't seen in twenty years, not since Dave the Deputy chucked the mother off his front porch. Here we were again on another porch, a woman holding the door inside who didn't seem to have a clue who I was, and Tristan who staggered right past her, and spoke to the woman on the couch whose eyes were like spaceships.

"Hi, Mom. It's me. It's Tristan. This is Bobby. He was a kid when you saw him before. Don't worry about it."

He went on telling her all about me and growing up and avoided all the shitstorm that was her marriage and his childhood, and she kept nodding her head as he talked, and her face had something that was nearly a smile, but that whole time the woman who opened the door just stood there in front of me, keeping the door half-open. She was not inviting me to enter. And she was so big, or hefty is probably a better word—broad shoulders, sleeves rolled back so I could see she had meaty tattooed forearms as if she'd spent her life bailing hay or delivering sheep.

When Tristan took a pause in yakking to his old mother, he turned just his head halfway back toward the door. Her hand was still on the latch, black hair streaked with orange, eyebrow thick across this face that was so familiar, but I couldn't remember meeting anybody but his....

"Bobby, that's Dot. My sister Dot. Remember?"

Nothing, not a word. She didn't say anything, and I really didn't remember her, but for some reason, I thought I remembered she might be damaged or delayed, or some kind of a psycho. She was just staring, burning holes into my eyes, and the flat line of her mouth bore no expression, until, suddenly, she spoke.

"You're forgiven now. It's alright, Bobby. It's alright. You can go. Goodbye."

She moved then, somewhat gingerly, still drilling that recognition into my eyes, and in slow motion brought the door to the point where I could see only her left eye, then she nodded, and it clicked shut. I could hear Tristan inside.

"Hey, Dot, he's okay, he..."

"I know, Tristan. I know. He's gone now."

The rain was coming down, just "spitting" as my own mother used to say, and I didn't want any more to do with those people, so I practically ran to my car, bolted into the seat, and I felt the wave then wash over me. I felt it. I knew it for the first time maybe ever. I *was* forgiven, I was washed clean by the blood of the lamb! And then I got the hell out of there before Tristan could squeeze past old Dot and invite me in to chat up his Space Odyssey mother.

Uncle Auguste comes out next and says, "BobbEE! Let me take your plate." I catch a tangy whiff of smokejumper's aroma, but he has a waiter's napkin over his gray left sleeve. It's midnight. "Bobby, I have a little job I need your assistance with, but first, perhaps Monsieur would select a slice of pie? Hey, I think it is your Papa, n'est, pas?"

Across the street, there he is. Dad running. He doesn't look like the same person I spoke with two hours ago. He looks frightened, mortally afraid of something, and running fast, that sheaf of "pocket papers" rolled up in his hand like a relay racer's baton.

PENELOPE

25.

HE HEARD HIS own breath, the thump of his heart in the dark, seeing next to nothing. He knew he was going up a hill toward houses belonging to people he did not know. Blue from the lit-up streets down there on his right. Nothing but people dancing. Where the girl was he didn't know who gave him the acid and smiled into smoke, in strobe, sharp teeth in that light. He was running away and now police car strobe bathing him, blue and dark, blue and dark. Running to the top of the hill, he realized they were flashing at him. But he was simply running. And tripping on windowpane acid.

The summer moon was up dust all over the forsythia. Was something missing? They were quiet for a second. They waved flashlights along the side of the hill.

"You were running."

They shone the flashlight in his face.

"Here's my wallet...I'm tripping...I'm going to sit down."

Dizzy, from the running as well as the strobe, the acid, from heavy breathing, he sat down, didn't look in their faces. Side by side; they were staring at him, one holding the wallet. They'd been driving around town, looking for something;

they didn't expect this. It took about a minute to decide what to do.

One was pale and thin. The other had a different head on the same uniform. The one who beat Cecile badly.

"Massimo Monroe Bacca," he said finally, reading from the driver's license. "We'll give this back in a minute," slowly, as though the man sitting on the ground couldn't understand English, or was deaf, maybe retarded.

He gave the license to the other one, who went into the car and cranked up the radio. He sat in front of their headlights. Standing near the hood ornament and looking down, the officer lit a cigarette.

Bacca incredibly cool, a face in a blur of hair. Like lots of people all over town. Gotta go by eye color, hair color, size, weight. Can't just look at somebody and tell who he is. Maybe that's what happened with Cecile. He couldn't tell.

"Can I ask you a personal question?"

The officer, and he remembered the man was called Deputy Dave, looked over toward the courthouse and smiled slightly when he said, "Sure."

After a pause, "No, never mind."

His eyebrows went up, he seemed disappointed. "Okay."

He should ask why a police officer beat his gentle sister-in-law.

"LET ME ASK *you*—we gonna find anything?"

Dave was pointing with his thumb to the car where the other was still on the ten-four.

"I don't want to see you fuck up your life with a thing like this."

Offended by the "fuck..."

Kicked her ribs. Broke her spleen. He was smiling. Teeth

like giant tablets. How do you forget teeth like that? I want to let you go. That's what the teeth meant.

If he didn't say so right away and acted strange, they'd have hauled him in. He was afraid and they came; what else could he do but tell them? They were the ones who knew. He didn't. His brain was shut off. They knew what to do, they were in charge. He was in their hands. They would take care of him—this wasn't his first acid trip; he could do things he was incapable of.

"Why do you wanna do that stuff?"

He didn't answer. His eyes said it, the corners of his mouth turned up. Perhaps Dave saw remorse. The creases in his black pants could slice someone's throat. He exhaled cigarette smoke, looked at Orion's Belt, then Scorpio setting on the southern horizon. A life he could not live.

The other one-handed back the wallet. They stared at the grass for the moment it took to agree. Deputy Dave leaned out the window as the car eased over gravel, making a disturbing noise combined with the airy dispatcher's growl. Skin so white, hair close to the scalp. Somebody's twin. Where was the other? Whoosh-whoosh, the flashers, in and out of his own face. Light made his teeth pointed.

"You be careful. Go home now. Okay? Go...home..." Dave's voice as they drove away.

THIS IS THE part everyone knew. He told everyone. At least for the next few weeks. And I heard the details over and over. "Bobby, you know all this already, but...": He was tripping, the cops stopped him, they let him go—and he got paranoid. My Dad. That's how he was. It had taken Moses a few years to work through Mac's papers and somewhere in the process, he came upon a letter Mac had written, and didn't send, to me, to tell what happened that night. Moses sent the letter, with one of his own cryptic sentences: "Not sure whether or not you want to read what's in here, but it *is* addressed to you, and I as your old Mentor feel it my duty to inform you 'beyond these gates lie danger.' Be well, Bobby. Moses."

In typical Mac fashion, he opened the letter with a macabre one-liner: "Bobby, if you're reading this, I'm already dead...No, not really. I've just always wanted to start a letter like that. I'm writing to tell you about the night I got stopped by the police for 'running uphill' as they told me, and then let me go, to wander around town, scared out of my mind they would come and arrest me anyway—wandered till dawn."

The irony is I did, in fact, receive it when he was dead. Buried among his papers, it never made it to the mailbox, although had I received it when he *was* alive, I could have told him I empathized about the unnecessary stress that night must have caused. I can still see him running past The Little Friend. The chaos, the terror, the way some payment had come due. I still wish I had been able to talk to him about that night, about that summer in fact, but he drove away in September. And planned to enter a war apart from the literary ones he'd been fighting. Nevertheless, he might very well have not mailed the letter to me because it wasn't intended to be sent. Perhaps it was a first draft of something he planned to publish in his literary magazine, and I was simply ghosting as the intended audience. I only heard about that magazine once that summer. He brought me with him to some artsy party and another guest mentioned the first issues of it, *Maverick,* the magazine Mac had founded. He went immediately into "interview mode"—*not a single issue is eclectic...I avoid all the elitist downfalls of any other one of these rags*—but he wasn't being interviewed, no one asked him to explain his editorial policies, nor expound any of his well-known theories on the American literary scene. In just that way, volunteering more than anyone might want to know, on he went in the letter, detailing the whole night, all the way into dawn when he's sitting naked at the piano playing maudlin tunes, while my mother slept nearby.

Apparently, he never told anyone what instigated his paranoia that night, what happened to his knife or finding my mom in the early hours. He never told his cronies that the police who left him under streetlights didn't say, "go home," or *be careful, take care,* any of that good stuff. Deputy Dave left Massimo Monroe Bacca throbbing from windowpane acid and a near police bust, and he wasn't about to miss a chance to plant fear in that hyper-charged imagination. He knew about the "poet who killed somebody in Albuquerque," the brother-in-law to his last "piece of shit" girlfriend; all he had to do was suggest a violent act to plague the poor bastard for the rest of his acid trip. What Dave really said was: "Last week we took in a guy high on that stuff. Stabbed his girlfriend with a knife," and then they shot out of there, "...off to some store robbery, wolf teeth blue under the flashers."..."Don't you do that, don't make the same mistake, Mackey!!" Deputy Dave's voice trailed off in Mac's head in the misery of night dust and starlight.

HE WAS STANDING in the gravel by the side of the road when their lights finally dissolved down the street, passing each overhanging tree lit by street lamps, turning blue and crimsoning branches and trunks. He half-believed the police car entered a tunnel, then pinpoints of their taillights disappeared. No one heard his voice. He waved his hand and each millisecond of the present broke into bone structure and fabric "the way cartoons are built in a studio one frame at a time. It was then all the houses took one step forward." My Dad, the acid-headed poet.

Soon he was lighting matches down the street in a stone corner of the old Customs House, a granite edifice where summer wind swept hysterically up from the bay. He tore up every piece of identification, tore his wallet to shreds, and tried to set fire to his money to get rid of every trace of himself, mash the ashes into the cracks of the sidewalk. He would have to leave town. The police set him up. They would circle back and arrest him for loitering or anything they could think of. He was certain they would not leave him out there; they were toying with him. He trusted them and they were gone, trusted them with an authority deeper than his own to protect him from himself, although that phrase they left him with penetrated, kept repeating among the clicks and squeaks in the cavernous echo chambers of his auditory nerve, needles scratching twenty different phonographs. He kept hearing: "Stabbed her, stabbed her, stabbed his girlfriend with a knife." He had to leave and had nowhere to go. "Stabbed her." And he killed her? Where were they? At the house he still owned but my mom was living there—and Cecile, and until tonight, sometimes Tommy. They would park in the bushes, wait for him to trudge up the hill. The little light on the dash blue, their faces cold—the hook was in his lip, and he was drowning.

The purpose of the letter, he wrote, was to tell me how much he loved my mother. He wanted me to grasp what it felt like for him to have loved her for at least half his life before they split up. "The proof I loved her," he said, "is in the drug and the suggestible nature of my personality. Both led me to believe what the police said—that, and my guilt over losing her seemed to be a prediction of where my own patterns of life had directed me."

But that driving accident, that death, if what Winston told me was true, showed how little he cared about the lives of others. He was too busy being famous to care. Obsessions and guilt re-emerged as he wrote that letter. He thought he wouldn't be able to prevent himself from stabbing her. He tossed away his worn-out Swiss Army knife. It *was* reading Moses's letters about their early days that put me on a mission to learn what happened to Mac. But Mac's letter, a guide, told me why he never really *came* home, even after he returned.

"How can that have been me?" he kept asking. "Well let's face it, Bobby, you probably noticed I had hit my own depth of self-hatred. I wasn't a drunk or a junkie like Burroughs, but like him, I loved my wife very much. I've always loved her no matter how bad things got between us. Burroughs pushed things too far with his little parlor trick—Billy Burroughs was no William Tell—but I don't think anyone can help but recognize how real was the love he felt for *his* wife, just like I felt for Natalie, but it *was* a low low time for me."

He'd lost track of whatever values they instilled in him in that very worthy education. Lost track of The Good, and now he shrank away from those essays, his petulant reviews. Shrank from even the person who *could* compose such distasteful, humiliating accounts about poets who only strove to do better work, to be better people. It was about innocence—that's what education meant. "Of course, it's meant to be lost. A certain way of life finally murders the beautiful innocent generous child within." His loss was layered: he lost it over and over in different and appropriate ways. At bottom—who he thought he was—he could expect nothing, could not justify his own addiction, his "depravity," as he called it. Then the car ran into a tree and killed the young man.

He was addicted to playing around with the lives of others; he interfered, he wanted to control the fate of a girl with a pretentious tattoo and a bogus young academic. He lost a certain innocence in that death and started taking whatever came as deserved. To do what the universe meant him to. When they said, "stabbed her with a knife," he thought it was a command.

He didn't know what "goodness" meant—those old shifting philosophies. It preoccupies some more than others. True to self after you've lost your innocence, *that* was goodness, but some never quit with the innocence. Without losing it, without doubting everything, you don't find out who you are. Can't lose innocence without gaining a kind of portal into yourself. Whether or not you enter. It's a loss of certainty, that old knowledge of good and evil—Goodness *can't* arise in someone who doesn't doubt himself. "When I finally came to doubt myself, my motives, my cynical convictions, it was because I knew what The Good is, but I can't name it and can't find it within myself. Doubt, doubt everything, doubt even why I'm doubting, and at least I'm putting myself in the way of The Good, of something. To know only good, a belief in utopia, it misses the point. You see yourself whole, see others the same, before you're experienced. Losing innocence is what self-awareness *is*."

THEN HE APOLOGIZED for leading me away from his narrative and getting a "little too preachy, probably," for my taste.

The accident was on Veterans Day, November eleventh. Of course, the old Citroen was totaled, but he kept it anyway and had it restored. He didn't say how he managed to locate a mechanic or a body shop for such a beast in New Mexico, and for all I know, he might have had the parts shipped from

Germany. Once he was ready, he drove out of Albuquerque and kept going for the next six months or so, sleeping in the car, living on whiskey and scraps of food. Sometime after his ramble, he showed up back home—among us but not with us. He took up residence in his old studio as I've mentioned. Didn't even try to patch things up with Mom although he did let her know how things stood with himself, with me and he would stay at arm's length from her life. She'd been seeing Tommy for several months by then; that is, before the whole ring thing. Tommy was no suitor—even Mac knew that.

He wanted to keep the accident, which he referred to as 'The Manslaughter,' uppermost in his mind when he abandoned his teaching assignments and drove away from New Mexico. He told me he stopped at almost every gas station in the Northeast to purchase $11.11 in gas. This shocked me a little since that numerical configuration has haunted me for years. I've assumed the clock will stop at that time when I die, but now I realize it already stopped for him. He thought of this gas gesture as not only a reminder of what he'd done on November 11th but as a tribute to that young man, who as I learned from Winston, was Jeff Fournier. The guilt, he said, had been insurmountable and he carried it with him in that old car.

He went back to what happened that night. They left him standing there like some Dickensian ghoul, huffing along, passing houses with curtained living rooms, quiet and dull. He thought of himself as guilty of manslaughter—though never charged as such—and now he was contemplating the murder of his estranged wife as if all that was required was a simple nod. Does contemplation make you a murderer? Still, he was running uphill toward my mother—*Stabbed her with a knife, stabbed her, stabbed her*—his head like a wind tunnel, and he believed an inevitable knife was ready to fly into his hands.

Had I gotten this letter before he died, I could have asked him why—why was he running toward the house where he knew he could find Mom? Maybe because the drug peppered him up so much he would have done whatever his imagination suggested. Compulsive and helpless to resist, he couldn't have gone anywhere but where *she* was. I would have asked him if he hated her. Years earlier he couldn't stop himself from tourettically yelling obscenities in a church, or in a movie theater or lecture hall, or at a poetry reading. Self-control, all but vanished, once meant he was not a piece of the crowd—he wouldn't acquire *its* hysteria: if hysteria was not his own, he was lost.

The knife flies to his fingers. He removed from his back pocket the old Swiss Army knife, flung it onto a lawn, and continued to run and mutter. A simple thud and he laughed about the futility of it. Kitchen knives still disturbed him, afraid of dropping one on his bare toes, accidentally cutting himself and not knowing until too late, nicking off a fingertip. But he's even more afraid when he gets there, he'll pick up a knife and there won't be a voice—his hand will just do it. Many people hear voices, they're insane. Sometimes they kill. This was different. He would go to the house, his acid head throbbing so loudly how could she not recognize what's wrong? Knives will be all over the place. He thought he might pick one up and start. Maybe more than one—her scream would stop him—prison would stop him. But why, Dad? When did this begin? I wish I could read his mind; in the letter, he writes it felt as though his head were glass, so I should be able to see what brought him to her. Did the acid amplify a residual hate? Was he the ultimate good-natured misogynist? Why did he try to ruin that tattooed girl's life? "Stabbed her with a knife!" It's just not the Dad I knew. Too late now to ask him why.

Yet he was able to tell me in that letter that he *didn't* kill her or cause her death; instead, he *chose* to give her back her life. He could honestly say, without fear of contradiction or of my telling him the truth—that this *act of mercy* proves he was deeply, deeply in love. And he was writing all this to *me,* their only offspring. He knew he was a good person. He hadn't strayed too far from being that genuinely loving husband he had tried to be when they were married, the husband he wished he still had a chance to prove to Natalie, Mom, that he could be. He was good. He hadn't lost it. What was it that proved that at bottom his human goodness prevailed? What else could it be? He was like everybody else in a struggle with the choice between good and evil. He knew it seemed bad that he spent most of that night wandering around uptown wanting not to go where she was and where he might do something he couldn't control and fighting with himself about whether to go there, about whether he really *would* do what those cops had planted in his imagination. He was struggling with a choice like lots of other people had to every day. Only for him, it was a decision, conscious—well maybe, he said, maybe it *was* seated in his own unconscious, but deep in his mind, in his own nature, and the decision simply came without in fact having to be decided. It was just his nature choosing the obvious without his rational mind having to enter it at all. And *that's what proves, Bobby, that's what proves that I really loved your mother, my simple natural disinclination to do her any harm.* The fact, he said, that I chose *not* to kill her, but that I chose to give her her life, and it was a life that wouldn't involve me anymore, that alone proves that I'm not only a good person who can restrain himself from doing something evil when the idea is presented to him and the drug could perhaps even wipe away his conscience, but it proves that I loved her; I *didn't* kill her. I let her go on with her life. I came to her, I think, to tell her that. So, you see? Goodness. *That's* the basis of our character, yours and mine. And hers too. Because I didn't do it—that means I'm a good person and I loved her freely.

If he had only given me a chance to speak to him about that night, I might have said, "Is that it, Dad, is that all? Do you really think that's true? Well, I don't think you and William Burroughs know what the fuck you're talking about. Did you totally believe you of all people were *capable* of killing? 'Choosing not to' does *not* prove you loved her. You were lying. You were incapable of loving anything but an idea. You didn't *choose* to do anything. You couldn't. You didn't even choose to go there; you just followed an inclination set off by the police. A fantasy. Your 'unconscious' led you to refrain from stabbing her? With a knife? And you lived with yourself all those years thinking that? Even though you walked around the whole night with the intention to do it, like a spike at the center of your mind? The cops woke up something; they didn't command you. How long did you poison your marriage until you got to a point you could tell yourself you couldn't trust your own actions and do this to her? To her? Of all people. Is it a hatred for the one you worshipped, a reaction to your own feebleness?"

He thought it might be some genetic instinct, and worried, he said, he might have passed this on to me. I didn't think so, but I do take sharply his memory of hiding in the bottom bunk of his childhood bedroom with his mother. She was clutching him tightly and they could look out through the opened door at the bare lightbulb on the ceiling of the kitchen. The walls and formica were a bright yellow, and the linoleum was in parts shattered gray and white. The two of them listened as the dishes were thrown against the walls, as the chairs were overturned and then he saw the long and sharp knife thrown into the kitchen floor and, he said, the memory is still with him of that twang as it flipped from side to side. His father, who was an excellent butcher, was yelling over that knife noise as it went back and forth, and still is, he wrote, still is.

I would have told him that memory didn't mean he had to be like my grandfather, or that I had to be either: he thought he could kill my own mother, yet he never once in that letter said he realized he would be taking her away from me. If I only could have faced him directly, I might have been able to say that even a traumatic memory, his scary knife, wasn't enough to make him turn into someone he was not. I would have said, "You congratulated yourself for proving what you thought love is: choosing not to kill the one you love! You never, never thought of me, or of her, the person she is, in this letter, so why did you even address it to me? For some literary triumph? You weren't in the least bit sorry for thinking you could have taken her away or for believing you could stab her with a knife. You should have begged me, and you should have begged her, to forgive you for even thinking you had that vileness in you, but now you can go rot in hell."

Of course, I don't believe in a hell, and I didn't want him to suffer—he had been in his own hell for several years by the time he wrote this letter, but I think, had I an opportunity to let him know he was plainly delusional, I might have let him see how foolish he was when he got to the part about standing in the dark room at the foot of a bed where two people he once knew were asleep. He broke into their house, through the unlocked kitchen door. He walked in. He knew them; they befriended him and Natalie long ago. He slept with the woman once, but that's not why he was in their bedroom. He needed them to stop him from going a few blocks more and doing what he was afraid he would do. What some inward twisted freak of his personality was planning, instigated, he was cool-headed enough to think, by police and window-pane acid. He stood over their bed watching them sleep. They would never have known he was there if he turned around and stepped softly back downstairs. They were asleep in their unfinished attic room with silver insulation running up the slanted ceiling. One day they would finish it. If they stayed together if he didn't wake them up. But he needed them. Needed them to stop him from doing what he thought about doing. Inside. Deep inside the realm of the accident, he told himself, before he climbed the stairs to their bedroom, as he walked around and around:

His body a hollow shell walking about their kitchen.

Under the light coming in from the street, turning in circles, waiting.

In the early morning before dawn, the acid—the acid—led him toward the knife.

Breathing louder than the refrigerator.

The comfort of the real life they had like the one he ignored all those years.

THESE WERE SETTLED people, he thought, as he stood at the foot of their bed. At peace with one another, with themselves, with their bodies; his crawl through the bar life—that recognition, a rebellious need to flaunt convictions in the sweet undomesticated scent of old urine—a corrupted freedom of mind his whole thing—all that, he had held it above this: the beauty and peace of two sleeping people.

Together, undisturbed, confident they belonged to one another.

All that mattered they could hold in their arms or squander, and he had lost that choice.

The thin blanket covered the grainy outline of bones.

A roundness of thigh in the man, of a shoulder in the woman, the quick shaft of her spine curled toward him.

She formed into an "S" and he the shape of an "L". And they moved: he became the letter "I," and she the crippled bow of a "C".

Standing over the bed, sweaty hands on the bedrail, an electric pulse transmitted from them.

I would have whispered to him then: *You lost it—the one opportunity offered. They could never have stopped you. Who were they? How could they have known your mind. What would 'stabbed her with a knife' mean to people who trusted each other? Who lived for and with one another as one soul? This was your last chance to make amends—I've learned a little something about amends recently. I know you could have forced yourself to go somewhere else. You could have made up for years spent ignoring who she was while you loved some exotic thing—her accent, style, her existentialist roots—you didn't know her, you couldn't have—that night on acid was your only chance. You saw her in the role where she existed in your light—knowing you would never do any such thing with knives, you pretended, and she protected: showed who you believed in—she didn't break the mirror. You pretended to go there to do her harm, but you went to find out who you were, and you lost your only chance. I would have whispered that what you lost, what was missing, and what you didn't even notice was missing, Mac, was devotion. You never had it, this same devotedness these two sleeping people have had for a decade or more, and which my mom had offered you from the very beginning, even before I arrived on the scene. Devotion, Dad. You lost the only chance you ever had to be one soul devoted to another, a soul exchanging a soul's life.*

She was just some Beatrice scribbled on a men's room wall.

We were both guilty of that, but I would have walked away from there. Instead, their faces turned to one another—carelessly, these bodies released their lives.

"Snoring like a potted plant," he said he thought, "the soul runs in and out like a child at play in snow who enters and re-enters its mother's kitchen to be unclothed of the frozen crusts until bare skin shines in her hands dripping on the floor."

They bent to one another under the sheet, a wave rocking its wrack of flotsam. They swam beneath his gaze; he glowed like a mad voyeur. When the man twisted again, a movement of annoyance ran over his mouth, mustache twisting, his gray beard snagged in the silver band of his wristwatch. His eyes opened and bulged. And he moved too fast to the lamp beside the bed. The white roar of sheets off her shoulders. "What? What?"

Her lips crushed and ruined, her face as if a bandage was ripped away.

He squinted beside the lamp, grunted like a dog in pain.

She awoke into shock and kept wiping her face.

He thought, "What were they saying, these poor things? Wrapped in that soft orange light, their whole room flooded with it, all their little patchworks everywhere in the shade. What a sorrow immersed this weird attic. Whose faces were these?" And then his strange voice bounced off the insulated walls and cobwebs.

"I took some acid...having a bad night.... I'm sorry. I'm sorry, can you help?"

They sat up, they stared.

"I...I better go, I..."

And their eyes. They should have done something, but

what? How, anyway?

Look, he wants to go. Let him. Why did he come here?

Voice quick, faraway, and harsh, stuttering and insistent, annoyance overflowed his body:

"...it's alright,...sorry..." again and again, "...please,...didn't mean to..., just needed to stop....don't worry, don't talk..." and he flew from that house like an embarrassed thief jammed between the flashlight and the wall. In the street were two squat houses. Abandoned trucks unencumbered by a stricter order under the russet light. To their insomniac neighbor as she peered through bent Venetian blinds and placed one cigarette after another to her cracked lips, he looked like some worrisome scabrous growth.

26.

ABOUT A MILE down the road from The Little Friend, beside the big lagoon, there were no other businesses but a lonely piddling grocery store growing into something that, because it was spilling packaged goods off its shelves, was getting close to being a supermarket long before the advent of Box stores. It hadn't enough space to hold all the snacks and tourist delicacies late-night customers knocked to the floor, but it did have five cash registers, which made it the busiest place in town by day, and a haunt for hungry wanderers after the bars closed. Beyond the reach of neighbor-to-neighbor or 'honk & wave' acquaintances, Tommy was treated to the same big city anonymity he sometimes yearned for. Though the girl they questioned later could tell he wasn't from around here by how he acted, *and* he dressed all in black, and "NO," she "... for the *friggin* third time, did not *reckanize* him," after all the questions especially from her mom who owned the place. She "*... di-n't* kno-*ow who he WAS!*" when he stepped in there, gun in hand, with his toothless smile.

It may have been the easiest heist he ever pulled off, certainly one he'd given little thought to. None of his buddies at the Little Friend could recall him saying anything about robbing anybody, let alone going to any damn store. To them, the idea "Sure 'nough musta just popped inta his haid when he went cruisin' past." Random acts. He stood across from the first of the cash registers waving his gun at the pretty blond girl, just out of high school, cigarette smoke forking out of her ash tray beside *TV Guide.* The other cash registers were closed. The two other customers at the back were too busy to notice Tommy, thinking they'd go with a six pack of *Beer-Beer* and slip a few extra cans of *Coors* in their pockets. Later, according to the news, she shook so badly Tommy had to count out the money himself and shove it into one of her paper bags. He went away with about three hundred dollars, told the young girl to sit down on the floor, don't call anyone, go home as soon as he left.

WHEN UNCLE AUGUSTE and I stepped out of the woods, we stood on a sidewalk beneath a madrona tree on a quiet street lined with even more lovely madrona trees, green husks spread like darts below them, gnarly roots littering the sidewalk. Beside Auguste was the most beautiful dog I ever knew—a collie, white, brown and black, calm and elegant eyes in her sharp face. We were looking at the house across the street from where we stood in the shadows. She sat beside my uncle as though they'd been together all their lives. And, I knew, because Uncle Auguste had told me already, that her master, Dave the Deputy, was home alone tonight in his well-lit house across the street. Noises arose from a party at his neighbor's house, one or two motorists slowly passing us and Deputy Dave's front porch.

Uncle Auguste began to appear in town every now and then since the year I turned nine; he visited on leave from forestry contracts in the North Cascades. He had arrived in town after dark that night, and here I was, enlisted for some "small chore," as he called it; he said it would help if I was along to watch. I looked up to him as always. His lively spirit, his deep French accent, his jokes, and his nodding shiny bald head were the contrast I needed to the giant nothing that was Mac.

We stood peacefully with the beautiful collie. Beauty, the dog, knew me, but I won't say she was especially interested in me, or that she did more than tolerate me, the kid who came along with Cecile. Neither Auguste nor my mother ever told me, when I was a kid, that Cecile had been rescued from her own mother and had been carried away to live in the homes of many families before she came to us, but I had surmised that her discomfort with any feeling of domestic contentment had its source in an early trauma.

The sound we could hear was from Dave's house—I knew his stereo was in the living room and it was playing The Rolling Stones, loud enough, the screen door open. The neighbors were dancing to music I didn't especially care for; they were laughing and whooping and some of them sang along with a bombastic AM radio station. Dave's Ford Mustang was parked outside his house, his "Bullitt car," the same as in the movie. My uncle turned his head toward me and nodded when the dance tune finished; before another one started, he held up his left hand. His big eyes opened wide, looking down at me. In his hand was the detonator he had built, and with his thumb, he pressed a small button. The Mustang made a popping sound and the back seat burst into flames. Auguste was holding tight to the leash and the dog seemed a little more nervous as flames shot up. The people who'd been dancing on the front porch were amazed, and someone started to scream. Dave stumbled onto his own front porch, then held up both hands, pulled his hair, started inside as if to get a fire extinguisher, but the engine and gas tank exploded. He stood back, away from the flames, turned to take in what was going on, and when he saw us with his dog, he came across the street.

"Oh, thank you. I'm glad she wasn't near the car."

"Or in the house," said Uncle Auguste.

"What?"

"Monsieur, you were just now in your house. You were alone, correct?"

"Yes, no one else is in there."

"No cats?"

"Of course not. I don't have a damn cat," he said.

Auguste held up the second detonator and said, "For Cecile."

A room at the back of Dave the Deputy's house burst into flames. When he turned back, only the dog, who loved Dave, but now also Uncle Auguste, stood beside him at the edge of those woods, her leash draped over Dave's foot.

AS UNCLE AUGUSTE and I hurried through the woods away from Deputy Dave's burning house, we heard the whine of police sirens competing with fire sirens. Right after the firetruck arrived, a cop car pulled up in front of Dave's burning Mustang. We heard the officer shout at Dave, "Come on, man. We got a robbery! Let's go!" and Deputy Dave and Beauty jumped in as the car shot out of there.

When we returned to The Little Friend, it was about two o'clock in the morning, and my mother was already ushering out what seemed like the last sleepy patrons. She had me sit on the stool behind the bar and away from the window while she finished the clean-up. Uncle Auguste cradled a bottle of wine he had bought from her and would take back to the smokejumpers; he told me not to say anything, but I desperately wanted to describe for her the look on Deputy Dave's face. I kept it to myself, and they chatted while she dried glasses with a spotless white towel. After a few minutes, Wesley Roblé, my Django tutor, was at the door knocking so insistently she had to let him in. Beside him was the young man Moses, then the only black man in our town. I hardly knew Moses at all, nor did most of the people we knew. Many of them had come from one city or another, but so many years ago that now any semblance of the big city told them it might be time to move to higher ground. And Moses seemed, simply because he was black, a fugitive of the bigger world out there. People were leery of him, and very few, other than Tommy and of course Mac, who was after all the connection Moses had to our town in the first place, were able to converse with Moses without a sudden though unconscious sense of distrust and suspicion. I already noticed that Moses was reticent, yet I had heard him make occasional jokes with Mac about fears of the middle class, and he said nothing that could be construed as overt hatred; I saw that he was deeply hurt by the ostracism that prevailed by default from our little group of white rabidly hip back-to–the-land rebels who seemed to be waiting for something from him that might never emerge—a way to accept him into the conclave, a gesture on his part that broke the ice. For it was real ice—frozen out, he refused to be more than himself, or to accept the role—our Black Man—and he himself waited, in vain as it turned out, for a sign that no one thought of him as somehow "other."

"Well, they popped him."

Moses was silent. Wesley was a wiry little man who always wanted to get to the bottom of a story as quickly as possible.

He said he followed in his Camaro and watched while Tommy's Galaxy raced cop cars along some side streets and into a cul-de-sac. He got close enough to see what was going on. The cop, who wasn't in uniform, only a white t-shirt because it happened to be Deputy Dave who just had time to take off his tunic when his house burst into flames, was patting down Tommy who assumed the position up against the cop car. The other officer was there with his gun out, and, oddly enough, Beauty the dog was in the back seat. Wesley never saw that before. Collie dog in a cop car.

He yelled out, "Hey, Tommy, you alright? You need anything?"

Dave half-turned toward him and told him he could keep moving right along if he didn't want to be arrested for obstructing, his gun waving kind of crazy in the air.

"'I'm okay, buddy. At least he didn't kick me in the kidneys yet.'"

Wesley said Deputy Dave pounded Tommy's ribs then, his hands still on the roof of the cop car. " 'That must make you feel like a man,' Tommy said, ... and Dave pounds him again, a fist to the kidneys. 'What's the matter, can't you do better than that?' And Dave slams Tommy's face down on the roof of the car. 'Hey, don't hold back, you motherfucker, it's not like *I'm* your girlfriend.' That's about when Moses told me to let's get the fuck outa there," Wesley added.

"Tommy's hands were cuffed the whole time and he never even tried to fight back. His mouth and ear were bleeding, but he never went down. Meanwhile, the other deputy tossed Tommy's back seat, front seat, and trunk. 'Okay, Tommy, where's the gun? Dave, no gun here.'

'Where'd you put that pistola, Amigo? Huh?' That's when that big empty smile comes on, and he had blood comin' out his mouth. 'Gun? What are you talking about, Officer? I abhor weapons.' That's Tommy for you. He's a character. He'll get out of this alright. I hope. Deputy Dave says, 'Get in the back seat, you cocksucker. Move over, Beauty.' What was he doing with a great big collie dog in the back seat of the cop car, anyway? Okay, I gotta go take a leak. Is that okay, Natalie? Before I go home?"

Wesley started to walk across the room, then noticed the hulking figures at one of the tables. The Night People.

"Hey, The Three Amigos! What are you guys doing up so late?" he asked, but nobody answered. They all went back to the various items they had on the table: a deck of cards, a thick notebook, and a small drawing on a bar napkin.

"Oh, oh, I forgot my friends." Said my mom. "I'm sorry, but tonight is not a good night for our after-hours, I am afraid. I will be closing the bar and going home, but I don't think I'm just now in the mood to talk. Our friend is... you know, don't you? He's..."

They all looked up at her. Somewhat hopefully, I thought, but still, they didn't say a word. "He has been arrested. I would like to try to help," she said.

I remember the squeal of the three chairs as they slowly stood, three shadowy figures, key chains, and ragged jackets clicking and scraping; each gathered what he'd been working on into some crinkly paper bag and nodded to my mom. They mumbled something and looked up quickly at her and at me and at Moses. I think they said good night or good luck.

My mother nodded at them too. She couldn't say any more. Uncle Auguste's face was a cross between sadness and inevitability; he always thought Tommy was going to snap. I came up to my mother and took one of her hands and looked up at Moses standing across the bar from her near the front door. His expression, too, seemed sad, but that hadn't changed from the moment he arrived and the whole time Wesley was telling us what they witnessed. Moses saw it all but didn't add any details. As soon as Wesley was out of earshot, though, he began to talk.

"There *was* a gun. The police didn't find it. Tommy tossed it out his car window. That's what most people would have done. So, I'd imagine it's still somewhere along the grassy strip between the store he robbed and that turn-off a couple miles from here. I think that's about where he took off into those side streets Wes was talking about. It's got to be along that strip of grass, where the ditches are, and that's the first place they'll look in the morning. They're gonna want that, so they can prove he threatened the cashier."

My mother stared at him. He had a deep voice, and he just rolled out these predictions, which seemed correct to me, probably to Uncle Auguste, too, who didn't say a thing.

"I was thinking your boy here, and me, could go out and look along that strip. I'm sure he's got the good eyes for that sort of thing, a black gun in the black grass won't be easy to find."

Then they both turned to look at me. I'd never seen my mother like that before, the recognition of all he just said and what Tommy did and what could happen to him, how many years he could be put away for, if they found the gun, and all of it on her, she may have thought, all of it her fault. She opened her hand, the one I wasn't holding onto, and we both looked down. The ring. It had gotten wet while she wiped the glasses, but there it was, shining like the moment he extended her hand out to me when they were both so happy.

"Rob-AIR," her voice uplifted, with a smile for me, "Will you be able to do this? Do you want to go with Moses? It might be dangerous, and I think against the laws, but if you can find that gun, I think you will save Tommy from going to prison for a long time."

27.

WHEN I WAS twenty-one or twenty-two and not living at home anymore, I stopped by a donut shop one night with my friend Joey for a cup of coffee. This was around the time Lou took over The Little Friend and changed its name, its mood, and she got a job someplace else. So, here she was, all cocktail-waitress in her skirt with matching bowtie, buying four cups of coffee and a few donuts. I could tell she was just beginning her shift; she was still beautiful. I didn't say, "Hi, Mom," because she kind of got the drop on me with, "Oh, Hello, how are you doing? How've you been?" Like we weren't related. I didn't get it, but later I thought she didn't want the donut shop guy to know any part of her life. All her secrets. Always there were secrets I had to keep from Mac or someone else. I never noticed she kept secrets from me. When she was ninety she had a very big secret. *"Mon Cher,"* she began. I don't know which felt worse, listening to her, or knowing I would have to tell her the truth. She'd been awake all night, thinking exactly what she could say. She didn't realize I was the one, helpless when her dementia seemed an open wound, who put her in the nursing facility. She believed she could just "retrieve," she liked to say, "her living situation"—her house—by having someone move in with her, or come and take care of her, but this, this *new* plan, the secret, would "reverse the table," she said. I could no longer have corrected her idiom, but I knew she meant she wanted to turn the tables on fate itself.

"I would not need anyone there at night. How would I not be safe at night, Rrrobair? I do not get up; I do not walk around. I stay in the bed. So! Nobody need be there."

Her plan was so simple. She could present the argument, one she'd conceived in insomnia, that, in the morning light, certainly must hold up. She had been preparing exactly what she would tell my *Papá,* word for word. She wanted to try it out on me, her little speech. How she could tell him they should let "bygones be bygones" and live together at Seven-Seventy-Seven where she believed he was still living, alone. She would tell him they could spend their last years together and she would keep an eye on him, and only one nurse would come occasionally to "take our temperatures, the blood press*ure* and be made certain we are eating, no broken bones. Hey? That's all we shall need. What do you think? Let us call him right now and ask. He won't say 'No.' What do you think, *Mon fils*?"

That eagerness on her face, so frail. She'd been planning to tell me this all night as she lay awake, morphine administered to others worse off, the woman in the next bed screaming again, the mops passing along the corridor, vacuums shifting over the rug—its patterns made her dizzy so she would not attempt to walk. She was the prisoner who found a way out through an air vent; that look on her face, the same, I should think, for escapees who descend a rope ladder before searchlights blast the perimeter. My role in this scene? To reveal how things really were.

"Mom, he died seven years ago."

And a switch seemed to click on, her excited expression dissolved, freedom itself vanished, succeeded by a cringing embarrassment.

"I could not have forgotten that. Could I? How could I have? Oh, *Mon Fils,* did I really forget he has died. So long ago. Like yesterday I knew him. Where? Where is he? Where is his body, I mean now?"

BUT SOMETIMES SHE had moments of lucidity, like flashes of herring filtered through the net of dementia. So, shortly after Moses sent Mac's letter, I asked her what she remembered from that night when he arrived at Sevsen-Seventy-Seven tripping on the acid and to tell me about the knife. Whether she *could* remember what really happened mattered less to me than that she may have been afraid, may have felt he was dangerous.

"He came into the house soon after I arrived from the Little Friend, and he was like a burning light bulb. He thought someone planted a knife on him, someone told him he was a killer, someone told him to pick up a knife and kill his girlfriend. He thought this meant kill me. He didn't know why he came to our house, but when he thought of women, only me, he said, was who he wanted. He did not have thoughts of killing but there it was—a 'smear on imagination,' he said he couldn't find how to wipe away, so every kitchen knife was fear, every glass breaks, cuts. I laughed. I knew I shouldn't, but if I thought he could do anything even a little bit violent—impossible and—what is that word?—ludicrous.

"'Why don't we take a walk?' I suggested.

"'It's almost morning, it's still very dark.'

"'Just step outside with me.'

So, we walked to the top of the hill. Full moon, crazy dog

barks. Strange dog. Tall, and thin. I think it's wolfhound, some breed like that, and we didn't go near. It was dark and eerie, misty a little, and this big brute of dog howls.

"'Hound of fucking Baskerville,' he said and, 'That's it! Enough, I want to go back inside.'

So, we did. But he was much calm now; we talked and talked about everything. About you, our lives together and since then, our two lives apart, about how he felt the accident was a part of his life and he relived it every day, and learning how to get along, but would not forgive himself.

"I was very tired. He wasn't, even though he was awake all night and had a lot to tell about the police. They stopped him, you knew that, yes? No, he wasn't tired, he said, but I lay down on the couch and covered myself over with the knitted blanket. I kept it there since you were a baby, remember? And he talked to me for quite a while, although I *was* falling asleep. He was sweet like his old self.

"You know, Bobby, before you were born, he used to bring me a big chocolate truffle in a box with its own white ribbon. He would wait for me to step off the subway train at that station in South Boston. I was tired, working all day long at the cosmetics counter of Filene's in the big city. His silly grin. Lit up the whole underground station and he glowed sitting there on that old wooden bench, 'festooned,' he said, 'in wads of pink gum.'

"So, that's how he used to be, and after we talked—you know: about the... knife.. and about the LSD... and about the police...oh about nearly everything: about you...about poor miserable Tommy...ha, that poor man...it was good, and he was himself, the old Massimo again.

"So, just before dawn I looked up from the couch and there he was, naked, sitting at the piano. The light was coming in through the windows and he was glowing in a way I never seen him before, playing something beautiful. I don't know what it was, but beautiful, and I had to stay awake while he kept playing for me, but I couldn't. He had an angelic almost innocent smile. First time I saw that smile since way back in days we first met."

28.

ALWAYS IT SEEMS those memories from the traumatic bright lights of childhood parlors, the yellow kitchens, stark hardwood dining tables, from the bunk beds and shattered bureaus where someone's hand came down too heavily; always these images keep arising and rearranging, as it were, the furniture and the people's faces, the shapes of their noses and the muscles twitching in a neck or in their difficulty with the formation of some precious, pertinent noun, the name of someone beloved or an object one takes for granted. The act of naming even now has become fraught with memories, and we attempt to say it right, to get it out so that others learn this moment won't be coming back, you can't return. You can't bring *them* back, those people who were trivial, or vital to you, yet their significance was not what you needed to recall to justify why *those* days, apart from others, why those days keep returning. And return as images, or as emotions, which flood the present. In literature and in movies, flashbacks occur for the mature central character. We're allowed to feel the recurrence of the colors of leaves, ice on the pond where it happened, tools left out in the weather, harsh or startling traffic noises, these created this person as he or she appears in the imagined realm. The pretense that past is prologue slides right over the immediacy of the past, not certain aspects of it, as it led to the present. It's nearly impossible to say "I am" or "I feel" without all I've witnessed, every morning held sacred, every night in dread, the whizzing-past of faces at the fringe of my meaningful life—the fly-by of someone's shoes, escaping tires in the rain, those neighborhood squeals from a forest, the thud of my weight against a desk to prophesy condemnation, all of it, the continuum itself, is what I am.

Let's call her Rose. This is how we met: we were both on the bus and she asked me if I had a quarter to pay the driver. In cities, I don't talk to anyone, usually. But she came to where I sat and asked if I could help her out with the fare. I dug into my jeans as she laughed and I did manage to pull out a quarter. When the bus dropped me off, she disembarked as well.

"Oh. Your stop too? Where are you going?"

"Wherever you are."

I hope I've learned by now that no one *is* a minor or fringe character, but back then both of us were—Rose was for me, and I was for her. She was the girl who loved the saxophone on "The Low Spark of High Heeled Boys." Played it off and on all day—the meditative piano, the steady drone of bass—and me in my best John Proctor outfit edging along the street and certainly invisible. I spent several years after she left learning how not to be boring, though no one noticed much difference. We called what we were in the "relationship," which meant "I'd never marry you, no matter what." She bought everything. I didn't have money: I was the Artist. She was the moneymaker, fascinated with my dad who did some acid. Later, after she moved from photojournalism to writing her fictitious memoir, she threw him in as a fringe character or a facsimile of him.

I found her three times after my night scribbling Dante on the Men's Room wall. Once, there she was on a city street. She had a dance class, but in an hour we could talk. I came back, but she didn't; the building she pointed out never held a dance class. Once, at a dedication of a building, she was with her fiancé, or so she called him; he was upset with her and when I heard that tone in her voice, that familiar tone, I stepped away, as if I was more interested in the entertainment. When I looked back, she was gone. Last year I found her after many internet searches. A picture from when I knew her, and one as a wizened old woman. She must have led a hard life. Of course, if I don't investigate a mirror honestly, I can say every moment in my own past makes the present unforgiving. But it wasn't that I was boring, although I certainly was. She left me stewing with my paintbrushes and canvases because of Isabel, unbeknownst wife of the son of the guy who dismantled my family twenty years earlier, the night my dad the famous poet tripped his brains out on windowpane acid.

She sat me on her lap, the way a mother might, although she indeed was the least motherly of women; she wanted to make sure I wouldn't lie. I would have lied, would never have let her know, didn't think she was owed that. But this had been all a part of my redemption, I thought, just like Tommy and the cops, Auguste and the rescued dog at the burning house, Tristan bone-breaking down the bathroom stairs, the wrath of his militant sister. I could have told her I met someone and that would have been it. Our two sham lives nipped in the bud before thirty years went by and we wound up boring each other into a dull grave. But she had to worm it out of me, the name, the description, the sex, the when and where and why until she was in fits of hysteria marching about the house like a derelict in bad need of heroin.

THE LAST NIGHT I spent with Isabel we both understood would be the last. Neither of us wanted this anymore and besides Rose finished taking photographs in Peru and would return the next day. We decided to take sleeping bags and lie on the grass under trees bordering the long driveway to my house. Usually, I would have been able to point out constellations and distant planets, or we would attempt to speak. The profound sense of a universe spread out before us. We were silent and did no more than lie there, separately relieved. After about an hour the car came up the driveway. Rose's Jeep—she was in a hurry. I watched as she pulled up, jumped out, and ran up the stairs. The house was dark, but she turned on all the lights and I heard her call my name—it was bright in there, and she was calling and calling until she gave up. We rolled up our sleeping bags and trudged along a trail through the dark trees, to Isabel's three-decker.

THE PHONE RANG.

"Don't answer it."

"I've *got* to answer it."

I nodded, and, even as she was picking up the receiver, I bent down to put my shoes on and collect my things. I could have simply waved as I went out the door while she was on the phone. I knew it was her husband.

"He wants to speak to you."

"He doesn't know who I am."

"No. He doesn't. He just said, 'Let me speak to that guy in there.'"

She held out her cell phone and mouthed the words "he's drunk" as I walked carefully across the rug she had salvaged from some yard sale. I squinted at her. I was distrustful now. Had she planned to have him call tonight?

"Listen—I'm in a phone booth out on Twenty. I've got a gun here and I'm gonna put it in my mouth and pull the fucking trigger."

"Hey."

"Shut the fuck up. I don't know what you're doing with her—listen to me—You're the one who's been with her a week or two longer than most of them. I'm through with the whole fucking thing. You understand? You get the fuck out. Get the fuck away from her. I mean it. I'm gonna fuckin' shoot myself if you don't. I know what it fucking means if you stick around, and I don't want..."

He started crying.

"Can I say something?"

"What? Shut the fuck up."

"Listen. I'm leaving here. I was already going. This was the end."

I looked across the room at Isabel, arms folded across her chest, gazing at the design on the worn rug.

"I was almost out the door when you called."

Silence.

"Say you won't hurt yourself. Right? Tell me. I'm ready to go. I already was. I swear to you. She doesn't want me. I can tell. Okay? She just wants you. Here, I'm gonna give her the phone."

I handed her the phone and she walked over to the window to talk to him. I couldn't hear, but her voice for the first time was soothing—those names and phrases they use when they talk. She turned toward me. "Yes. He *is* leaving. We already decided. Before you called. We said this is it. No more. We were just talking. He was almost out the door when the phone rang, and it was you. Do you want me to come over?"

29.

"DO THEY ALWAYS let you stay up so late?"

Moses was driving us to the spot where he thought the gun might be.

"Who? My parents?"

"Yeah, you know. Your Mom, your uncle—I know your dad's not always in the picture. So."

"Oh, I go to sleep when I'm tired, I guess."

"Oh. What grade you in?"

"Me? I'm going into 9th."

"Oh, you're starting high school."

"Yeah."

"I remember one thing about the first year of high school."

What?"

"I remember I got a good grade on one essay I had to write for my English class. It was a crazy class. Mostly. Well, I was the only black kid. And I sat in the front row. The teacher was all the time apologizing because his boss told him to play this tape recording of *The Adventures of Huckleberry Finn,* while we were supposed to be reading along in our seats. I read along, but the rest of the class wasn't even looking at the damn books they had in front of them. You ever read it?"

"*Huck Finn*? No. My dad keeps telling me to, but I figure I'll get it in high school so I might as well read other stuff now."

"Like what? What do you read?"

"Comic books. Sometimes I read Dante."

"Dante?"

"My Dad practically forces me to read some of it every time I'm over at his place."

"Oh. Well, anyway I wrote this essay, see, because the teacher kept apologizing to me because he played that tape. And I liked the book. I would have read it on my own, probably, but that recording started to wear me down every time it said 'nigger' and me the only black kid in a room full of white faces. So, my essay was on the topic of 'interdependence.'"

"Wait. What did you say? Wait a minute, what grade did you get?"

"I got an A. I just hoped it wasn't because the damn teacher was feeling sorry for me for having to hear that one word all day long. And I said I thought good old Mark Twain wasn't interested in writing this big antislavery book and he wasn't writing about fairness or hoping to change the lives of enslaved people, but he *was* telling you what it was like to be a human being. By using two opposite human beings as the only characters in the book that know exactly how the other one feels and how to be themselves."

"Oh. Yeah, I get it. You got an A, hunh?"

"Uh-huh. A. Yeah. You know, you should read it. The book, I mean, not my own essay."

"Oh, I will. I will."

"I'm surprised Mac didn't make you read it already. Mac and I once met a man whose parents were enslaved. Now, Jim, the black man in the book, is this enslaved human being, you know? Who is *owned* by some sweet little old lady who's gonna sell him and as a runaway he could be killed any time in the whole book, and Huck, he's like, "I'll go to Hell, but I'm gonna help you get free, Jim." Just a kid. About your age. Pretty cagey, though—was imprisoned, faked his own murder.. Yeah, so, we met this man back in high school, your dad and me; his parents were somehow set freed when they were children, and I don't know what happened to his grandparents. Slaves all their lives, I imagine, and maybe died in enslavement. That's a whole different life, my friend. You and I can't imagine what that would be like. I mean, I know what's real about being the only black kid in school or the only black man in this little hick town, but to be enslaved? Bought and sold? Sold down the river? Beaten? Starved? Your daughters and wives raped whenever the Mastah gets the urge—yeah, we can't really know what any of that could have felt like, day in day out. Sorry, you probably don't want to hear all my opinions on all this."

"Oh, yeah, I do. You're right, though, I don't understand it. Were kids slaves, too?"

"Yeah. Just kids until they were old enough to split up from their mom's and dad's, trained to work like animals, man."

"Oh. But there's no slavery now, right?"

"Not supposed to be. I looked it up once, though; how many people you think are enslaved around the planet? Take a guess."

"Um. I don't know. A thousand?" I had no idea, of course.

"Forty million."

"Oh."

We drove on for a bit in silence. The night air swimming across us through both windows.

"So, did you like high school?"

"Of course not. Now, what kind of question is that? I told you I was the only black kid not only in that class full of white kids but in the entire school. So, no, I *did* not like high school. Oh-oh. Here we are. I think this is exactly where you're going to find Tommy's gun. You ready?"

"How do you know it's here?"

"Because I know. He's smart. Look, we're less than a hundred yards away from that store, not near any streetlight, and there's a good size drainage ditch right there. You go ahead, and I'll park up that way a little."

He left me there for a few minutes by the side of the road. It wasn't raining, but the summer grass was damp. I was glad I at least had on my flip-flops. Who knew what else could have been tossed into these weeds? Pretty soon Moses came walking along the slope that fell into the ditch.

"You find anything?" He said in a loud whisper, but I could hardly see him, it was so dark.

"No, not yet. What about you?"

"Yeah, I found something. I think it's a condom. No, wait, that's mud. Found some baby shoes. Where are you?"

"Right here. I'm in the tall grass."

"Oh, it ain't gonna be in there. Look up closer to the gravel, just below the gravel there in that grassy part next to the breakdown lane. That's where he would have tossed it."

"Oh, okay. What's this?"

"What? You see something?"

"Diaper. A load of cigarette butts. This is ugly. I don't like this. Wait, I think I found something. No, coffee cup, full of... more butts. What you got?"

"Oh, shit. Sorry. Found a wet pair of socks."

"The grass is real wet. Can't we go home now. I don't think we're gonna find it out here. Dammit. Stepped in something.

Maybe they won't even come looking for it."

"Hey, watch the swearing. Okay. Just a little bit longer. The grass is wet 'cuz it's dewy along in here. Don't worry about it. It's going to be sun-up pretty soon and those cops will want to come out here to search in the daylight."

"Alright. Oh, yuck. I stepped in something again. Wait, I feel something here. It's in the tall grasses. See, Moses, I was right all along. Wait. Here it is. Oh my God!"

A distant headlight flashed our way, and he saw what I had in my hand.

"Shit, Tommy. Oops, sorry, again. I shouldn't swear in front of a kid. But, Jesus, how do you walk into a store and rob them with a plastic gun?"

"Looks real, though. I think."

"Yeah, that looks like a real gun. But even so, if Tommy can get a good lawyer, he might be able to argue, she probably knew it *was* plastic, so she was just giving him the money? It was her money, after all, or her Momma's, so maybe she was just donating to one of Tommy's favorite charities."

"Like the Food Bank?"

"Yeah. The Humane Society. Or she might have been the one pilfering the cash so Tommy would give it to Toys for Tots, or Planned Parenthood, who knows?"

I CAN'T BE CERTAIN, but my best guess about the way it happened is this:

"We gotta swing by my house," said Deputy Dave. "I gotta take Beauty home. Or drop her off with the neighbors for a while till I figure out a few things."

"What? We got a prisoner here. We can't take no detours now, Dave."

"Look, I can't take her into the station. You don't mind all that much, do you, Tommy? Listen, Jake, some asshole set my car on fire, then my house. You saw it burning when you stopped to pick me up, remember? I think maybe my neighbor will watch Beauty, while I quick check on the fire and make sure some of the place got saved. So, let's go there."

"Alright, alright. But I'm not getting in the middle of this for you, okay?"

"Right, Jake."

WHEN THEY GET to Deputy Dave's inferno, the fire department has just about turned his living room to rubble and smoke. He jumps out of the police car from the passenger side, walks all the way around to the rear door on the driver's side to let out Beauty, but has to get the key from Deputy Jake, who turns off the engine, gives him the key, gets out of the car and stretches.

"Dave, you're fucked," Jake says as he walks across the street to talk with his cousin Lou Oates, who just emerged from Dave's house, coughing on the front lawn.

"Yeah, I know. I'm really going to hurt somebody for this. I just don't know who it was exactly, that's all, but I got a pretty good idea."

While he's saying this, Deputy Dave unlocks his unit's back door. Beauty goes charging out, her leash jangling on the pavement, Dave runs after her, "Beauty. Hey, Beauty, come back here..."

That's when Tommy recklessly makes his move. He wiggles out the back door Dave left open, reaches behind his back, his hands still handcuffed, for the keys Dave, chasing Beauty away from the fire and smoke, left in the door; darts around the other side of the car, and plunges into the same woods where Uncle Auguste and I went to hide when Deputy

Dave's house incinerated.

Tommy had a little experience with locks and keys, so the handcuffs take only a moment before he's back to being a free man. Free and determined then to sneak through the woods and crawl up the hill to my mom's house. He would have thought she'd overlook his vicious remarks earlier that night. He would tell her he had too many beers with the boys. At any rate, she would know how to take care of such a tricky situation and how to sneak him out of town. Small town cops, he thought. No problem really. Natalie will know how to get him out of this one. Maybe that Auguste can hide him in the trunk of his car when he heads south. Or if he had to go to trial, she would stick by him, he thought. If they did catch him, she would come visit him. They would remain friends, he felt sure. But several years later, Mom and Cecile went to Los Angeles to find Tommy at a small rundown apartment building on Venice Beach. She learned he had a heroin habit, and knew she could persuade him to get help. When she knocked on the front door, she called out his name in her mellifluous voice. He panicked and climbed over the railing of the small veranda and fled down the beach.

IT WAS STILL dark enough to blend with the shadows of fir and hemlock along the side street where Seven-Seventy-Seven protruded from its perch on the hill. The sun would be up soon. Yet all the house lights were blazing, and I could see the sliding glass doors on the front porch, the huge picture windows, and even the little pantry window was lit up.

Moses and I sat in his car because under those glaring lights my mother and father were yelling in the house together. It was the first time Mac was there, as far as I knew, since we came back from France, and went our separate ways.

"What d'you think, they fighting?"

"No, they don't fight. They just do a lot of talking."

"In French?"

I had to stop and think about that. And then remembered that yes sometimes they'd go back and forth in both languages. But one of them always gets frustrated by being unable to explain clearly in the other's tongue.

"That makes sense. I think my parents talked in two different languages too, although both were English. That's why they split up when I was your age. I always had dreams like they were back together, my dad sitting at the kitchen table reading something, but with his coat and hat on. Look."

A short distance down the hill Deputy Jake and Deputy Dave back their police car into an alley, its nose protrudes, and its lights dim.

"They lost Tommy, I bet."

"I was always a little afraid about having Tommy around. I don't know why, but I thought something bad's gonna happen. And then, when he proposed to my mom, I knew it would be bad."

"What? Tommy was going to marry your mom?"

"Yeah, I think. He gave her the ring and all."

"Oh. Well, that might mean something or nothing. You never know with Tommy. Besides, I thought she was still married to Mac."

"I...I don't know."

Soon we could hear the piano start to play, and we could see my Mom lying on the sofa next to it. She looked as though she'd gone to sleep. A first bird chirped as the sky began to lighten. It reminded me that I hadn't been to sleep in a long time, and old dreams popped into my head. Flashes of one must have come back from talking about Tommy:

"I had this dream once about Tommy being in prison. I dreamt they gave him a lobotomy and he came back to protect us all. I felt real safe around him in the dream. He was standing at the bottom of some stairs and all around him were these sweeping plains. Endless space. But there wasn't any sunlight: it was all still and silver like moon covering the town, and Tommy in the middle of the moonlight with a big smile on, hands in his pockets. A bunch of kids outside playing some game. Every once in a while, he takes the hands out of the pockets like he was getting ready to help anyone who came running toward him. I remember I woke up feeling so afraid. Tommy was like this robot Catcher in the Rye guy who was going to have to control our minds soon too since he didn't have any mind left to control himself. He could never get angry again. He could only help, and all we could do was keep from letting him see what we were thinking, so he couldn't help us if we did the wrong thing."

"Yeah, sounds about right. Tommy and your dad. They're Natalie's Angel-headed hipsters."

"What's that?"

"The Beatific Vision."

"Oh. You their Angel?"

"Yeah."

"Angel demon Death?"

"Wha? No way, man. I'm a black man with nothing but light in these shoes. But your dad, now he's always got some kind of dark angel going on inside him. Look at the way he's sitting up there right now, in fact. He's a naked man playing a piano to a sleeping woman. I mean *look* at your dad *and* your mom in the window up there. It's the Juggler story. You know that story? It's French, some old Medieval tale, religious of course, 'Le Jongleur Nostre Dame.' Your dad ever tell it to you?"

"What are you talking about? I don't get it."

"The Middle Ages? You know the Middle Ages, right? He makes you read Dante or something, right?"

"Yeah, I know about Dante. He was a poet."

"Right. Also Catholic like this story. Anyway, you might read it some time. There it is, though, your dad and your mom, they're a perfect portrayal of the story in its secular version."

"The what?"

"The not-religious version, you know? Well, the arrangement of the two of them up there. Look at them in that big window. Your Dad would see this, I think, if he wasn't all fucked up right now to begin with. Wait a minute. You know he took some acid tonight, right?"

"Yeah, I thought so. I mean I *knew* that I guess."

"Yeah, some time tonight. Anyway, my point is they are in that same symbolic setup as that Juggler story. It's allegory, I guess. I know you know what allegory is, right?"

"Yeah, I guess."

"Dante's loaded with them. You'll get that sooner or later. Doesn't matter. The Juggler in the story can't please anybody because he doesn't know any damn Latin."

"My Dad knows Latin. He knows all about Latin. Hey, how do you know all this stuff, anyway?"

"We learned it together, your dad and me. I told you that, right? We were in high school where they made us learn Latin and Greek and all kinds of other shit? Oops, sorry. Stuff. I even learned the story from him. All the Juggler had was this little talent. It wasn't even juggling at first, the first version of the story. It was tumbling. You know, acrobatics? And he had to roll around naked in front of this statue of the Mother Mary because that's who he was.

"Wait. Was this after you wrote the Huck Finn paper you

got an A on?"

"Yeah, yeah, after that."

"But..."

"Listen, doesn't matter. I got an A on everything. That was why they let me into private school. That's where I met Old Mackey up there."

"What did you mean you learned the story from him. From my dad? He told it to you?"

"No, I read it in one of his books. I found it somewhere after I lost contact with him. *The Juggler and the Life of the Heart.* I found it in some bookstore somewhere. A book of poems, you know? Like he always does. But this one was poems about dead poets nobody ever heard of. He was praising these people who had disappeared, and writing in their voices, and telling the story of how they ended up on the trash heap. Anyway, then there were two other monks watching like you and me sitting out here watching your Dad and Mom. There he is, up there playing the piano for her, and dammit he really *is* naked—and of course, she can't hear a thing; she's sound asleep. Just like the holy lady statue. Couldn't hear a damn thing or see this guy tumbling around. And those two monks watching him—us—were just about to stop him when...Well, I don't want to spoil it for you, but if your mom were to wake up right now the way the statue of the Madonna came to life, and if she wiped the sweat off your dad's forehead, that would be the perfection of their own particular version of this same old-timey Juggler story. *I* think so anyway. Though come to think of it, there is one version where she shoots breast milk at him."

TOMMY WAS SLOUCHING up the hill. And Deputy Dave and Deputy Jake, as noiselessly as they thought they could be, emerged from the cop-car in the laurels. They had guns drawn, handcuffs held high, and they crept slowly up the hill behind him.

"Tommy?!"

He stopped, but he didn't turn around to look at them; he put his hands on his head and looked up at the sky. He saw me staring out from the passenger side of Moses's car and pointed his fake gun-finger at me, smiled his toothless fallen angel recognition. Then, keeping his hands above his head, he turned his finger to point toward my mom and dad in the picture window.

"Look at that, Bobby. Look up there!"

It had been his last hope to be taken in like all the other strays she allowed at her round oak table, a place to hide for the night. But she was asleep on the couch, and Mac was in there now, and—how it must have surprised and in a way delighted Tommy—Mac was naked as a songbird and playing the piano as the sun came up.

I was thinking of him just that way when I looked down at my hand where it hovered above the railing at the dark bridge over the Neponset, my hand gray and the lines along my palm caked by his ash. Human flesh, his human flesh, father flesh, a famous man's flesh, and bone. Half his ashes left my hand, a silken veil puffed out and flowing onto that windless night out over the quiet river, muddy as it was, as it always was I think, muddy stillness itself. Just as, in memory, there he still sits at that piano; the wraith of a murderer chased away from his consciousness by dawn light. It poured into the room, covered his bare chest, his gray hair long and stringy and sparkling—even his teeth, his eyes, sparkling in first spears of light the sun flung over downtown rooftops, glazing windows, gliding over uncut lawns, picket fences, gates hung open. First light spiked clouds across the bay and burned them nearly to the shape of a choir in magenta robes. The front windows of Seven-Seventy-Seven shimmered, and down our living room walls crept a new color, like crimson but not, a color we have no word for; it found my mother asleep on the couch and set her awash in light too immaculate to hope for, smoothed her shoulders beneath my childhood blanket. And it baked my father, finally without a trickle of fruitful beginnings, where he hovered naked above the piano keys, striking them more benevolently than perhaps he ever had, as if to create for the first time that tune, the only tune he played throughout my childhood in every country, wherever we alighted, something he made up years before; and the wicked sunlight sculpted his already old delicate face, which even then I swear knew everything, reassured me fear was pointless, that being uncertain or certain, really didn't matter, which was all I could think of when I heard his piano and his raving smile crinkle with light.

The End

MICHAEL DALEY is the author of a book of essays, *Way Out There* (Pleasure Boat Studio, 2007), and several books of poems and translations. His most recent collection of poems is *Born With* (Dos Madres, 2020). He is a retired teacher, and the publisher of Empty Bowl.

BOOKS BY MICHAEL DALEY

The Straits
Angels
Amigos
Yes, Five Poems
Original Sin
The Corn Maiden
Horace: Eleven Odes
To Curve
Way Out There: Lyrical Essays
Moonlight in the Redemptive Forest
Alter Mundus by Lucia Gazzino (tr MDaley)
Of a Feather
Born With
True Heresies
Telemachus
This Is How Good Your Are: New & Selected Poems

"While the unexamined life is not worth living, the examined life extends its benefits to us all. And this book is such a record, in prose that is often but a breath away from poetry, shards of watery glass collected from the wake of a deeply-felt and honestly-lived life."

-BILL PORTER (RED PINE)

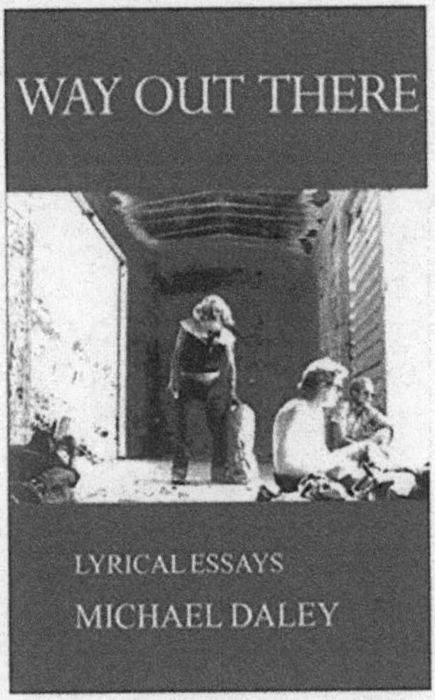

CULTURAL WRITING. ESSAYS. These entertaining and insightful essays are gathered from Daley's years traveling, working, writing, and finding his way in America's far west and beyond. With lyric grace and disarming honesty, he captures the optimism, experimentation and self-discovery that marked the 1970s and 80s for a generation. Traversing the shifting ground between meditation and memoir, Daley offers a unique take on our time and culture. Whether traveling by freight-train, fishing boat, boot leather or thumb, his perspective is always fresh and inviting. Daley's language is tuned the music of the moment, and his poet's eye is alert to details that bring his essays to life. Looking back over his own life—from early seminary days in Boston, poetic rambles "on the road" in the West, teaching English in Hungary—he scrutinizes our culture and offers a disarming portrait or an artist coming to terms with his and our history.